W9-APL-621

Sea Glass

Also by Anita Shreve

The Last Time They Met
Fortune's Rocks
The Pilot's Wife
The Weight of Water
Resistance
Where or When
Strange Fits of Passion
Eden Close

Sea Glass

A NOVEL

Anita Shreve

BOOKSPAN LARGE PRINT EDITION

LITTLE, BROWN AND COMPANY
Boston New York London

This Large Print Edition, prepared especially for Bookspan, Inc., contains the complete, unabridged text of the original Publisher's Edition.

Copyright © 2002 by Anita Shreve

All rights reserved. No part of this book may be reproduced in any form or by any electronic or mechanical means, including information storage and retrieval systems, without permission in writing from the publisher, except by a reviewer who may quote brief passages in a review.

The characters and events in this book are fictitious. Any similarity to real persons, living or dead, is coincidental and not intended by the author.

ISBN 0-7394-2577-3
Printed in the United States of America

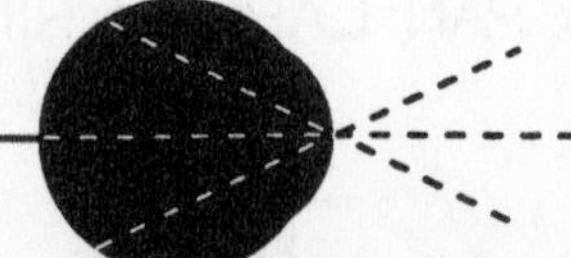

This Large Print Book carries the Seal of Approval of N.A.V.H.

for Betsy

Honora

Honora sets the cardboard suitcase on the slab of granite. The door is mackereled, paint-chipped—green or black, it is hard to tell. Above the knocker, there are panes of glass, some broken and others opaque with age. Overhead is a portico of weathered shingles and beyond that a milk-and-water sky. Honora pinches the lapels of her suit together and holds her hat against the wind. She peers at the letter *B* carved into the knocker and thinks, *This is the place where it all begins.*

The year is 1929. A June day. A wedding day. Honora is just twenty, and Sexton is twenty-four.

The clapboards of the house are worn from white to flesh. The screens at the windows are ripped and flapping. On the second story, dormers stand like sentries keeping watch over the sea, and from the house a thicket sharp with thorns advances across the lawn. The doorsill is splintered, and she thinks it might give way with her weight. She wants to try the pitted knob, though Sexton has told her not to, to wait for him. She steps down into the dooryard, her pumps denting the springy soil, unleashing a scent that collapses years.

Sexton comes around the corner then, his palms upturned and filled with dirt. He is a man with a surprise, a stranger she hardly knows. A good man, she thinks. She hopes. His coat billows in the breeze, revealing suspenders snug against his shirt. His trousers, mended at a side seam, are loose and ride too low over his shoes. His hair, well oiled for the wedding, lifts in the wind.

Honora steps back up onto the granite slab and waits for her husband. She puts her hands together at her waist, the purse she borrowed from her mother snug against her hip. Sexton has an offering: sandy soil, a key.

"The soil is for the solid ground of marriage," he says. "The key is for unlocking secrets." He pauses. "The earrings are for you."

Honora bends her face toward the pillow of dirt. Two marcasite-and-pearl earrings lie nearly buried in Sexton's hands. She brushes them off with her finger.

"They belonged to my mother," Sexton says. "The soil and the key are an old tradition your uncle Harold told me."

"Thank you," she says. "They're very beautiful."

She takes the key and thinks, *Crossing the sill. Beginning our life together.*

The man came into the bank with a roll of tens and fives, wanting larger bills so that he could buy a car. He had on a long brown coat and took his hat off before he made the transaction. The white collar of his shirt was tight against his neck, and he talked to Honora as she counted out the money. A Buick two-door, he explained. A 1926, only three years old. It was the color of a robin's egg, he said, with a red stripe just below the door handle. A real beauty, with wood-spoke wheels and navy mohair upholstery. He was getting it for a song, from a widow who'd never learned to drive her husband's car. He seemed excited in the way that men do when thinking about cars that don't belong to them yet, that haven't broken down yet. Honora clipped the bills together and slipped them under the grille. His eyes were gray, set deep beneath heavy brows. He had a trim mustache, a shade darker than his hair. He brushed his hair, flattened some from the hat, from his forehead. She had to wiggle the money under the grille to remind him of it. He took it, folded it once, and slipped it into the pocket of his trousers.

"What's your name?" he asked.

"Honora," she said.

"How do you spell it?"

She spelled it for him. "The *H* is silent," she added.

"O-*nor*-a," he said, trying it out. "Have you worked here long?"

They were separated by the grille. It seemed an odd way to meet, though better than at McNiven's, where she sometimes went with Ruth Shaw. There a man would slide into the booth and press his leg against your thigh before he'd even said his name.

"I'm Sexton Beecher," the handsome face dissected by grillwork said. At the next window, Mrs. Yates was listening intently.

Honora nodded. There was a man behind him now. Harry Knox, in his overalls, holding his passbook. Growing impatient.

Sexton put his hat back on. "I sell typewriters," he said, answering a question that hadn't yet been asked. "The courthouse is one of my accounts. I need a car in my job. I used to borrow my boss's Ford, but the engine went. They said it would cost more to fix it than to buy a new one. Don't ever buy a Ford."

It seemed unlikely she would ever buy a Ford.

The courthouse employed at least half of the adults in town. Taft was the county seat, and all the cases went to trial there.

"Enjoy the car," Honora said.

The man seemed reluctant to turn away. But there was Harry Knox stepping up to the grille, and that was that. Through the window at the side of the bank, Honora caught a glimpse of Sexton Beecher buttoning his coat as he walked away.

* * *

Sexton tries the switch on the wall, even though they both know there is no electricity yet. He opens doors off the hallway so that light can enter from other rooms with windows. The floorboards of the hall are cloudy with dust, and on the walls a paper patterned in green coaches and liveried servants is peeling away at the seams. A radiator, once cream colored, is brown now, with dirt collected in the crevices. At the end of the hall is a stairway with an expansive landing halfway up, a wooden crate filled with a fabric that might once have been curtains. The ceilings, pressed tin, are nearly as high as those in public buildings. Honora can see the mildew on the walls then, a pattern competing with the carriages and footmen. The house smells of mold and something else: other people lived here.

She enters a room that seems to be a kitchen. She walks to a shuttered window and lifts the hook with her finger. The shutters open to panes of glass coated with a year or two of salt. A filmy light, like that through blocks of frosted glass, lights up an iron stove, its surface dotted with animal droppings. She twists a lever, and the oven door slams open with a screech and a bang that startle her.

She bends and looks inside. Something dead and gray is in the corner.

She walks around the kitchen, touching the surfaces of shelves, the grime of years in the brush strokes of the paint. A dirty sink, cavernous and porcelain, is stained with rust. She gives the tap a try. She could budge it if she leaned her weight against the sink, but her suit is still on loan from Bette's Second Time Around. The butter yellow jacket with its long lapels narrows in nicely at the waist and makes a slender silhouette, a change from a decade of boyish dresses with no waists. She shivers in the chill and wraps her arms around herself, careful not to touch the suit with her hands. There are blankets in the car, but she cannot mention them so soon. She hears footsteps on the stairs and moves into the hallway just as Sexton emerges from the cellar, wiping his hands on a handkerchief.

"Found the furnace," he says. "In the fall, we'll have to get some coal."

She nods and gestures with her hand to

the kitchen. He trails his knuckles along her arm as he passes her.

"What a mess," he says.

"Not so bad," she says, already loyal to what will be their home.

In April, the typewriter salesman returned to the bank. He came through the door so fast that Honora thought at first he might be a robber. The wings of his coat spread wide around his trousers as he made his way to her station. She resisted the urge to touch her hair, which she hadn't washed in days.

"Want to go for a ride?" he asked.

"You bought the car."

"It's a honey."

"I can't."

"When do you get off work?"

"Four o'clock."

"Banker's hours."

The clock on the wall said half past two. The sound of a woman's high heels could be heard on the marble floor. Sexton Beecher didn't turn around to look.

"I'll be outside at four," he said. "I'll give you a ride home."

I don't even know you, she might have

said, except that Mrs. Yates was leaning in Honora's direction lest she miss a word. Honora was silent, which the man took for acquiescence. She noticed this time that his eyes weren't really gray, but green, and that perhaps they were set too close together. His forehead was awfully high, and when he smiled, his teeth were slightly crooked. And there was something cocky in his manner, but that might just be the salesman in him, she thought. Honora laid these flaws aside as one might overlook a small stain on a beautifully embroidered tablecloth one wanted to buy, only later to discover, when it was on the table and all the guests were seated around it, that the stain had become a beacon, while the beautiful embroidery lay hidden in everybody's laps.

Sexton returns with a can of oil from the car. Honora finds a piece of castile soap wrapped in a tea towel in her suitcase. He removes his jacket and rolls his sleeves. His left forearm is already tanned from leaning it out of the window of the Buick. Honora feels a small ping in her abdomen and looks away.

The tap retches and sprays a stuttering dome of brown water into the sink. Honora jumps back, not wanting the water on her suit.

"It's the rust," he says. "They said the water was turned on, but I didn't know for sure. A valve was stuck in the basement."

Together they watch the water clear.

His shirt is dirty at the back. She reaches over to brush it off. He leans against the lip of the sink and bends his head, letting her touch him in this way. When she stops, he straightens. She holds out the soap and together they wash their hands in the bulbous stream of water. She scrubs the marcasite-and-pearl earrings. He watches as she puts them on.

"Should I bring the picnic in, or do you want a nap?" he asks.

She feels herself blush at the word *nap.* "I haven't been upstairs yet," she says.

"There's a bed. Well, a mattress. It looks clean enough."

So her husband had looked for a bed even before he searched for the furnace.

"There are blankets in the trunk," she says.

After a time, Honora stopped thinking of him as "the typewriter salesman" and began to think of him as Sexton. He drove over from Portsmouth eight times in the three months that they courted, telling his boss that he was onto something big in Taft. He was from Ohio, he told Honora, an American heading in the wrong direction. He'd had a year of college on the co-op program, but the freedom of traveling and the possibility of fat commissions had lured him east, away from the classroom. He made good money, he said, which might or might not be true; she couldn't be absolutely sure. Yes, there was the Buick, but she couldn't ignore the too-tight collars and a sole coming loose from a shoe. The sleeves of some of his shirts were frayed at the cuffs.

They courted in the Buick with all the typewriters (Fosdick's Nos. 6 and 7), her mother's house too small for any sort of privacy. Sexton was charming and persistent in a way Honora had never experienced before. He told her that he loved her. He also told her that he had dreams. One day there would be a Fosdick in every household, he said, and he would be the man to put them there.

"Will you marry me?" he asked her in May.

On his sixth visit, Honora noticed that Sexton could hardly contain his excitement. A stroke of luck, he said in the Buick when finally they were alone. His boss knew someone who knew someone who knew someone. An abandoned house, but upright nevertheless. All they had to do, in place of rent, was take care of it and fix it up.

"It's a way to save," he told Honora, "for a house of our own."

When they announced their engagement, no one was surprised, least of all her mother. She'd seen it in him from the very beginning. In fact, she'd said so early on to Harold—wasn't that so, Harold?—that this was a man who would get his appointment.

Honora reaches down to touch the fabric in the carton. Faded chintz, curtains after all.

And something else. A framed photograph tucked into the side of the box, as if snatched from a dresser at the last minute. A photograph of a woman and a boy. Years ago, Honora thinks, studying the dress that falls nearly to the ankle.

The stairs creak some under her weight, which even with the bedding isn't much. The sound embarrasses her, as if announcing her intentions. A crystal chandelier hangs rigidly over the landing, and she sees that the ceiling of the second floor has been papered like the walls. At the top of the stairs, a sense of emptiness overwhelms her, and for the first time she feels the enormity of the tasks that lie ahead of her. *Making a house liveable,* she thinks. *Making a marriage.*

It's just the empty rooms, she tells herself.

The second floor is a warren of tiny chambers, a surprise after the spaciousness of the floor below. Some of the rooms are painted pale blue; others are prettier, with printed paper on the walls. Heavy curtain rods sit naked over the windows. On the window seats are cushions—frayed and misshapen from overuse.

At the end of the hallway, she finds a suite of three rooms with a series of dormers facing the sea. In the bathroom there is a sink and a bathtub. In the bedroom she thumps a mattress with her fist, making a small cloud of dust in the salt-filtered light of the window. Why did they take the bed but not the mattress? She tucks in the sheets, crouching at the corners, and listens for sounds of Sexton below, her heart beating so erratically that she has to put a hand to her chest. She unbuttons the yellow suit jacket, only then realizing that there aren't any hangers in the shallow closet by the door. She folds the jacket inside out and lays it on the floor next to her shoes. She slips off her skirt, turning that inside out as well. She sits on the edge of the mattress in her blouse and slip, and unrolls her stockings.

The kitchen was unseasonably hot and close for late June, steam rising from the iron and making droplets on her mother's nose and brow. Her mother wore her purple cotton dress with the petunias, her low-slung weight seemingly held up only by her pinafore as she lifted the iron and set it down again on the tea cloth over the butter yellow suit. Honora sat on a chair at the kitchen table, writing labels for the canning, both of them silent, aware of change. Her mother's hair was done up in a bun with combs and hairpins, and the stems of her glasses dug into the sides of her head. On the stove, there was the white enameled pot, the funnels and the jars, waiting to be filled with spring onions and asparagus and rhubarb jam. Even at the beginning of summer, the kitchen was always awash in jars, the canning going on late into the night, as they tried to keep one step ahead of the harvest from the kitchen garden her mother kept. Honora, who hated the peeling and the preparations she was expected to do after she got home from the bank, nevertheless admired the jars with the carefully inscribed labels on the front—*Beet Horseradish Relish, Asa's Onion Pickles, Wild Strawberry Jam*—and the way that, later, they'd be lined up in the root cellar, labels facing out, carrots to the north, wax beans to the south, the jars of strawberry preserves going first from the shelves. But this year her mother had cut the garden back, as if she'd known that her daughter would be leaving home.

Her uncle Harold, blind and papery, couldn't walk the length of the aisle of the Methodist church and so he stood by the front pew with his niece for half a minute so as to give her away properly. She was the last child to leave the house, the boys gone to Arkansas and Syracuse and San Francisco. Her mother sat in her navy polka-dot silk with the lace collar, her comfortable weight caught primly within the dress's folds. She wore real silk stockings for the occasion, Honora noticed, and not the tan stockings from Touraine's. Her mother's black shoes, serviceable rather than pretty, were the ones Harold always referred to as her Sunday-go-to-meeting shoes. Her mother wore a navy cloche, the silver roll of her hair caught beneath it with mother-of-pearl combs.

Just before they'd left the house, her mother had polished her gold-rimmed glasses at the sink. She'd taken her time at it and had pretended not to cry.

"You look very pretty," she said to Honora when she had hooked the stems of her glasses behind her ears.

"Thank you," Honora said.

"You let me know, won't you," her mother said. She took her hankie from inside the cuff of her dress. "About what you want me to do with the suit, I mean."

"I will."

"Some women, they like to keep the clothes they get married in. I had my wedding dress with me right up until Halifax."

Honora and her mother were silent a moment, remembering Halifax. "Your father would have been so proud," her mother said.

"I know."

"So you let me know about the suit. I'll be happy to pay for it, you decide to keep it."

Honora took a step forward and kissed her mother's cheek.

"Now, now," her mother said. "You don't want to set me off again."

Sexton walks into the bedroom with the picnic basket in one hand, the suitcase in the other. He looks at Honora sitting on the mattress, her stockings and her shoes and her suit folded, her garters peeking out from beneath a girdle to one side of the bed. His face loosens, as if he'd come prepared to tell his new wife one thing but now wishes to say something else. Honora watches as he sets down the picnic basket and the cardboard suitcase. He removes his coat and lets it fall from his arms, snatching it before it hits the floor. He yanks the knot of his tie sideways.

She slides backward and slips her bare legs under the cool sheet and blanket. She lays her cheek against the pillow and watches her husband with one eye. She has never seen a man undress before: the tug of the belt buckle, the pulling up of the shirttails, the shoes being kicked off, the shirt dropped to the floor, the trousers—the only garment removed with care—folded and set upon the suitcase. He unbuckles his watch and puts it on a windowsill. In the stingy light of the salted windows, she can see the broad knobs of his shoulders, the gentle muscles through the chest, the surprising gooseflesh of his buttocks, the red-gold hairs along the backs of his legs. Sexton kneels at the foot of the mattress and crawls up to his new bride. He puts his face close to hers. He slides under the sheet and draws her to him. Her head rests on the pad of his shoulder, and her right arm is tucked between them. His knee slips between her thighs, causing the skirt of her slip to ride up to her hips. He kisses her hair.

"What makes it so shiny?" he asks.

"Vinegar," she says.

"You're shaking," he says.

"Am I?"

He presses his mouth to her shoulder. "We'll take our time," he says.

McDermott

McDermott sits at the edge of the bed and smokes a cigarette. Behind him, near the window, the English girl is counting out the money. She counts slowly and moves her lips the way some people have to do when reading to themselves. The room has a sink and a chair and a window open to the street, silent now, everyone on his lunch break, thirty minutes, not enough time to eat a proper meal, never mind have a proper fuck.

The girl counting the coins is framed by the window and in it, she is almost pretty. Maybe she has spoken and he hasn't heard her. The looms have made McDermott deaf. Well, not deaf exactly, but they have changed sound, damaged sound, so that sometimes spoken words seem to come from the bottom of a well, and others have halos around them, gauzy halos that slur sound. The girl has thin hair and glasses, blue eyes and a long face. He once asked her why she did it, and she said simply that the money was better than in the mills and she didn't have to work as hard. He thought it was the most honest answer to a difficult question he had ever heard.

The air coming through the window is soft and cool. There are nine, maybe ten days a year like this, days that leak out between the tight cold of winter and the suffocating humidity of summer. Days that make him think of picnics as a boy, when his mother felt well enough to make the meat pies and the iced tea. Before Sean died. Before his father pissed off.

McDermott can tell simply by his inner clock (never wrong) that there are eighteen minutes left in the lunch break. Eighteen minutes before the mill horn sounds and everyone comes out of all the doorways along the street below him, rolling shirt-sleeves, slipping arms into jackets, still chewing their food. The bosses lock the gates at 12:45, and anyone who is out stays out and forfeits a day's pay, if not the job itself.

"I count only a dollar and forty-seven cents," the girl says. Her voice floats up to him from the bottom of a jar.

He bends and fishes through the pockets of his pants on the floor. She is nineteen, the same age as his sister Eileen. She has a thin cotton robe wrapped around her body. Her nipples are hard, but McDermott knows it has nothing to do with excitement. More to do with money. He lays the copper pennies on the chenille bedspread, hastily pulled up and lopsided. He wants silence and he wants to sleep, but the pain the start-up horn will cause him isn't worth the exquisite pleasure of the stolen oblivion.

He watches the girl squirrel the money away under the bed.

"All right then," she says.

She takes her glasses off and lays them on the windowsill. She has a large eyetooth, just the one, and it makes her mouth crooked. The tooth sticks out a bit when she smiles, which isn't often. She has on a vivid orange lipstick that he sometimes asks her to take off. She stands and lets her robe fall from her body. She tugs the blue spread from the bed with the dexterity of a housekeeper. If they are quick about it, he'll have five, six minutes left of peace and quiet.

Alphonse

Every day Alphonse gets up and rolls off the galvanized bed and goes to the outhouse, and if he is lucky and there isn't a line, he is in and done in no time and can get a head start on the lunch pails for his two brothers and three sisters. He especially wants a head start because if they see him making the lunches in the buckets they will complain and one will be sure to say I don't want the potato, give it to Augustin, and then it will begin and he'll have nothing but trouble.

It is his job to make the lunches and to scrub the floor in the morning because he is only working bobbins and makes the least money, and besides, he is the fastest sprinter and can get to the gates inside of a minute, which leaves him five or six anyway to scrub the floor after the girls, who are the laggards, leave the house.

His mother has the night shift and has to sleep in the mornings, so it is his job to get everybody off even though he is the youngest. Well, not the youngest, Camille is still in school, but the youngest of those who go to the mill.

They live on the top floor of number 78 Rose Street and have only the back stairway in and out. Last winter his father slipped on the top step and went all the way down the three flights, and if it wasn't for the ice he might not have broken his neck, but the mill doctor said the steps were brick hard because of the ice and that was the problem.

After that, his mother, who hadn't worked in the mill because of having six children, started on the night shift, and that was when Alphonse's troubles started and the chores got worse.

Marie-Thérèse should be doing the lunch pails, but she wouldn't and then they wouldn't have any lunch at all. You can't make Marie-Thérèse do what she doesn't want to do.

It is forbidden to speak English in the house because his mother is afraid that America will swallow her children, but sometimes words slip out and she hits him if he says *newspaper* or *milk* or *thirsty* by mistake. But then when he is doing the bobbins, he isn't allowed to answer in French because the second hand is American, or maybe he is Irish, and he pretends he doesn't understand you even if you only say *oui* or *non.*

On Sunday mornings they all go to mass at St. André, and once in a while he will see Sister Mary Patrick from a distance. She tried to keep him out of the mill and threatened (for his own good, she said) to tell the bosses that he was only eleven, which is illegal, but then she didn't, probably because she forgot.

On Sunday afternoons now that the weather is good Alphonse takes the trolley to Ely with one of the two dimes he keeps from his pay packet. He walks the rest of the way to the beach. He doesn't have a proper bathing suit, but that is just as well because he's afraid of the water. He likes to sit on the sand and search for shells and look at the ocean and feel the sun on his face and get burned and not come back until it is very late so that he doesn't get asked to do one of the Sunday-night chores.

He wears overalls and a shirt and a cloth cap, and his mother prides herself on keeping everyone in shoes, even though Alphonse is still wearing Gérard's old ones and they are too small and lost their laces months ago. He doesn't pack a pail for himself but instead puts a piece of bread and a hunk of cheese and a boiled egg in a sack that once had coffee in it. He can run better with a sack than a pail.

He hears his mother stirring in the bedroom. He rinses the scrub brush and gets the rag out and tries to damp-mop the water away with the rag under his foot the way his mother taught him. He wants to go in and see her and say good-bye and he knows she won't mind if he wakes her up—she says she loves to see his face—but he has only a minute left and if he goes into the bedroom he will find it hard to leave.

When he gets off his shift and runs home, he has fifteen minutes to see his mother before she has to go to her own shift. Usually she just gives him instructions. Once in a while she calls him My Boy.

Alphonse grabs his sack from the table. He lays the rag over the wooden railing on the back stoop and flies down the stairs, taking only three or four steps each flight. There is no one on the street, but he will make it to the gate before it closes. He always does.

Vivian

"I'm absolutely certain there has been a mistake," Vivian says.

The desk clerk, a weasely looking Franco, consults his pebbled-leather register for the third time. "It says here that you are due to arrive on the twenty-fourth, madam."

"I can't have been due on the twenty-fourth," Vivian says patiently, "because I am here now."

She sets her train case on the mahogany desk and pulls off her gloves. She wants to shed her town clothes and slip into a lighter dress—the cowslip yellow might be good, she thinks. Over by the doorway, a porter waits with her eight glazed-linen trunks. She tucks a strand of hair under her cloche. She hates the humidity. Her hair is frizz now, just frizz.

"I believe you are two days early," the desk clerk says in his horrid accent. His suit is shiny and bears traces of dandruff all along the shoulders.

"Impossible," Vivian says.

"I am sure we can arrange something, madam."

"Thank you," she says. "But I want my usual corner room. And it's miss, not madam."

"Which corner would that be?"

Vivian suppresses a sigh. "The southeast corner, fourth floor," she says.

"Yes, of course," the desk clerk says, catching her eye. And she is certain that he is smiling.

The insolence. As if she'd just stepped off the street. As if she hadn't been coming to the Highland for twenty years, ever since she was a girl. She turns, searching the lobby for a familiar face, and sees Asa Whitlock, who's been summering at the hotel at least as long as Vivian has, huddled under a tartan blanket in a wicker wheelchair by the window. In the corner a woman in a frost green suit is standing next to a man in a panama hat and natty pants. The woman has smart town welts on her feet. The couple, like Vivian, seems to have just gotten off the train.

Vivian takes in the old horsehair sofas, the oil portraits on the walls, the carved pillars around which velvet banquettes have been placed for the guests, and she thinks how tired and dowdy the lobby looks, which, she supposes, is the point. Upstairs in her rooms there will be the old iron bed with the lilac sateen coverlet, the bureau with thin slats at the bottoms of the drawers that loosen on dry days, the sage tin ceiling she's been known to stare at for hours at a time. Over the bureau will be the spotted mirror in which she will be able to make out only a partial image of herself (just as well at twenty-eight, she thinks) and on a low table by the window will be a chamber set—for show, thank God, and not for use.

Through the window over that low table, Vivian will be able to look at the ocean from her bed. Her favorite time of the day is shortly after her tea has been brought in the morning, when she props herself up against the pillows and the rattling iron headboard and gazes out to sea and empties her mind. Follies of the night before can be erased. The day to come not yet imagined.

"Vivian."

A tall man bends and kisses her ear. "Dickie Peets," she says.

"You just got here?" he asks.

"They're being very rude about my room," she says.

An exotic combination of lime and coconut lifts from Dickie's skin. He holds a skimmer like a plate under his arm. Beyond him, through large double doors, the dining room is already set for lunch. Starched linen, polished silver, white crockery. It hasn't changed a whit in twenty years, Vivian thinks. Dickie draws a silver case from the pocket of his linen jacket and offers her a cigarette.

"Who's here?" she asks.

"John Sevens," he says. "And Sylvia." Dickie thinks a minute. "That makes a tennis party. You on?"

"I've got to unpack," she says.

"You're looking very well," he says.

"Since when have you had specs?" she asks.

"Got them around Christmas. Blind as a bat, actually. Smashed my car."

"Not the Freschetti."

"The Isotta Fraschini. 'Fraid so."

"How awful," Vivian says. "Were you hurt?"

"A knee thing," Dickie says with perfect nonchalance. "Spent most of the winter in Havana, recuperating. You should try it. Havana, I mean."

"I'm not very good on boats."

"Fly," he says. "Only forty-three hours from Boston—train and plane."

"Really."

"Jai alai. The casino. Rooftop dancing. Just your thing, Viv."

She takes a long pull on her cigarette. Is he mocking her?

"How long are you here for?" he asks.

"The usual. Until September. How about you?"

"Bought a house here," he says.

"You're not serious," Vivian says, aware of the desk clerk needing her attention. She deliberately ignores him. "Where?"

"The coast road. The Cote place. Had to fix it up and so forth. They're nearly finished, though. I've got rooms here in the meantime," Dickie says, stubbing his cigarette out in the glass ashtray on the reception desk.

"Miss Burton?" says the desk clerk.

"Got the makings of a sidecar in my room if you want a cocktail before lunch," Dickie says.

Vivian thinks of icy drops of water sliding down the outside of an aluminum cocktail shaker.

"Make it very, very cold," she says.

Vivian walks through pale azure hallways to her rooms. The porter opens the door and stands aside to let her pass, and as soon as Vivian enters her own suite, she feels the bristle leave her skin. Her duster slides from her shoulders, and she tosses it over the back of a chair. She unpins her hat and pats her hair. She takes in the delicate white light through the gauzy curtains floating in an east window, the old walnut desk with the pigeonholes in which she will put her invitations and her writing papers, and the mauve settee with the rose silk throw. She peers into the mirror. Her penny-colored hair has risen up around her head like a copper nimbus. Her eyebrows need plucking, and her lipstick has worn off. Dickie looked both smug and happy. He must have a girl, she thinks.

She tips the porter, and he leaves her suite. She walks into the bedroom, sits on the bed, and slips off her shoes. She lies back on the lilac sateen coverlet. The air and the light are worth the filthy train ride from Boston, she decides. She pictures the empty house she left this morning in Boston, the dark brick town house overlooking the Public Garden. Her father had sailed for Italy with his new wife just the day before, and Vivian, unable to stand the empty rooms, decided to travel up to the hotel early. There are friends she might have visited—Tilly Hatch in Lenox, Bobby Kellogg on Nantucket, Lester Simms in Banff—but she wasn't in the mood to be a houseguest so early in the season.

She stares at the pattern on the tin ceiling. *Oh, I'm going to be so bored,* she thinks.

She gets off the bed and opens a suitcase. The porter has laid her luggage out on trunk stands all against the walls. She removes her perfumes and her atomizers and sets them on the bureau. She puts her silk stockings and her lingerie in the top drawer and hangs her Maggy Rouff evening gown in the closet. She glances at her watch. Dickie Peets said a sidecar. A sidecar might be just the ticket.

Alice Willard

Dear Honora,

I still have the ironing to do, you know how Harold likes his sheets, but I will try to write a line or two so that you won't think we have already forgotten you here at home. After you left today, I picked the first of the peas, it is so unusual to have peas before the Fourth of July, and I see that the beans are coming along nicely too. It looks as though this will be a good year for the garden.

How is the house? How are you and Sexton? He is a fine man and will make you a good husband I think and Harold says the man has gumption. We are all right here. Except that Harold had a coughing fit and I worry for him, but at least it is summer. As you know, he does poorly in winter. I know that it is always warmer by the sea in winter, so I guess we will have to envy you this year.

The reason for my letter is that Harold and I have been wondering if you and Sexton will come to visit on Labor Day weekend. I know you have just left, but it is never too early to plan. Maybe you and Sexton could manage four or five days here in Taft. I am hoping I can persuade Charles and his wife and baby to come from Syracuse as we have never met Evelyn or Baby Emma. Charles says Emma is very pretty. So our little family grows again. One grandchild and another on the way. Though Phillip's letter was very sad as May has discovered a lump on her breast and has to have it (the breast) removed. It is probably already gone. I didn't want to mention this to you just before your wedding day even though I got the letter two weeks ago. It was some time before May told anyone and now the doctor says he can't promise her a cure. Phillip begged me in the letter to go over to Estelle's house to call him on the telephone. I won't go into details about that conversation except to say that it has been some time since I have heard a man that upset. Anyway, I thought you should know, and I hope you don't mind that I waited until after the wedding to tell you.

But enough of unhappy news. We want to hear that you are well and are settling in fine. There were some aspects of married life I might have discussed with you, and I have been feeling poorly I didn't do that, but marriage is its own teacher I have always thought and I trust Sexton Beecher is a gentle man.

It was a lovely wedding and you looked very pretty. As soon as you mail the suit to me, I will take it back to Bette's. You have another two weeks, so there is no hurry. Let me know if you decide to keep it after all. As I said, you might like it for sentimental reasons.

I just realized that I have never had occasion to write you a letter since you have never gone away from home, which explains why this feels a little strange.

Write and tell us about Labor Day as Harold and I would like something to look forward to.

Love,
Mother

McDermott

"You heard about Gastonia," Ross says.

Ross's voice is hard to hear in the din. McDermott watches his mouth. "I read about it," he says.

The speak is crowded with the day shift—warp twisters and slasher tenders and mule spinners and carders—all drinking away their pay packets. Mahon makes the drink in Exeter, brings it over in a bread truck to the speak. The first whiskey always hurts McDermott's stomach, and he's pretty sure he has an ulcer. The noise in the mill has ruined his hearing, ruined his nerves. Lay off the drink, the mill doctor said, and gave him a bottle of white pills to take. Sometimes McDermott shits blood.

"They're on trial now," Ross says.

"So I hear."

"They'll get off."

Ross has bad teeth, horrible to look at, but McDermott has to watch his mouth in order to understand him.

"The police chief was killed," McDermott says.

"Lackey for the bosses," Ross says, and spits on the floor.

"You think it'll happen here?" McDermott asks.

"I know it will happen here," Ross says.

Though McDermott is just twenty, already he is a loom fixer. He reports only to the second hand. He has been in the mills since he was twelve, since the day his father pissed off. Every day except Sundays, the din rises up around him and makes a hollow sucking sound in his ears, as if he had dived into the ocean and was trying to come up for air. He repairs broken looms and checks others to make sure the cloth is weaving properly. He is supposed to report weavers who aren't doing their jobs, but he hardly ever does. In return, any weaver in McDermott's section tries hard to keep up. McDermott is careful not to take advantage of this goodwill or to take credit for a job another has done. A boastful loom fixer, he has seen, never lasts too long.

Still, the work is difficult and McDermott, like almost everyone in the mill, hates his job. Especially since the speed-up. For three months now, the bosses have ordered the machines to go at a faster speed. If the machines produce more cloth for the same amount of wages, the argument goes, then the northern mills might be able to compete with the southern mills that are taking away all the business. Already the Hookset Mill has closed because of lost business. The Dracut Mill has announced a 10 percent pay cut.

All his life, McDermott has lived in company housing, eight kids in a two-bedroom apartment. The babies, when they came, slept in bureau drawers. When he was thirteen and got his growth, he slept on three chairs in the kitchen. When his father left the family without a note or a word, his mother moved into a cot in the kitchen to let the three older girls, who needed privacy then, have the double bed in her bedroom. Now his mother is gone—a stroke, the mill doctor said—and Eileen, who is nineteen, is in charge. McDermott moved into the men's boardinghouse nearby, but he gives Eileen half his pay packet. He brings food when he can and eats with Eileen and his brothers and other sisters two or three times a week, mainly to keep the boys, who are a handful, in line.

McDermott, like everyone else in the mill, second hands and overseers alike, lives for the breaks. Even in December and January, when the weather is raw and freezing, McDermott likes to go outside during the ten minutes the workers are allowed in the afternoon. He once discovered a trapdoor that leads onto the roof, and as soon as the horn sounds, he pretends to head for the lavatory and instead takes a quick turn near the back stairs. On the roof he smokes a cigarette and looks over to the falls because he needs the quiet like some men need drink. He can see across the rooftops of the mill housing—every brick building precisely the same: four floors, one chimney, three dormers on each top floor—to the railroad bridge that crosses the river. On good days, he can see all the way to the ocean, a thin, hazy blue line on the horizon. When the weather is poor—when there is a blizzard or it is raining so hard he can't open his eyes—McDermott stands in the shelter of the air shaft, shivering, just so he can see the sky.

There isn't a day that goes by that McDermott doesn't think of taking off like his father did. He imagines his father in Iowa or Saskatchewan, working a combine in an enormous field, stopping every now and then to watch the wind make waves in the wheat and the clouds point still farther west—not a building or a chimney stack or a rickety wooden fire escape in sight. But then, as if it were a daily ritual he needed to observe, McDermott will think about Eileen and about his younger brothers who are a handful. He is determined to keep Eamon and Michael out of the mills. It's no place for a man, never mind for a boy. All you have to do is look at the faces around you when you go back in from the break—faces waxy with exhaustion or resignation or grim determination. The women's faces are the worst. When the men get off work, they head for a meal or a drink. The women go home to hungry children and cramped apartments that need tending. Some of the women weavers have admitted to McDermott that they count to themselves on the looms to pass the time—to eight, say, repeatedly; or to four thousand and eighty. They swear it makes the clock move faster. McDermott thinks about entire lives spent counting simply to make the days go faster, and that fact, out of all the miserable facts he knows about mill life, seems to him the saddest one of all.

"There's a meeting," Ross says.

"What about?" McDermott asks.

"The speed-up."

"What about it?"

"It's killing the men," Ross says. "No one can keep up. Everyone is getting docked. They can't feed their families."

Left unmentioned is the money the men in the speak are pissing away on whiskey. McDermott doesn't want a family of his own. Since the speed-up, the men are taking their sons and daughters out of school and putting them in the mills. What's the point, McDermott wants to know, of having children at all?

"We want the elimination of piecework," Ross says, ticking off the demands on his fingers. "We want the clock system out. We want a standard wage scale. Forty hours, five days a week, minimum of twenty dollars a week. We want decent housing. We want a reduction of rent and light charges."

"You'll never get it," McDermott says.

"We won't if we don't demand it," Ross says.

"Where's the meeting?"

"Nadeau's. Make sure you're not followed. Last time, Hurd stood outside and made a list of everyone going in."

"I don't know," McDermott says. He means he doesn't know if he will go to the meeting. He means he doesn't know if he wants to get involved. He sucks on one of the white tablets the mill quack gave him. The English girl is sitting on a stool.

"They're starving in Gastonia," McDermott says.

"You get relief," Ross says. "There's organizations that send relief."

"Communists," McDermott says.

"It's the unions," Ross insists. "It has nothing to do with Communists."

"If we starve, it'll be the Communists who'll feed us. Tell me there weren't Communists in Gastonia."

Ross downs his shot, signals for another. "They're sending someone named Mironson from the Trade Workers Union," he says. "They want rolling strikes like they had in the south. Break the backs of the mills in New England."

"Great," McDermott says. "Then none of us will have jobs."

Honora

Beside her, Sexton is snoring, his arms thrown up against his pillow as if he'd just been robbed. She slips out from under the blanket, pulling the sides of her blouse together. When she stands, Sexton, still sleeping, rolls away from her. The smell of his skin is on her neck and arms. She looks for blood and finds a smear on the sheet, random spots on her slip. Not as much as she'd been led to believe. *A massacre,* she remembers Ruth Shaw saying at McNiven's, though Ruth was given to exaggeration. Her mother never mentioned it, never said a word.

She crosses the room, the floorboards cool on the soles of her feet. She snatches up the picnic basket and her suitcase and Sexton's coat. The latch makes a soft click as she closes the bedroom door.

She finds a towel in her suitcase and washes herself at the sink in the bathroom. She puts on a nightgown, draping the blouse and slip and brassiere over the lip of the tub. She slides her arms into the brown overcoat, pushing the long sleeves up to free her hands. If she doesn't eat something, she thinks, she will die. She walks into an empty room, sits on the floor, opens the picnic basket, and looks inside. She puts the heels of her hands to her eyes.

She is on the other side of something now, removed forever from who she was only yesterday. Removed from her mother's home. She thinks of her mother rising that morning with only Harold in the house, Harold who wakes up every day coughing.

In the basket, carefully arranged, are bowls of potato salad and coleslaw, a wax packet of fried chicken, a loaf of wheat bread, a jar of wild strawberry preserves, two bottles of Moxie, and two small peach pies, individually wrapped. In a tissue packet, she finds a tablecloth, hand embroidered with her new initials, HWB, Honora Willard Beecher. She holds it to her face, then sets it down on top of the basket. She removes a pie with fluted edges.

As she eats, she walks through the house, taking huge ravenous bites, careful not to get any on Sexton's coat. The sunlight pushes at the frosted windows and makes her want to be outside. She runs lightly down the center stairway, the coat skimming the broad steps. In the hallway, she is momentarily disoriented, but then she finds a passageway to the front of the house. She opens the door.

She has to put a hand up to ward off the light. It is diffuse but intense. The room is long, with floor-to-ceiling windows facing east. Six pairs, she counts, her eyes adjusting to the glare, the world beyond the salt-encrusted windows a temporary mystery. The room is empty save for one item, a grand piano in a corner. Honora stands at the keyboard and picks out a tune, the notes muffled, as if small puffs of air prevented the hammers from striking the strings. One key doesn't sound at all. Her fingers are sticky from the pie, and she licks them.

She walks to a window, trying to see out the margins, but the view is slivered and unrewarding. She tries the front door and, surprisingly, it gives. She steps out onto the porch.

And, my God, there it is. The ocean. The sun seemingly rising from its surface even as she watches. The color of the water a splintery white, too painful to look at for any length of time. The dune grass is overgrown with sweet pea and beach roses and something else she cannot name. To the south is a long crescent of sand with intricate lacings of seaweed, and to the north a scarred bit of earth, dotted with new growth, a darkened slab in its center. She makes her way to the porch railing, its wood long weathered, rotted out in places. Beyond the front steps is a boardwalk that leads to a wooden deck overlooking the water.

She walks the length of the boardwalk, the wood weathered dove gray. All along the beach's span, there are cottages and one hotel. She draws the coat around her for warmth, letting her hands slide up into the sleeves. She steps off the deck onto the sand.

"Honora."

She turns. Sexton's face is sideways in

the slit of a second-floor window, stuck open from the damp.

"Come back to bed."

His face leaves the window and then immediately reappears.

"And bring the picnic."

The shout startles a flock of seagulls. They spread out in a fan pattern from the roof of the house and then swoop down low and skim the dune grass. In the wet sand by her foot, a bit of color catches her eye. She picks it up and studies it. The glass is green, pale and cloudy, the color of lime juice that has been squeezed into a glass. The edges of the shard are weathered and smooth and do not hurt at all. She brushes the sand off and presses the sea glass into her palm, keeping it for luck. She thinks that she and Sexton might need the luck.

Vivian

Razors of light flicker behind the shades at the windows. A stale metallic taste is in her mouth, and her temples are caught in a vise. Still the knocking continues.

"Go away," Vivian calls faintly from the bed.

She lifts her head from the pillow and a wave of nausea ripples to the back of her throat. She has no memory of returning to her room last night, or was it actually this morning? She *does* remember seeing the ugly scissored scar on Dickie's knee, and then, later, finding him in the bathroom, naked, dozing on the black and white tiles in a fetal position. And, oh God, did she really sleep with the man?

The images come with the jerking motions of a Movietone newsreel: emerging from Dickie's room at eight o'clock in the evening and changing into the rose opaline while Dickie sat at the end of her bed, smoking and recounting a story about a woman who drowned in the Hotel Plaza rooftop pool in Havana; Sylvia crying at dinner, she was that drunk, and John saying to her, in his affected drawl, *You're stinking;* walking barefoot into the hotel from the beach, her wet feet covered with sand, while the weasely Franco desk clerk pretended not to notice her. Under the covers, Vivian moves her legs and notes with dismay that her underwear is missing.

She sits up sideways from the bed, not straightening her neck until she is certain she won't be sick. She will have to pretend it didn't happen at all. Dickie will do that for her; he is good at dissembling. If she encounters him today, she will simply suggest she was elsewhere and see if he takes the hint and runs with it. Is it too much to hope that he has already moved into his new house?

She studies the skirt of the rose opaline with its hundreds of new small wrinkles, tributaries of streams surrounding the lake of a stain. When did she spill the highball? At dinner with John and Sylvia?

There is one shoe beside the bed. She has no idea where the other is. She thinks briefly of packing, of leaving the hotel altogether, but where exactly would she go? Her head hurts terribly, and the sun threatens behind the shades.

Sexton

"I'm going to get supplies," he says, and leaves the house as if he's done it all his life.

His breath is high and tight inside his chest, and he wants, ridiculously, to shout. It isn't the sudden east wind, against which he raises the collar of his coat. No, he feels like a kid again, a kid with a new bike, riding it hard over a bump, soaring, getting air under the wheels. He's left Honora sleeping on the bed, her hair mussed all around her face, the flawless white skin of her back begging to be touched. Hard to walk away from.

He slides into the driver's seat of the Buick, more gray than blue now with road dust. He will have to buy a bucket, give the car a wash, maybe Simoniz it afterward. He puts the clutch in and adjusts the power lever. He stabs the starter button on the floor with his foot and feels the familiar lurch and purr. He picks up a crumpled napkin and tosses it out the window. He likes to keep the Buick tidy.

The only stores he's seen are in the mill town they drove through the day before. He remembers a five-and-dime where he could get cleaning supplies, a market where he could buy food. And he ought to get gas there as well, he thinks, at the Texaco station.

But first he wants to check out the coast road. An open road always tempting, promising surprises, the possibility of luck. It's why he is a traveling salesman, why he chucked it all back home. Nothing better than to find an unfamiliar road on the map, see where it takes him. He got the Claremont Bank account that way, and the Mutual Life account in Andover. It's how he found Honora, for that matter—that bit about the courthouse true only after he had met her.

He looks at the fuel gauge. A quarter of a tank, more than enough for a spin.

Sand drifts across the cracked pavement like blown snow, but the Buick handles well, the weight of the typewriters in the backseat giving it welcome ballast. He likes the products that he sells, understands their value and knows that he can convince almost anyone of their necessity. But he likes the typewriters as objects even more: the enameled keys with their silver rings, the gold engraving on the black casing, the satisfying thunk of the carriage return. The Fosdick is a good and serviceable machine, heavy as a son of a bitch.

Christ, he thought the house would have some furniture: a table, a couple of chairs, a bed. He and Honora would have brought furniture with them if they had known, and surely Honora's mother would have given them some household bits and pieces, just to get them started. Sexton has eighty dollars saved from his commissions—a fat one just last week, though he had to shave off a bit for the earrings. He thinks about Honora's face when she saw the earrings in his hands. Smiling, but still there was that solemn thing in her eyes, taking in the ritual. He couldn't remember exactly what old Harold had said and so he'd had to make it up as he'd gone along. Odd that bit about unlocking secrets, he thinks now. Where had that come from?

The coast road hugs the contours of the beach, leaving only the cottages between the Buick and the water. Beautiful they are, even boarded up before the season starts in July, as if their eyes and mouths were taped. Old dames facing the sea. The houses mute till someone comes and rips the tape off.

He turns a corner and skids a bit on the sandy pavement.

Take it easy, he thinks.

The road is a ribbon now, threading through the beach on the right, a marsh on the left. A marsh and something else, he sees, as he pulls out from the shadow of a house. A tidal pool, maybe half a mile across, and at its entrance a feisty current tossing whitecaps against the banks of a narrow channel. There are boats anchored in the pool, half a dozen lobster boats and someone's yacht, its mast tilting wildly in the chop. A channel has been dredged.

He hadn't planned on getting married so soon. Jesus, he's only twenty-four. And for a while there he thought he might not ever get married, the thrill of the open road too deep inside his bones. But he knew, even that first day at the bank, with Honora behind the grille, that this might be something different, something worth staying put for. He will never forget the sight of Honora's hands, long fingered and slender and white, so white, slipping out beneath the grille, as if she were a nun and that was all she would allow him to see. The hands snagging his thoughts—practically the only thing that could take his mind off the car, the shine of the paint job a gleam across the front of his brain.

He looked up then at her face, the dark eyes blanketed with lashes. Her hair shingled back from her cheekbones. A beautiful jawline, almost masculine, and a long neck. She had on that day a low-waisted dress that was pinkish beige with complicated buttons along one side. He couldn't see her legs and he remembers wanting to. Wanting to know if the skin there was as perfect as the hands. Was that what made him go back that second time—driving from Portsmouth to Taft with a pressure inside his chest, trying out phrases all the way, finally relying, in the end, on that old salesman's trick: announcing the time of the appointment as if it had already been agreed to? I'll be outside at four, he said, knowing instinctively that she was not the type to tell him to buzz off. The nerve of him when he thinks about it. How had he known for sure she wasn't married? Of course—the hands. White and unadorned. Then afterward, before she got off work, scurrying for appointments at the courthouse in case she asked, casually, for a name.

The legs were as good as he'd hoped.

He comes to a slight hill and a fork, the road pulling away from the beach. He takes the left fork down to a wharf and a tiny village with a sprinkling of houses and shacks, a fish house near the end of the road. There's a stiff breeze from the east, blowing a flag straight out. Across the street, against a storefront, an old man is sitting in a rocking chair. There are signs in the window: Nehi and Za-Rex and Old Golds.

Sexton's coat, when he gets out of the car, billows out behind him. He crosses the street, holding his coat closed and his hat to his head. When he reaches the steps of the porch, the wind stops abruptly, as if someone had shut a door.

He lights a Lucky Strike and crumples the empty pack.

"Hello," he says to the man.

The old geezer is dressed in summer garb, a light suit, his legs spread wide, the trousers riding high over his ample belly. He has on a bow tie and a straw boater, and a medal is pinned to his lapel. Sexton can see the loop of the chain of his pocket watch but not the watch itself. Without the wind, Sexton realizes, it's pleasantly warm on the porch. He tosses the empty cigarette pack over the railing.

" 'Lo," the old man says. The one syllable without inflection. Welcoming or not, it is hard to say.

"Not a bad day," Sexton says.

"Not 'tall." The old man's hands, one holding a cane, the other a handkerchief, are dense with liver spots and moles. Sexton takes a deep pull on his cigarette. "East wind today," the old man says.

"Nice on the porch, though," Sexton says.

"That your car?"

"It's a Buick."

"A twenty-seven?"

"A twenty-six."

"How many miles on it?"

"About four thousand."

"Hope you got yourself a bargain." The New Hampshire accent, a deadpan lilt, is thick on the man's tongue.

"I think I did," Sexton says.

"What are you doing in these parts?"

"My wife and I have been asked to look after a house," Sexton says, the words *my wife* giving him a pleasant jolt.

"What house would that be?"

"It's at the end of the beach. Three stories high. White with black shutters. In pretty bad shape."

"That would be the old convent."

"Convent?" Sexton asks.

"Thirty-five, forty years ago now," the old man says. "The house used to be a convent. That salt air, it'll age a house before its time."

"The house is empty. We didn't expect that."

"Don't know why not. Been empty four years now."

"Guess I got some bad information," Sexton says.

"Guess you did." The old man starts to rise.

"Don't get up," Sexton says. "I'll just go inside and look around. Is the owner in there?"

"You're looking at him."

Sexton watches the tortuous unfolding of the old man's limbs.

"Name's Hess. Jack Hess."

"Sexton Beecher." The man's hand in his own is all bones—fragile bones, like those of a bird.

"Don't have much in the way of furniture," the old man says. "But if it's hardware you're looking for, I reckon I can help you some. We got staples and whatnot too."

Sexton holds the screen door while Jack Hess pulls himself into the store with a hand hooked around the doorjamb. His walk is stooped, and just looking at him makes Sexton want to arch his back.

It takes a moment for Sexton's eyes to adjust to the gloom after the bright light coming off the water. The store is a marvel of bins and boxes and tin trays and hooks holding all manner of hardware and food. Lightbulbs, brooms, doorknobs, boat winches, birdcages, enameled pots, fans, axes, knives, brushes of all kinds, paints and varnishes and oils, spools of string, cheese graters, meat grinders, jelly glasses, toilet plungers, ice skates (ice skates!), and even a wire chair held upside down on a hook. Despite the clutter, the store appears to be spotless, the wood floor varnished to a high sheen, the mahogany counter with its jars of screws and hinges and buttons seemingly clean enough to lick. Behind the register are tins of food. Raisins and flour and cereal. Coffee beans beside a grinder.

"Guess I'm set," Sexton says.

"Don't have it in here you probably don't need it."

"No, I probably don't."

"I got the one chair you can have for seventy-five cents."

"I saw that."

"I can fix you up with some wood crates you're desperate."

"We're desperate."

"What line a work you in?" The old man takes his position behind the counter, ready to fetch whatever Sexton might ask for.

"I'm a typewriter salesman."

"You don't say."

"That's right." Sexton steps outside to crush his cigarette with his foot.

"You go around in that car of yours and sell typewriters?" the old man asks when Sexton has come back through the screen door.

"I do."

"Don't reckon I have any use for a type-writer," the old man says, pronouncing the word as if it had four syllables.

"Don't reckon you do. Though one might be a help with the bills. And the orders."

"Easier just to write 'em down."

Sexton laughs.

"Who you sell 'em to?"

"Pretty girls," Sexton says.

The old man grins, revealing yellowed teeth.

"You want to go for a ride?" Sexton asks the man.

"In your Buick?"

"You could show me around."

"Don't want to keep you from your er-rands."

"I've got time."

"Don't want to keep you from your wife. She mind if you take your time?"

"Don't know," Sexton says. "I've only been married a day."

"Oh, Lord," the old man says, and takes a step toward the door.

Jack Hess sits with his legs splayed. Either his belly has simply grown too big or he has lost the use of the muscles in his thighs. "You should try the mills over to the Falls you want to get rid of them typewriters," he says.

"Your store do a good business?" Sexton asks.

"In the summer it does. Duller than a preacher's sermon in winter. That there's the Highland Hotel. They do a dandy rice pudding."

The Buick rounds a rocky point. To one side of the road is an inhospitable stretch of coastline; to the other are some of the largest houses Sexton has ever seen. He whistles appreciatively.

"More money than sense," Jack Hess says. "That one belongs to Gordon Hale. He owns one of the mills over to Ely Falls. That one there is George Walker's house. His grandfather started the Walker Hotel chain, don't you know. That one there, that's Alice Beam's house. Her father made his money in shipping. She'll stay on over the winter. About fifty of 'em do. You got heat?"

"I think so," Sexton says. "I hope so."

"Well, they had to for the home, didn't they?"

"The home?"

"Folks you're rentin' from, they didn't tell you much, did they?"

"Not much," Sexton says.

"There was a woman came here when she was a girl—oh, thirty years ago now—and she got herself involved with a doctor, and, well, that's a long story for another day, but she went away and then came back and started a home for other girls who had gotten themselves in the family way, don't you know. Marvelous enterprise too. Never a complaint from anyone on the beach, even though the place was full of what you would call high-spirited girls. Closed down four years ago."

Sexton pulls to the side of the road to let a beach wagon pass. "The home was a convent?"

"Years ago. French nuns from Quebec."

Beyond the wild growth of beach roses, the ocean spreads to the horizon. A deep twitchy blue with whitecaps. Sexton reaches for a new pack of Luckies from his pocket and expertly tears it open even as he drives. "You want one?" he asks Jack Hess.

The old man sighs and shakes his head. "Under doctor's orders now. Had to give it all up—this, that, and the other thing."

Sexton puts the cigarettes back in his pocket.

"My wife died in twenty-four," Hess says. "Haven't been the same since. I don't eat right, and I don't sleep right. A good marriage, Mr. Beecher, that's all you need in life. I envy you just startin' out. I do. Some fun to be had you keep your head on straight. And times is good now, aren't they? Boom times, so they say."

"We're trying to save up for a place of our own," Sexton says.

"What do you get for them typewriting machines of yours?"

"Depends. Sixty-five dollars for the Number Seven."

"And how much of that do you get to keep?"

"Eight percent, five dollars and twenty cents for the Seven."

"Gonna take you a while, Mr. Beecher."

Sexton smiles. "Of course we'll get a mortgage."

"Them banks," Hess says. "They whistle a good tune, but they're out to make money, pure and simple. It's no service they're offering. They're selling a product just like you are with them typewriters. Best not to forget that."

Sexton nods politely.

"Tell you something else," Hess says. "Don't take your boots off in a house you owe money on. Renting or caretaking, whatever you're doing now, that's different. You're saving up, and that's respectable."

Sexton nods again. These old duffers, he thinks. They can't catch up. Full of advice from another era.

"So that's my speech for today," Hess says. "Sometimes an old man, he just don't know when to shut up. You come back to the store now. We'll get you and that bride of yours all fixed up. She a good cook?"

Sexton shrugs. "I have no idea," he says.

Vivian

Vivian draws her baku as close to her head as it will go. The straw hat has a wide brim, but she wears her colored glasses anyway. She has managed two aspirin, which haven't so far made a dent in her headache. Lying on her bed earlier, she thought that what she really needed was fresh air. Bravely, she decided to make peace with the smug sunshine on the beach.

A waiter brings her a canvas chair and a striped umbrella, and she sits gingerly, each movement a painful jar. She should have eaten, she thinks. If the man comes back, she will order something sugary. Tea with sugar. Yes, that might be just the thing.

The tide is out, the beach flat for a good distance. The air is cool and moist, and if she shuts her eyes and sits perfectly still, the pain is almost bearable. What she should do, she knows, is dive into the ocean. It's the best cure for a hangover she's ever known. But to do that, she'd have to go back into the hotel and change into her bathing suit, and she doesn't have the necessary stamina. She can smell coconut oil, and around her there are voices, punctuated by children's squeals. On the porch, the pre-lunch crowd sips martinis behind the railing. Just the thought of a martini makes her put a hand to her stomach.

She opens her eyes a fraction and squints, and, oh God, there's Dickie Peets walking a dog at the shoreline, holding his shoes, getting his feet wet, his white flannels rolled. She bends as if to search for something she's dropped in the sand, hoping that he won't glance up and recognize her. She stays in that position until she thinks it is safe, even though it makes her head hurt.

"Viv?"

She sits up and shades her eyes with her hand. "Dickie," she says, pretending to be surprised.

"Didn't expect to see you up so early," he says. A small dog the color of the sand puts its paws on Vivian's skirt. Dickie lifts the dog away from her.

"Lovely morning," she says, ignoring Dickie's comment. "What kind of a dog is that?"

"A mutt, I think."

"It looks like a sheep. What's its name?"

"Don't know. Think I'll call him Sandy."

"How original," she says.

"It's not mine," he says.

"I didn't think so."

"Found it whimpering in the stairwell this morning."

Dickie looks remarkably fit, Vivian thinks, considering he kept pace with her, maybe even outdid her, last night. She remembers him lying naked, in a fetal position, on his bathroom floor. "I'm not terribly good company at the moment," she says.

"Nor am I, so I think we'll suit each other just fine."

Dickie sits on the sand, favoring the injured knee. He has on dark glasses too, and she can't see his eyes.

"I'm not sure I can carry on a conversation," Vivian says.

"Won't say a word," he says. Beside him, the dog is panting.

"I think he might need some water," Vivian says.

"He's fine," Dickie says. "I'll take him inside in a moment. You all right?"

"As well as can be expected," she says. She pauses and then she sighs. "God-awful, if you want to know the truth."

"Me too, if that's any consolation."

"Not much, but thank you." Vivian rubs a small circle in her forehead. The surf looks even more inviting now. Perhaps she should excuse herself and get her suit.

"We did tie one on," Dickie says.

"So we did," she says. "I don't want to think about it."

"Found your shoe," he says. "In the corridor outside my room."

She puts a hand to her temple. "Mail it to me," she says.

"I gather they had to carry Sylvia to her room."

"Really? What was all that crying about at dinner, anyway?" The ocean smells like "beach" today, she reflects. It's a certain smell of sea and sand and suntan oil.

"John's got a girlfriend," Dickie says. "He's deliberately ignoring Sylvia. Finally had to tell him to cut it out. Man's sadistic, if you want my opinion."

"Funny, I don't remember that part," Vivian says. The surf, though it pounds, provides a comforting sound. Gulls, encouraged by a hapless child who is feeding them, swoop low over the sand.

"Daresay there are whole conversations you don't remember," Dickie says.

"You insolent shit," Vivian says lightly.

"I am rather."

Vivian smooths the skirt of her white linen dress. She puts her hands to her eyes. "What are we doing, Dickie?"

"Don't know, Viv. What are we doing?"

"We're behaving terribly. And we've only been here a day."

"Isn't that the point? To behave terribly? In the summer, I mean?"

"There has to be something better," she says.

"Like what?"

"You have no imagination."

"Possibly not."

"Something that's not such a waste. Not so self-indulgent."

"We're who everyone wants to be, Viv."

"How sad," she says, glancing out at the

haze at the horizon. She loves diffuse light—light in which objects have no edges.

"Unbearably sad, really," Dickie says. "You fancy a martini? Hair of the dog and all that?"

She digs her toes into the sand. "Go away."

"Tea with ice?"

She shrugs. Dickie looks around for the waiter, catches his attention, and orders two iced teas. "About last night," he begins.

Vivian puts a hand up. This is a conversation she doesn't want to have. "Sorry to disappoint you, Dickie, but you're not the first."

He fingers a shell and begins to use it to scoop the sand between his legs. "Didn't think so," he says quietly.

"Nor the eighth either, if you want to know."

He seems mildly surprised. "As bad as all that?"

"I'm afraid so," she says.

"How come, Viv?"

She stretches her bare legs out and burrows her feet into the sand. "I'm twenty-eight. Twenty-nine in September. I've missed my chance."

"Poppycock."

"Besides," she says, "I don't believe in marriage."

"Really not?"

"Name me a good one."

He thinks a moment. "Jean and Eddie?"

"She's a simp. Doesn't count."

Dickie ponders her question.

"See?" Vivian says.

"Brain's not up to par this morning," Dickie says. "You've had proposals, surely."

"Oh God, yes," Vivian says. And it's true. She's had dozens. Well, not dozens. Maybe six or seven. Two of them serious.

"You come across as hard-boiled," Dickie says, "but I'm not sure you are."

"Count on it," she says.

"I have a girl," he announces suddenly. "Actually, I'm engaged. To be married."

A small jolt runs the length of Vivian's spine, and she sits slightly forward. Dickie engaged? She monitors the shock. She ought to be upset. Furious, really. Should she act furious? But, oddly, Dickie's announcement feels good, like diving into the ocean does. Painful at first and then refreshing.

She lowers her dark glasses and peers at the man beside her. “A small detail you forgot to mention yesterday afternoon, perhaps?” she asks.

Dickie looks away.

“I hope she’s liberal minded,” Vivian adds. “Who is she?”

“Someone I met in Havana,” Dickie says.

Vivian registers a small ping of jealousy and then a larger one of intrigue. Anyone in Havana is bound to be interesting. You can’t go to Havana and not be interesting. She lays her head against the canvas back of the chair, as if she might doze off.

“Not sure I love her, though,” Dickie says. “That’s the thing.”

“Don’t whine,” Vivian says. “I can’t stand a man who whines.”

Dickie throws the shell toward the water. “Just trying to explain about last night,” he says.

“Not loving someone is no excuse for being disloyal.”

“You believe in that, do you? Loyalty and vows and so forth?”

“Not sure,” she says.

“It was just that you looked so . . .

so . . . I don't know . . . *smart* standing there at the reception desk," he says. "No one's as smart as you, Viv."

"Don't be smarmy. It's beneath you."

"But it's true," he says.

She glances over at Dickie's shins, long and bare and sandy. A waiter appears with two glasses of iced tea with lemon pinwheels on their rims. "I hope you're not falling in love with me," she says, sitting up. She takes her glass and sips.

"Don't think so," Dickie says honestly. Too honestly, Vivian thinks. "What's your story, Viv?"

"How do you mean?"

"Rumor is that your mother went off with another man. A French industrialist or something."

"A contradiction in terms," Vivian says. "But yes. She did. When I was eight."

"Poor Viv."

"I hardly knew her, so don't feel sorry for me."

"Never feel sorry for you, Viv. You're probably the last person I'd feel sorry for. I'd probably feel sorry for myself before you." Dickie puts his glass in the hole he's dug in the sand so the dog can drink from it.

"When are you getting married?" she asks.

"At Christmas."

"I'll send you a present," she says. She thinks a minute. "A nice glass lamp."

"Viv . . ."

"I'm quite serious," she says. "I know where I can get some terrific glass lamps."

"Want some lunch?" he asks.

"What's on the menu?"

"Haddock, I think," he says. "And strawberry shortcake."

Vivian shakes her head.

"I'm sure we could get some sandwiches," Dickie says.

"Cucumber sandwiches?" she asks. She pictures a cold cucumber sandwich.

"Your arms are getting pink," he says.

She slouches back down into her canvas chair, and for a moment her head swims. "Yes, I do need something to eat," she says.

Dickie stands and brushes off his trousers. He takes her hand, and she lets him help her up. She rests her forehead on his chest. "What are we doing, Dickie Peets?"

"I don't know, Viv," he says. "I just don't know."

Alphonse

Alphonse sits on the sand in his short pants and watches the dark-haired woman and the man lying on a blanket on the beach, though he has to turn his eyes away when the woman lowers the straps of her brown bathing suit over her shoulders. He digs his feet into the sand and buries them. He's sweating so much that his skin is slick.

He watches the woman fix her straps and stand up and begin to walk to the water, slowly at first and then faster, so that when she gets to the water's edge she is almost running. She stops and puts one foot in the water and takes it out immediately. The man calls out *Honora,* and the woman puts her arms out wide for balance and high-steps above the waves and then dives into the ocean. The cold is such a shock that she immediately stands up and hollers simply because she has to. The man runs to the water's edge and dives in and swims toward the woman underwater. Alphonse wishes he knew how to swim and he tries to imagine what it feels like to hold your breath and plunge into the water. Do you close your eyes or do you look for fish?

The woman stands a moment, but a wave hits her and her knees buckle. She rubs her eyes and then begins to laugh. She laughs like his mother does sometimes when she's on the verge of crying. Hysterically, the notes of the laugh rising into the air and then floating away. A wave carries the woman into shore, bumping her along the sand, and then begins to pull her out again. Alphonse pretends that the woman is drowning and that he will have to rescue her.

The woman digs her fingers and knees into the sand and holds on even though the ocean tries to pull her out. She crawls to the waterline. She turns and sits on the sand with her knees drawn up and her arms wrapped around them. Her dark wavy hair is straight now from the water and lies flat to her head like a cap. The boy watches the man point his body toward the woman and throw himself onto a cresting wave. He slices through the water like a shark.

Honora

After their swim, Sexton washes the salt from the first-floor windows while Honora scrubs the kitchen cupboards. She gives him a broom with a cloth tied over it, and he sweeps the cobwebs away. As she bleaches the mildew from the walls, he uses a chisel to open the swollen windows. She rinses the grit from the radiators, and he rakes up coal that has fallen onto the cellar floor. She lays the tablecloth her mother made for her over an assembly of wooden crates and puts the mismatched plates and flatware Sexton bought at the local store on its surface. She arranges beach roses in a glass, and she and Sexton share the one remaining glass for drinking. For supper, they have tinned pork-and-beans and brown bread and Indian pudding.

In the days that follow, Sexton constructs a platform bed on which they lay the mattress. They use wooden crates for bedside tables, and Honora makes curtains from the fabric she found in the carton at the foot of the stairs. Sexton removes peeling strips of wallpaper, and Honora polishes an abandoned set of andirons.

Each evening, after they have done their chores, Sexton and Honora take their baths. Honora likes to bathe alone, but Sexton says he prefers company. He bends slightly forward, and Honora soaps his neck and shoulders and spine. As she washes him, she thinks about how fate contrived to have Sexton Beecher open a map and select a route and drive to Taft, New Hampshire, and walk into a bank and find Honora Willard on the other side of the grille. What if it had been her lunch break? she wonders. What if he'd seen the sign for Webster and taken it instead? What if he'd gotten waylaid in Manchester? What if his tire had gone flat?

One evening, after Sexton and Honora have bathed and eaten, they go for a walk along the beach. The sun, just about to set, lights up the cottages and the water with a rosy hue. The surf at the waterline is pink. Honora stops and bends to pick up a piece of pale blue glass. She rubs her fingers along the edges, which are smooth. The glass is cloudy, as though a fog were trapped within the weathered shard.

"What's that?" Sexton asks.

"It's glass," she says. "But not sharp. Here. Feel it."

Despite his bath, Sexton's fingers still have white paint in the creases. He holds it up to the light. "It's being in the ocean gives it that effect," he says. He hands the shard back to her. "The color's nice," he says.

"Where do you suppose it came from?"

"It's trash," he says. "It's garbage. Other people's garbage."

"Really?" she says. "I think it's kind of beautiful."

"I have to go back to work," Sexton says early in July.

Honora has known all along that this will

happen, but still, the announcement takes her by surprise. "So soon?" she asks.

"Someone's got to make a living."

This is said genially, without arrogance or irritation. Honora has worked, at the courthouse and then the bank, since she was fifteen, but there has been no talk of her taking a job. It is assumed by both of them that she will stay behind and make a home. There is enough work to occupy any woman for months.

"I could go with you," Honora says.

"It's against company policy," Sexton says. "They would fire me."

They are sitting at the kitchen table, having just eaten a turkey loaf and an onion pie. For practical reasons, she has replaced the embroidered tablecloth with a rectangle of blue-checked oilcloth bought at Jack Hess's store.

"How will this work?" she asks.

"I'll give you money," he says.

She glances at the headlines of the newspaper beside his plate. *CELEBRATION OF FOURTH COSTS 148 LIVES.* She turns the newspaper around so that she can read the article. There is a grid next to the report. Seven people died from fireworks, seventy-one in automobile accidents, and seventy drowned.

"How much do we have?" she asks.

He looks up and thinks a minute. "Eighty dollars," he says.

She reaches across the makeshift table and puts a hand on his forearm. "Just thinking about having you gone, I need to touch you," she says, surprising both of them.

His skin is warm through his shirt. Already, she has washed and ironed the shirt several times. By her count, he has six dress shirts, two work shirts, two suits, one pair of work pants (stained now with paint), and a navy sweater that has pilled.

The touch seems to move him. "I could take you with me," he says. She watches him ponder the idea as if it were his, as if he had just thought it up. "You could be my assistant. You know how to type, don't you?"

"I had to learn for my job at the courthouse."

"You could sit down at the machine and demonstrate," he says, musing. "No one could resist those hands." He thinks a minute. "I certainly didn't," he says.

"You didn't?"

"The day I met you. When I walked into the bank. It was your hands I noticed first. Under the grille."

As if to prove the truth of this assertion, he takes her hand and holds it above his empty plate. Her skin is only slightly roughened from the laundry soap. "You could use some Jergens," he says.

Sexton likes to say he covers the three P's—Portland, Portsmouth, and Providence—and everything in between. He shows her on the map exactly where they will go, and she traces the route with her finger. From Ely, they will drive to Portsmouth, then travel out Route 4 to Dover and to South Berwick and to Sanford. From there, they will take the 111 to Saco and then stay on Route 1 all the way to Portland. On the return south, they will head west by way of Hollis Center and Shapleigh and swing by Nashua and Lowell and Worcester. They'll go to Boston and to Woonsocket and to Pawtucket and finally to Providence. After that, they'll see.

"You can keep me in clean shirts," he says.

"Where will we stay?"

"Cabins."

Honora knows all about cabins. The one-room buildings with counters for kitchens and communal bathrooms out back are popular destinations with tourists visiting the lakes near Taft.

Still, though, it's an adventure.

Sexton passes her off as Miss Willard, his assistant. She wears her butter yellow wedding suit and removes her ring. In a routine that takes shape as the days unfold, she shakes the client's hand and very slowly draws off her gloves, finger by finger. She sits in front of the typewriter and feels the tiny ovals with their silver rings. She can type nearly as fast as Sexton can speak, and her hands are a blur over the keys. Her husband keeps up a running sales pitch with the customer, and when he is done, Honora offers up the beautifully typed page like a magician pulling a rabbit out of a hat. She will have typed a verbatim transcript of the conversation that has just taken place.

A thing worth having is worth having now, she will have typed.

The sooner you get it, the sooner it will start earning you money, Sexton will have said.

Putting it off is like paying more for it.

Decide now, when it will cost you the least.

Honora watches the customer's face begin to work its way toward a purchase. No client fails to be impressed by the transcript.

"Which carriage would you prefer?" Sexton asks. "The wide or the narrow? Which stand do you think would be best—the high or the low?"

The customer chews the inside of his cheek, all the while watching Honora's flying hands.

"Would you prefer to take a discount?" Sexton asks. "Or divide the amount into four monthly installments?"

Perhaps thinking about the uses of dictation for himself, or a pretty assistant of his own, the client is silent for a moment.

"This is a description of what you want," Sexton says, moving in for the kill. "May I take your order now?"

Sometimes, however, a customer is recalcitrant. “Yes, but . . . ,” the customer says.

“That’s the very reason why . . . ,” Sexton counters.

“I’m not sure about . . . ,” the client adds, waffling.

“I’m coming to that,” Sexton says. And then, with precisely calibrated insistence, Sexton asks, “What’s the real reason for hesitating?”

As soon as the client puts pen to paper, Honora rises and slips her gloves back on. The most important part of a sale, Sexton has impressed upon her, is to get out of the room once the deal has been made. Nothing is to be gained by lingering. The customer might change his mind.

Occasionally, Honora worries about Sexton’s sales pitch. Is it true, for example, that a thing worth having is worth having now? That the sooner one buys a typewriter, the sooner it will start earning money? It seems to her that there might be a flaw in this logic, that it might not be absolutely accurate that putting a purchase off is like paying more for it.

She worries too about the slow drawing off of the gloves and the absence of her wedding ring. When she and Sexton thought up the routine, it was fun and frivolous, a lark that made them laugh. But by the third or fourth time they perform it, the gestures seem to have grown more serious, and Honora feels uneasy. There is the undeniable implication that Miss Willard—or the *idea* of Miss Willard—might go with the typewriter.

On their first road trip, Sexton sells twenty-three machines for a total sales commission of more than $135. It seems to both of them a fortune. In the cabins, in the afternoons, with the smell of mildew in the blankets, Sexton and Honora make love to the sound of the occasional car passing by on Route 4 or 111. The beds sag in the middle, the pillows are as thin as quilts, and when they are finished, they have to sleep squashed against each other because the beds are so narrow.

"You're very long," Sexton says to her one afternoon.

Honora feels his breath at the tip of her ear. Her nightgown is rucked up and down so that it seems that only a flimsy bit of cloth covers her stomach. When she shifts position even a little, fluid spills from her body and onto the sheets. She is awed by the intimacy, something her mother, even if she had wanted to, could not have told her about.

Sexton

"They say that Bill Stultz was drunk when his plane crashed," Rowley says. "You ever been up, Mr. Beecher?"

Sexton catches a whiff of whiskey breath across the bank president's desk. It isn't even eleven in the morning. Kenneth Rowley is youngish for a bank president—thirty-eight, maybe forty. He must have inherited a job he didn't want, Sexton decides, letting his eyes slide around the room: mahogany-paneled walls, window-sills so high he could rest his chin on them, an oddly immaculate desk.

"No, I haven't," Sexton says. "But I certainly would like to."

Actually, Sexton isn't sure if this is true. He likes adventure well enough, and the open road more than most, but what exactly keeps the plane aloft? he has always wanted to know.

A secretary of indeterminate age enters the room carrying two tall glasses of iced coffee on a silver tray. She sets the tray down, smooths the skirt of her summer-weight tweed suit, and eyes Sexton. Miss Alexander, her name is, if memory serves. Sexton winks at her as she leaves.

"Cream?" Rowley asks Sexton.

"Yes, please."

"Bizarre the way they're all going for a record of some sort," Rowley says. "Portsmouth to Rome, I hear now."

Sexton watches the ivory liquid swirl through the coffee and wonders when he should begin his pitch.

"What are you driving?" Rowley asks, stirring the cream. He slides a glass on a coaster across the desk toward Sexton.

"A Buick," Sexton says. "A twenty-six."

"Like it?"

"Love it," Sexton says.

"Have you seen the new Essex?"

"Not up close."

"Bought one for my wife last week," Rowley says, leaning back in his chair. "Hydraulic shock absorbers. Four-wheel brakes. Radiator shelters. Air cleaner. Paid six hundred ninety-five."

"How's it drive?"

"Smooth as a fucked mink. You married, Mr. Beecher?"

"A month tomorrow."

"Congratulations."

Sexton takes a sip of coffee and thinks of Honora back at the cabin. He likes to imagine her still in her nightgown, the one with the loose straps that slide over her shoulders. When they woke earlier in the morning, the sheets and the pillows were damp.

Rowley sets his coffee glass down. "So what have you got to show me, Mr. Beecher?" he asks.

"Well," Sexton begins, divesting himself of his glass of iced coffee and sitting slightly forward. "We're awfully excited about our nineteen thirty line. Of course, we still carry the Number Six and the Number Seven, and we have another model I'd like to tell you about—I'll get to that in a minute—and also a terrific new tool called a Copiograph machine that will just knock your socks off, but the machine I think you'll be the most interested in is our new flat-surface accounting-writing machine." Sexton pauses for emphasis. "It's a machine that will allow you to keep in touch with every transaction from every department without adding an extra man to the payroll," he says. "It consolidates accounting methods into a simple, unified plan. I've got a picture of it right here." Sexton reaches into his leather case and pulls out a catalog. He finds the page and hands it across the desk.

"What do you think about those Athletics?" Rowley asks as he looks at the brochure.

"I think they can go all the way," Sexton says. If Rowley reads the description of the accounting-writing machine all the way to the end, Sexton knows he'll have his sale.

"Boston's pitiful," Rowley says. He puts the catalog, description unread, down on the desk. "What's this thing going to cost me?"

"I've got one in the car," Sexton says, evading the money question. "Why don't you let me bring it in and demonstrate it for you?"

Rowley is silent, as if he's just remembered an important appointment.

"A thing worth having is worth having now," Sexton says.

Rowley pushes himself away from his desk on his roll-away chair. The chair seems to travel pretty far, putting some distance between him and Sexton.

"Putting it off is like paying more for it," Sexton says, trying to relax his shoulders. "I've got that new Copiograph machine I was telling you about in my car too. Which would you prefer I bring in? Should I bring in both?"

Sexton makes as if to rise from the chair.

The bank president wheels himself back to the desk. He studies Sexton for a moment. From a drawer, he takes out two shot glasses and a bottle. "What do you say we chase that coffee?" Rowley says.

Honora

In Portland, Honora and Sexton have a bathroom with hot water in the room. They flip a coin to see who will get the first bath. When steam clouds the mirror, Honora rubs a spot clear with the end of her fist. Her hair is matted to her head, and her skin is pink from the nearly scalding water. She cannot discern any physical differences between her married state and her single state—no obvious contentment or niggling unease. Her eyes are still wide and biscuit brown, and her eyebrows definitely need plucking. Possibly her mouth looks looser than it was, and she thinks, on balance, that this is a good sign. Unhappy women, she's observed from her years spent behind the grille at the bank, often have pinched mouths with vertical lines shooting upward to the nose.

* * *

On the road, Honora washes the stains from the butter yellow suit and rinses out underwear, which she hangs discreetly from the bottom rungs of wooden chairs. Sexton likes to eat in diners or in cheap restaurants, explaining to Honora the mathematics of expense accounts and commissions. If a man is allowed fifty cents a day for food and spends more than that (or if he *and his wife* spend more than that), then the $5.20 he's made in commissions that day might only be $4.70, correct?

If there's a client who has direct ties to the home office, Sexton goes alone to the appointment. Honora stays behind in the cabin and reads, propped up against the quilt-thin pillows. The headboards sometimes jiggle, and the smell of mildew rises up from the woolen blankets. She reads magazines—*Woman's Home Companion* and *The Saturday Evening Post*—and books she has bought on the road at filling stations or near the diners where they eat.

Dark Laughter. An American Tragedy. Point Counter Point. If it is cold, she reads in her pink sweater; if it's hot and the cabin doesn't have a fan, she sits by a window. She imagines she can almost hear Sexton's pitch several miles away, and she wonders how he is faring without her. Sometimes she stands at the window of the cabin, a semicircle of other cabins spreading out to either side of her, and watches for the Buick to turn down the drive.

If the weather is fine, Honora goes for a walk. She strolls through towns that seem little more than a school, a church, a town hall, and a bank, which she passes trying to catch a glimpse of Sexton. She has household money in her purse, and if the town has a five-and-dime she buys a rubber-coated dish drainer or a juice glass with oranges and green leaves painted on it. Once she buys a recipe book and spends a day in a cabin composing menus on the back of one of Sexton's triplicate forms. In the cities, she walks the streets until her feet hurt. She makes her way down to the harbor and climbs back up to a city square and rests on the benches in the parks with other women in hats and gloves. She walks faster in the cities than she does in the towns, a mantle of anxiety riding her shoulders, and it isn't until she reaches New Bedford and is walking along a street that parallels the harbor that she realizes that cities remind her of Halifax. What she feels along her shoulders, she realizes, is a hunching against impending disaster.

Honora likes to walk the tracks. She puts her hands inside the pockets of her dress, sets her cloche on her head, and points herself north or south along the railroad tracks. She appreciates the way they stretch out seemingly forever—the ultimate open road. No stop signs, no traffic, seldom an encounter with any other person, though there is plenty of life. The backs of houses that no one ever sees. Wash on a line. An old Ford up on blocks. Summer tea in a jar on a picnic table next to a well. An open garage filled with rusted bits of machinery. Sometimes she passes another woman in an apron and a head scarf, hanging out her laundry, and she and the woman wave to each other. But if Honora sees a man on a back stoop smoking a cigarette, a man who is home in the middle of the day, she doesn't wave. When a train passes, she steps back from the gravel bed and waits for the engineer to give her a quick salute.

"What did you do today?" Sexton asks, flushed from a recent sale and running his fingers through his well-oiled hair. Snapping his suspenders off his shoulders. Yanking the knot out of his tie.

"I went walking," she says.

"It's from my mother," Honora says.

"What's new?"

"May isn't doing well." Honora is holding her own breast through the cotton of her blouse. She puts her hand down.

"I'm sorry to hear that," Sexton says.

When they returned to the house, an air of reproach had permeated the rooms, like that of a once-favored dog who'd been left alone all day and hadn't yet been walked. Honora moved from room to room, holding the letter that was waiting for her on the floor of the front hallway, and it wasn't until she'd inspected the entire house that she had allowed herself to sit at the kitchen table and read it.

Sexton pours himself a drink from a bottle of illegal bourbon a client gave him to celebrate a deal. Six No. 7's at a 4 percent discount to a textile manufacturing company in Dracut, Massachusetts.

"And Mother asks again if we can go there over Labor Day," Honora says.

"You want a sip?"

She nods. He hands her his glass and pours liquor into a coffee cup for himself. They are silent, just drinking.

"I should do the laundry," she says.

"I'm going to buy you a washing machine," Sexton says.

"Really?"

He sets the bourbon down and bends to kiss the underside of her chin. "Forget the laundry," he says.

The blouse rises above Honora's arms as if it might fly away. Her clothes make a heap on the floor. Sexton likes to see her naked and has her stand a table length away. It is understood that he will tell her what to do, that she doesn't have to think about or guess at his desires. As for her own, they are buried deep inside her, bulbs that might one day send up strong shoots through a dark soil.

Vivian

"I'm so hot I can't drink," Vivian says.

The air is motionless, a phenomenon she has never observed so close to the water, not in all the years she's been coming to Fortune's Rocks. Beyond the beach, the Atlantic lies as flat as a wrinkled sheet. In each tiny wave, Vivian takes hope.

"Let's get out of here," Dickie says.

"Where would we go?"

"My house," he says.

"Now?"

"You've never seen it," he says. "There might be a breeze. Something of a breeze, anyway. Normally the place is crawling with workmen, but no one will be there now."

"We should say good-bye," Vivian says. "Whose house is this?"

She glances into the sitting room of the shingled cottage. Near the French doors, a Spud cigarette is burning a notch in a mahogany desk. Another butt is ground into the Persian rug. Ima Thurston is blotto, hanging over the arm of a silk settee as if she might be sick. Someone ought to put a bucket under her. In a corner, a sober quartet is playing a round of bridge. Laughter, melodious and feminine, returns her attention to the porch.

"Floyd Holmes, I think," Dickie says.

"I don't even know him."

"No, of course you don't."

It is the eighteenth or twentieth party Vivian has been to since arriving at the Highland. Some of the parties have been at the hotel itself, and others, such as this one, have been held at the cottages along the beach and then have moved on to one of the grand houses around the point or to the country club nearer to the center of the village. The guest lists include nearly all of the same people. Cedric Nye and his wife, Natalie, up from Raleigh, North Carolina. The brothers Chadbourne, Nat and Hunt, who invented a ball bearing that has made them millions. Cyril Whittemore, a radio actor whose mid-Atlantic accent is so pitch perfect that it's impossible to tell which side of the ocean he is from. Dorothy Trafton, whom Vivian knows from Boston, and whom she avoids as best she can because Dorothy was present at a tennis match at which Vivian, thoroughly fed up with Teddy Rice's arrogance, threw a racquet across the court and dinged Teddy on the ankle. And there's Harlan Quigley, from New York, and Joshua Cutts, who lives here year round, and Georgia Porter, from Washington (her father is a senator? a representative?), and Arthur Willet, who is said to have millions from a diamond mine in South Africa. His wife, Verna, wears sapphires as a statement of independence.

Honestly, if only they could all go naked, Vivian thinks. She has on the least amount of clothing she can possibly get away with—a meringue sundress with no back and made of such thin, gauzy material that it's nearly indecent (only two beige grosgrain ribbons keep it up)—and still tiny rivulets of perspiration trickle from her neck to her breasts. She has already run through all her dresses and will have to start again. Dickie, after an enigmatic absence of two weeks, about which he has so far said little, showed up just the week before, announcing cheerfully that his engagement was broken. The announcement didn't surprise Vivian, since she and Dickie have been together almost every day since that first morning on the beach, but *why* they are together remains a mystery to her. They certainly don't love each other, and she isn't sure they even like each other very much. They quarrel occasionally when drunk, and once they argued publicly at a dinner party at the Nyes', an argument that ended when Vivian called him a lush and Dickie deliberately dropped his highball onto the tiles of the Nyes' kitchen floor, Edinburgh crystal and all. Dickie was profusely apologetic within seconds of the stunt, but she sensed in both of them a certain pleasure in the event. And in that way, she thinks, they are similar types.

"I'm not sure I'll like drinking as much when it's legal," Vivian says as they make their way around the back of the cottage to Dickie's car.

"Oh, not at all," Dickie says. "Not at all. Imagine being able to walk into a corner grocery store and buy a bottle of gin. It'll have all the glamour of, I don't know, Moxie."

"It'll never happen," Vivian says.

Dickie starts the engine of his new car, a particularly low-slung Packard. Vivian lays her head back against the seat. The rush of air that the car produces is worth the trip. "Don't stop," Vivian says.

"We could drive to Montreal," he says.

He is joking, but the idea appeals to her nevertheless. She imagines the drive north through the night, slipping through the mountains, the air growing cooler and cooler until finally they have to shut the windows. And then they will be in Quebec and no one will speak English and that in itself would be heaven.

Dickie rounds the point and pulls up to a house clearly in mid repair. It sits on a small bluff overlooking the ocean, just at the juncture between the beach and the rocky point. Even before she emerges from the Packard, Vivian can see the water straight through the house's windows. Scaffolding makes it hard to discern the contours of the building, but she likes the absence of landscaping. The dunes run right to the foundation.

"I hope you're not going to put in any lawn or anything," Vivian says.

"Haven't really got that far," Dickie says.

"Leave it wild," she says. "Plant shrub roses if you must."

"Come see the inside," he says.

When he opens the car door for her, she takes his arm. Already she can feel a slight breeze. Her dress is an inch too long, and she snags the hem when they step up to a boardwalk that runs across what might normally be a front lawn.

"When was it built?" she asks as she picks up her skirts. "I'm giving up dresses, by the way," she says.

"You'll look swell in pants," Dickie says. "It was designed in eighteen ninety-nine for a doctor and his wife, but on the day they moved into it, she discovered that he'd been having an affair with a fifteen-year-old girl. A whopping big scandal. Well, for then. Not sure anyone would care now."

"Fifteen?" asks Vivian, interrupting. "Oh, people would care."

"He was run out of town, and the wife and children moved up to York. A writer, a poet, I think, no one you've ever heard of, bought the house for a song. But then he went broke almost immediately and the house was abandoned for years. I've had heat put in." He glances at her. "Thinking of staying on a bit after the summer is over," he says.

"Really? Whatever for?"

"Take my hand," Dickie says. "Dangerous around here with all the unfinished woodwork. Last week a plumber stepped backward off the upstairs landing. The railing hadn't been installed yet."

"What happened to the plumber?"

"Died, actually," Dickie says. "Not right away, but after he'd got to the hospital. Internal injuries or something. Not sure I was ever told."

"What happened to the girl?"

"The fifteen-year-old? I've no idea."

"Sad," Vivian says.

"Everything makes you sad," Dickie says.

"You're sounding kind of petulant tonight."

"Really, Viv, I don't think you give a toss about what happened to some ruined fifteen-year-old girl in eighteen ninety-nine. Or to the plumber, for that matter."

She thinks a minute. "I like to know the ends of stories," she says.

And suddenly Vivian realizes why she

and Dickie are together. He's the only person who makes her tell the truth. "I like the house empty," Vivian says as they walk into what appears to be a front room. Sandy, the dog, greets Dickie with a series of back flips. Dickie, after advertising for Sandy's owner and receiving no response, seems more or less to have inherited the pet. "It's too bad you have to have furniture," Vivian says. "The rooms are just right as they are."

"Won't put furniture in, then," he says. "That's settled. We'll eat on the floor."

Vivian hears the *we.* She watches Dickie feel in his jacket pocket for his cigarette case. He takes one out and tamps it down. "Not sure I've ever felt this way about anyone before," Dickie says.

She turns away from him and walks to a window. She examines the view. "Don't get mushy on me, Dickie," she says lightly, crossing her arms over her chest. The tide is dead low, and the sun, setting behind them, lights up the sand flats with a tangerine light that reminds her of that horrid Tangee lipstick she sees advertised in all the magazines.

"You never take me seriously," he says.

"Give me a cigarette, will you?" she asks. "You aren't going to play the thwarted lover, I hope. Because it doesn't suit you."

"For God's sake, Viv. Give it a rest."

She sits on a window seat and traces the diamond pattern of the windowpanes with her fingers. "Your house has charm, Dickie. It's magnificent, of course, with all the windows and the ocean outside and the surf roaring, but, truthfully, I'm a little sick of looking at water."

Dickie walks to the window and holds out a lit cigarette.

"Of course I take you seriously," Vivian says. "I take you dead serious, as a matter of fact."

"Because I was wondering if when the house is finished you might want to move in with me," he says. He pauses. "Till November, say? Then I thought you and I might go down to New York for a bit. Stay at the Plaza and so forth. Take a side trip to Havana."

Vivian struggles not to show her considerable surprise. She takes a long pull on the cigarette and suppresses a cough. Dickie smokes Chesterfields, which are too strong for her. "Are you proposing?" she asks lightly.

"You need me to?" he asks.

She exhales and studies the skirt of her sundress. She can see her skin through the thin material. "Not really," she says.

"Then it's a deal?"

"What I like," she says, looking up and gesturing to take in all of the house, "are all the windows open to the sky. It's an aerie. It's inspired. It makes me want to lie down and sleep."

Dickie moves toward her, but she pushes him gently away with her fingers. "It's too hot. Don't come near me."

Could she make a go of it with Dickie Peets? she wonders. She's been dreading the return to Boston. She is simply too old to live with her father, and what future is in that? Far better to live with Dickie, even if it would cause a scandal. Perhaps she could go bohemian, she thinks. Espouse free love and all that. For a moment she contemplates that idea as she allows Dickie to kiss her neck. "What on earth would we do all day?" she asks.

"Look at the ocean," Dickie says. "Don't

know. Got something I've been working on. Something I've been painting."

"Not seriously," Vivian says too quickly, and she can see that she has hurt him. She wraps his tie around her hand and pulls him closer to her. "I thought you were in stocks or something," she says.

He is silent a moment. He takes her breast in his hand. "Stocks all the way," he says.

McDermott

McDermott pauses at the entrance to the apartment building.

"Come on come on come on," Ross says, wiping his face with his handkerchief. "Don't hang about."

"I'll be right with you," McDermott says.

"Suffering Jesus, it's hot," Ross says, putting his filthy handkerchief back in his pocket.

A movement catches McDermott's attention, and his eyes travel across the facade of the brick tenement to a fourth-floor window. A boy sits on the windowsill, watching him. All week, the heat has been stifling, nearly intolerable inside the mill. For a moment, McDermott feels sorry for the boy and thinks of sailing him a coin so that he can go to the movies. Two coins, so that he can take a friend. Ross tugs at the sleeve of McDermott's shirt. "You don't want to be seen," Ross says from the bottom of the well. "The last thing you want to do is end up on someone's list."

Alphonse

All afternoon Alphonse has watched the men come and go through the door with the peeling red paint. Arnaud Nadeau's father, who keeps coming to the door to wave the men inside, is a mule spinner at the mill, and what all the men are doing in the Nadeau apartment Alphonse has no idea. The men move toward the door and pretend they aren't actually going in, and then they slip across the threshold with a sneaky movement that reminds Alphonse of Sam Coyne, who was always arriving late for school and trying to slide into his seat without Sister Mary Patrick noticing. Trying to pull a fast one. As if Sister Mary Patrick, who sees and hears everything, wouldn't catch him. It would be better, Alphonse thinks, for the men to walk up to the door as if they were going visiting, because anyone can tell there's something up.

He doesn't know the dark-haired man in the blue shirt who looked at him, the man who had his sleeves rolled and paused a moment on the steps. Alphonse is frightened because who knows what the men are up to inside Nadeau's? Maybe they are gangsters and are planning a robbery, though he really doesn't think gangsters would be so obvious. Besides, there are an awful lot of men going into the apartment. At least twenty that Alphonse has counted.

When the man with the blue shirt goes inside, Alphonse gets off the sill and kneels on the floor and peers over the ledge because he doesn't want to be noticed by anyone else, just in case. Marie-Thérèse comes into the room then and says, *Look at Alphonse, he's praying,* and he stands up quickly. *Didn't get enough at mass?* Marie-Thérèse asks in that horrible taunting voice that she has, and his mother, who is cooking a stew, laughs with her. And then, because of Marie-Thérèse, his mother is reminded that Alphonse doesn't have anything to do on the hot Sunday afternoon and tells him to go wash the sheets in the tub. Alphonse is so mad at his sister that he gives her a kick on her anklebone when he passes her, which makes Marie-Thérèse scream (she exaggerates everything), and then his mother cuffs his ear.

After he has scrubbed the sheets against the washboard—the sheets so heavy in the tub they make his arms tremble—he puts them through the double wringer and then hangs them on the line over the back deck. He hops down the stairs before his mother can ask him to do anything else. Alphonse thinks he should have one afternoon off a week, though it is pretty clear that his mother doesn't even get that and so he feels a little guilty leaving her alone with Marie-Thérèse, who is practically useless.

He thinks of going round to Louis Desjardins's house to see what he and his brothers are up to, to see if they want to go to the beach. Louis's mother works a second job at the rectory on Sundays and so Louis and his brothers and sisters usually have the place to themselves and you can count on it to be pandemonium over there. Alphonse reaches the bottom of the back stairs. Normally he'd cut through the alley to get to Louis's but instead he finds himself moving around the wall of the tenement to the front. He hugs the bricks and hopes no one will notice him, but that's just as stupid, he realizes, as the men who've been sneaking through Mr. Nadeau's front door. He wonders if the men are still inside. It has taken Alphonse at least a half hour to do the sheets and so maybe they have left already. He could go up to the door and knock as if he were just looking for Arnaud. That would be a perfectly ordinary thing to do, and then he could get a quick peek inside while Mr. Nadeau tells him Arnaud isn't home.

But when Alphonse reaches the front of the building he loses his nerve. The street is deserted. Even the women aren't out and about, which is unusual. Sunday is visiting day whether it's stifling or not. Sometimes his mother keeps her Sunday dress on and goes to visit his father's cousins on Fourth Street.

The front door opens. The dark-haired man in the blue shirt with the rolled sleeves comes out. Alphonse sucks in his breath. The man has his hands on his hips and his head bent and he steps off the cement stairs and walks in a small circle on the sidewalk in front of the tenement. His tie is loosened at his collar and his shirt has sweat stains in the armpits. You can tell the man is thinking about something. Maybe he is mad. The man raises his head to the sky, and Alphonse takes a step backward, thinking that two more steps and he'll be around the corner and out of sight, but on the second pass around his circle the man looks down from the sky and runs his hands through his hair and that's when he sees Alphonse.

"Hey," the man says.

Alphonse cannot move or breathe.

"You're the kid in the window," the man says.

Alphonse shakes his head.

"Come over here." The man beckons with his hand. "Come on, I won't bite."

Alphonse takes a breath as if about to drown. The man laughs and beckons again. Common sense tells Alphonse to run, but the man is smiling. Though Marie-Thérèse smiles a lot and she is a snake.

Alphonse puts his hands in his pockets and moves toward the man, who squats down in front of him so that they are more or less face to face. "What's your name?"

Alphonse can't speak.

"It's okay," the man says. His hair is parted in the center and his eyebrows go almost straight across. He has the bluest eyes Alphonse has ever seen.

"Alphonse," he says finally.

"I'm McDermott."

Alphonse nods. "Is that your first name or your last name?" Alphonse asks.

"It's my last name," the man says, "but it's all anyone ever calls me. Except my family."

"What do they call you?"

"Quillen."

Alphonse nearly laughs.

"You speak English pretty good," McDermott says. "I'm a little deaf, so I have to look right at you when you're talking."

"All right," Alphonse says.

"What did you see from the window?" the man asks.

Oh Jesus, Mary, and Joseph.

"It's okay," the man says, reaching out a hand and briefly touching his arm. "I'm not going to hurt you."

Alphonse heaves a great breath of air. "I saw men going inside," he says.

"Right," the man says. His smile vanishes, but his face doesn't look angry. "Best not to talk about what you saw, all right?"

Alphonse shakes his head violently. He makes fists with his hands in his pockets to keep them from trembling.

"How old are you?" the man asks.

"Twelve," Alphonse lies.

"You work in the mills?"

"Yes."

"Which one?"

"The Ely Falls."

"Doing what?"

"Bobbins," Alphonse says.

The man stands up and stretches his back. "The men in there?" he says. "They're trying to make it so your pop will have more money and you won't have to earn."

"I don't have a pop," the boy says.

"You have a mother?"

"Yes," Alphonse says. He nods vigorously in case the man hasn't seen his lips.

"In the mill?"

"She's a weaver."

"What's her name?"

"Evanthia. Blanchette."

"Your mother works on my floor," the man says.

Oh, Jesus, Alphonse thinks.

The man puts a hand on Alphonse's shoulder. "I want you to do something for me," he says. "I want you to run to Tsomides Market and get me some cigarettes. Lucky Strikes." McDermott hands Alphonse the coins. "I'm going back inside, but I'll come out in fifteen minutes," he says. "There's an extra penny there, so get yourself some candy."

Alphonse puts the coins in his pocket. "I'll be back before then," he says, looking at the man intently, making sure he can see his mouth. "I'm very fast." Immediately, Alphonse feels the color come into his face. What a stupid thing to say.

The man smiles. He reaches over and musses the hair at the top of Alphonse's head. "I knew that," he says.

McDermott

"Where you been?" Ross asks when McDermott returns to Nadeau's front room.

"I needed air," McDermott says.

For reasons of security, the two front windows have been shut, and McDermott can hardly breathe: the heat plus the cigarette smoke have made the room nearly airless. The man named Mironson, who has come up from New York City, is still talking. He's a sweet-faced man, small boned, with delicate hands and small feet. A thick hank of dark hair keeps falling in his face. Physically, he seems the least likely of men to inspire a crowd.

Twenty loom fixers in a room no bigger than a good-sized automobile. McDermott thinks of animals in a cage. Just the smell of the men is testament to a kind of animal-like restlessness. He has the sense that Boutet and Tsomides and O'Reilly and Ouellette and all the other Francos and Greeks and Irishmen want to flex their muscles, and he wonders if caged anger produces its own smell. Maybe the choice of a small room for the meeting was deliberate on Mironson's part, a kind of strategic move that will make the men nervous, anxious to break free.

"We have to . . . faster and . . . ," McDermott hears as François Boutet gestures with his hands. Boutet is short but powerfully built. His arms bulge below the short sleeves of his Sunday shirt. McDermott can catch only a portion of what is being said in the room because the words seem heavier than the air. He can see the anger, though, as sharp and as clear on the men's faces as if it had been etched.

"Doing the work of . . . or three," Paul Tsomides adds. Tsomides's brother owns the market to which McDermott has just sent the boy.

"They've changed the wage rates . . . wife . . . piecework, and she gets less for that," says a drunk named McAllister. He works in the Penderton mill, but McDermott has seen him often in the speak.

Some of the men are standing, while others are sitting on wooden chairs or on the floor up against the wall. All the furniture except for the kitchen chairs has been moved into the hallway. The room itself stinks of wet and onions. McDermott wonders where Nadeau's wife and children have gone.

"It's too easy . . . laid off," says Ouellette. "If I get . . . who's going to feed my kids? I have eight kids."

"You're . . . about a strike," a man called Schwaner says to Mironson, "but if we strike, they'll bring in scabs, and we'll lose our jobs. I can't afford to lose my job."

"You can't afford to . . . current wage," Mironson says quietly.

McDermott has to strain to hear the man. He watches his mouth carefully.

"You can't afford . . . no . . . security. You can't . . . long hours."

"But you go back to New York," Schwaner says. "Meanwhile . . . and our kids will be on the streets. Jobs are scarce now. Where am I gonna find . . . lose my job?"

"Jobs *are* scarce," Mironson says. "The mill owners . . . running scared . . . competition from the southern mills . . . cutting corners. It will only get . . . It's just a matter of time before *you*"—Mironson points at a man—"and *you,* and *you,* have no jobs at all. But with a union, your jobs will be secure. Your children should be in school, not in the mills," Mironson says, looking right at McDermott.

I don't have any children, McDermott almost says.

"And how we gonna do that?" asks a man named Delaney, his snarl coiling around the room.

But Mironson doesn't seem to fluster easily. "By securing a . . . wage," Mironson says evenly. "By making sure . . . child labor laws are enforced."

The men grumble, talking out of the sides of their mouths. Some of them, McDermott knows, have three or four kids earning in the mills. The last thing they want is to have the child labor laws enforced.

"Yes, there are going to be sacrifices," Mironson says. "In some cases, terrible . . . No conflict is . . . risk. But my question . . . this: Are you willing to . . . health and your . . . and the health and security of your wife and children, in the hands of . . . whose only goal is to make another dollar? If that dollar comes at the cost of . . . clinic, what will you do? If that dollar comes at the cost of more hours a day . . . *what will you do?*"

The sudden shock of Mironson's raised voice produces a temporary silence in the room. No man wants to appear to be a coward. Mironson is brilliant at this, McDermott thinks.

"So what happens now?" Ouellette asks finally.

"Open the windows, for God's sake," someone shouts.

Two windows and a door are immediately flung wide. McDermott edges his way closer to the window to get a breath of air. He thinks the men might agree to form a union just so they can leave the room. He ducks his head down to the open window, and when he does he sees the boy standing across the street at the corner, as if he were waiting for a bus. The boy has a Franco hairline, his stiff brown hair pointing forward all around the face. He badly needs a haircut.

* * *

Wisely, the boy does not come to McDermott, but waits for him to walk across the street. Together, they turn the corner, out of sight of the Nadeau apartment.

"You *are* fast," McDermott says.

"Tsomides wasn't open," the boy says, only slightly breathless. He hands the Lucky Strikes and the penny change to McDermott. "I had to go to the candy store on Alfred Street."

"You went all that way?" McDermott asks. "How come you didn't want the change?"

The boy shrugs. He has on short pants and a cotton shirt that once had long sleeves. It's mended just above the pocket. The boy's shoes have no laces. McDermott thinks about his own younger brothers, Eamon and Michael, who are a handful. They'd have kept all the money, would never have shown up with the cigarettes at all.

"Well," McDermott says. In the shadow of a tenement, there is at least the illusion of shade. McDermott can almost convince himself that there is a breeze. "What will you do with the rest of the day?"

The boy is silent a moment. "I like to go to the beach," he says finally.

"The beach over to Fortune's Rocks?" McDermott asks. The boy nods. He has wide eyes, nearly bug eyes, McDermott thinks. "How do you get there?" he asks.

"I take the trolley. Then I walk."

"Kind of hot today for that long of a walk," McDermott says.

The boy shrugs.

"You have money for the trolley?"

"I keep two dimes from my pay packet."

McDermott lights a cigarette, drops the match on the sidewalk. "You know how to swim?"

The boy shakes his head.

"You ever been fishing?"

"A couple of times," says the boy. "With my father."

"I like to fish," McDermott says.

The boy nods.

"Your father take off?"

The boy shakes his head and scuffs at the sidewalk with his shoe. "He died," he says.

"That's too bad," McDermott says. "When?"

"Last winter."

"Sorry to hear that," McDermott says, and after a moment adds, "I could take you fishing sometime if you want."

The boy looks surprised, as if McDermott has said something that doesn't quite make sense. McDermott can feel through his feet the creak and rumble of large wheels over cobblestones. The ice man, McDermott guesses. Working on a Sunday. He'll be doing a good business in this heat.

"Tell you what," McDermott says to Alphonse. "I want an ice cream, and I want you to go get it for me, but I don't want it unless you get one for yourself."

The boy looks puzzled at first, as if there might be a trick. "All right," he says after a moment.

McDermott feels in his pocket for the coins. "If I decide to go fishing, I know where to find you," he says.

Alphonse nods. He turns and begins to run. McDermott has never seen anyone sprint that fast. Too bad the kid isn't in school, he thinks. He'd be a natural for any track team.

But the boy isn't in school. He works in a mill. McDermott lights another cigarette and waits for the boy to return.

Honora

Honora stands in the kitchen, unpacking groceries from a cardboard box, the back of her rayon blouse sticking to her shoulder blades. She tries to lift the fabric away from her skin. Sexton walks into the kitchen with a letter in his hand. He sits down as if his legs have suddenly given out.

"What is it?" she asks.

"It's from the owner," Sexton says.

"Of the house?" Honora sets a tin of cleanser on the tabletop. "Is it bad news?"

"I'm not sure," Sexton says. "It could be great news. He wants to sell. In a hurry."

"He wants to sell the house?" Honora asks. She puts a hand on the back of a chair and sits down next to her husband.

"For four thousand dollars. And he wants to know if we would be interested in making an offer before he puts it on the market." Sexton stands and walks to the window. He begins to pace. He puts a hand to his forehead. "That's a great price," he says. "Even with the house in such bad shape. The guy must really need the money." Sexton reads the letter again. He brandishes it like a sword, slicing the air in his excitement. In his gestures, he is athletic and precise. Even in the wilting heat, Honora thinks of him as having snap. Watching him, she is reminded of the feel of crisp beans straight from the garden and the sound they make when her mother prepares them for the pot. *Snap* go the heads, and *snap* go the tails. "We could almost do this," he says.

"How?"

"We'll need twenty percent down," he says. "Eight hundred dollars."

"Where on earth will we come up with eight hundred dollars?" she asks, a little breathless.

"The Buick's worth four seventy-five," he says. "I could use that as collateral for a loan—say for four hundred dollars. We've got a hundred in savings. That's five hundred."

"And what about the other three hundred?"

"I don't know," he says. "I'll think of something. Maybe I could get an advance against commissions."

"Is that wise?" Honora asks, running her hand along the slick oilcloth.

Over the summer, Sexton has sold a great many typewriters. Honora and he have been to Littleton and to Lebanon and to Cranston. To Pawtucket and to Worcester and to Springfield. They've eaten ice-cream cones in the Buick and deviled-ham sandwiches beside lakes. They have played miniature golf and gone to see Mary Pickford in *Coquette.* They have dined in hotels and gone dancing in roadhouses. They've bought roller skates and an icebox and a settee and a radio, and at night, when they are at home, they listen to Lowe's Orchestra and to *The Dinner Hour.* Sexton checks the baseball scores and listens for the Motorists' Bulletin and the racing results. Sometimes Honora feels like one of the legendary bank robbers whose exploits fill the headlines. She and Sexton go into banks. They make quick getaways. They hole up in cabins.

"Business is great," Sexton says. "I've made more money in the last month than I made all of last year. And my line has expanded. I'm doing all business machines now—not just typewriters."

"Thank you very much, Honora," she says from the table.

Sexton bows. "Thank you very much, Honora," he says. He glances around the kitchen. "Just imagine," he says. "This could be ours one day."

Honora follows her husband's eyes. The kitchen has a kind of rudimentary cheer now. She has tacked brightly patterned oilcloth to the shelves and put on rickrack as an edging. The walls have been painted yellow, and she's made gingham tea towels that complement the oilcloth. The dishes on the shelves, though mismatched, are neat and tidy.

"It feels like ours already," she says.

She picks up Sexton's newspaper, intending to fold it and use it for a fan. She glances at the headlines. *204 KILLED BY ENFORCING PROHIBITION,* she reads. *SOUTHERN COTTON MILL STRIKERS START RIOTS.*

Alice Willard

Dear Honora,

I will write you just a quick note before you come. I don't think it would be a good idea to bring pies. Unless you are coming directly, they would not keep well in this heat. Yesterday, the temperature reached 100 degrees, which as you know is quite a record for Taft. I was in the garden digging out the potatoes and I had to sit down because I felt a spell coming on. Estelle has had the heat stroke, and I never knew how dangerous it was, but she has been laid up all week with strict orders not to go outside. Richard had to buy a fan to keep her cool, and he has been down to the ice house any number of times. If it is too hot, you and Sexton will want to sleep on the porch. I will make up the divan there just in case. It is a narrow bed and not too comfortable, but I think you won't mind too much. Sleeping upstairs has become very unpleasant. I rigged up that old fan Myra gave us in the attic, and at night we get a bit of a breeze running through the house. This heat can't last much longer I don't think and maybe by the time you get here we'll have had a storm and the heat will have broken.

I have that recipe you wanted out and a few others besides that have been in the family for some time. I used to make your father the Company Chicken and he liked it very much. It will be a change to have people to cook for, even though it is hot. Harold eats hardly anything these days and never seems to want a real meal.

I wish I could tell you to take your time with buying the house, but if Sexton is determined and thinks you and he can afford it, then who am I to tell you different? You have a good head on your shoulders, Honora, and sometimes a wife has to be the voice of reason in a family, though it is always best to do so in such a way that the husband doesn't feel that he is not the boss. Also you don't want to be thought of as someone who wears the pants. You know what that's like from watching Estelle and Richard. The poor man, he is run off his feet sometimes.

I'm glad you've decided to stay home more and let Sexton do the traveling. Automobiles have always made me nervous.

It is just too hot to eat. I think I will make up some cucumber sandwiches. Harold doesn't like them too much, but I feel in the mood for them today.

We might get a radio. What do you think about that?

Love,
Mother

Sexton

Sexton parks the Buick behind a J. C. Penney store. A large elm tree provides a canopy of shade. The parking lot is nearly deserted on this Friday afternoon before the Labor Day weekend.

"How long will you be gone?" Honora asks.

"Forty-five minutes at the most," Sexton says. "Want some gum?"

"I'm set."

"Cigarettes?"

She holds up her pack of Old Golds. "I've got my magazines," she adds.

He leans across the front seat and kisses his wife. She is happy. She is going home to see her mother. Her mouth tastes like Wrigley's Spearmint gum. Her hair has lost its sheen in the heat, and her skin is damp. Lately, they have taken to sleeping outside, on the porch. At night, there is sometimes the suggestion of a breeze from the water. The mosquitoes are fierce, but sleeping inside these days is unthinkable.

Honora waves him away with her hands. "Go," she says, smiling. "I'm fine."

Sexton lifts his jacket from the hook in the backseat. He has packed the Buick for the trip to Taft and has rigged up a kind of icebox so that Honora can take her pies. If this appointment goes well—and then the next—they will be on their way to Taft by five this evening. With any luck, they will get there before eight, and already he is planning to go swimming with Honora in the lake shortly after they arrive. They will wait through all the visiting and for Harold and Honora's mother to go to bed. Then he'll take Honora down to the lake. He'll tell her to forget her suit.

He tosses his jacket over his shoulder. He turns and gives Honora a quick wave through the windshield. Because of the reflection in the glass of the dappled shade, he can see only part of her face. He thinks that she is beautiful. She isn't classically beautiful and she isn't magazine beautiful either, but she is wife beautiful. He loves catching her face when she is ironing or making a bed. In those moments, she will look content, and contentment suits her features.

As Sexton walks, he rehearses his speech. Everything depends upon timing. He is counting on Rowley being half in the bag, getting a head start on the long weekend. The weekend itself is part of Sexton's plan, and he prays that Albert Norton, the loan officer at the Franklin Institution for Savings in Franklin, won't decide to leave early for his summer house. If Sexton can get in and out of Rowley's office before three-thirty, he can make it to Franklin by four, which is when he told Norton he would be there. It's a risky plan, and in odd moments it takes Sexton's breath away, but it's the only way Sexton can see to raise the money for the house. Besides, the deception is a minor one, isn't it? Merely a matter of dates.

And Sexton wants the house. He wants it so much that it sometimes makes his hands shake. He can't explain the feeling to himself rationally. Rationally, the house is no bargain. It's too big, too hard to heat, and in a community that virtually shuts down during the winter. And yet, if he can just secure this one thing, have this one possession, he will feel that somehow he's ahead of the game. That he's gotten the jump on life.

The stone entryway to the bank feels cool, and for a moment Sexton savors the sensation. He slips his jacket on over his shirt, nearly soaked through with sweat. He tucks in his shirttails and sets his hat on his head at an angle. As he opens the large glass door to the bank's lobby, he has a sharp and visceral memory of opening the door of the Taft Savings and Loan last March and seeing Honora across the room. Her shiny walnut-colored hair snagged his attention, and he found himself moving in her direction, even though another teller was closer to the door. Her hair was cut in a neat shingle that seemed to elongate her long white neck. He took out the roll of tens and fives and put it in the trough under the grille, and he watched her hands, the skin like smooth white silk, as she counted out the money. The urge to touch those hands shuddered through him like a punch. He left only reluctantly, knowing for a certainty that he would soon be back.

"Hello there," he says to the secretary who once brought him an iced coffee and to whom he has sold three of his machines. "How's the Number Eight?"

"It's just fine," Miss Alexander says. The secretary has on a green sleeveless dress today that shows the chicken wattles under her arms.

"And the Copiograph machine?"

"It's made my job a lot easier."

"Well, that's what I like to hear. Say, that's a pretty dress you have on there."

"Oh. Well," she says, blushing. "Thank you."

"I think I've got an appointment with Mr. Rowley," Sexton says, putting his face close to hers. Miss Alexander, flustered, consults her book. Needlessly, Sexton thinks. How many appointments can Rowley possibly have on a Friday afternoon before Labor Day weekend?

"He'll see you now," she says.

"Thank you very kindly," Sexton says, winking.

As he opens the door to Rowley's office, Sexton catches the briefest movement on the desk, a neat stack of papers quickly centered, a pen raised. But Sexton can see that the stack is too neat, the cap still on the pen.

"Mr. Beecher," Rowley says, looking up and then standing, pretending to be caught in the middle of his paperwork. He holds out his hand.

"Mr. Rowley," Sexton says.

"It's a pleasure to see you again. Take a seat, take a seat. How have you been?"

Sexton listens for—hopes for—a slight slurring of words. "Just fine, Mr. Rowley. And yourself?"

"Excellent, Mr. Beecher. Excellent. Apart from this infernal heat, that is."

And there it is. *Thisinfernal.*

"This room isn't too bad, though," Sexton says.

"No, it's not," Rowley says, moving the stack of papers to one side of his desk. "So what brings you out this way? Hey, by the way, my girl says that accounting-writing machine you sold us is just the ticket."

"Glad to hear it," Sexton says, reflecting that the girl is forty-five if she's a day. "No trouble with it, I trust?"

"Not a hint of trouble far as I can tell. Of course it's my girl who uses it. That's her department, don't you know."

And doesn't Sexton just know. If it weren't for the girls in the outside offices, Sexton would be out of a job.

"So what can I do for you?" Rowley asks.

Sexton sits forward. "Well, actually, I've come here on a—"

"Heeeey," Rowley says, pointing a finger at Sexton. "Those Cubs, huh?"

Sexton nods and points a finger back. "Really something."

"Charlie Root?" Rowley asks.

"The best," Sexton says. "And Rogers Hornsby?"

"Fantastic. Say, you headed out for the weekend?"

"As a matter of fact, yes I am," Sexton says. "Headed for the in-laws in Taft."

"Where's that?"

"A bit north of here. Near Conway."

"Oh, yes," Rowley says. "My dad used to keep a boat up there. This your last appointment?"

Thiz your las appointment?

"Yes," Sexton lies.

"Well, here, let's start the weekend off right, then. You care for a shot of my best whiskey?"

Sexton smiles and relaxes his shoulders. He sits back in the chair. “Thank you very kindly, Mr. Rowley. I surely would,” he says. Sexton watches the now-familiar ritual with the shot glasses and the bottle that has been squirreled away in a drawer. “My wife and I just bought a house over to Ely,” he says after his first good pull. The drink tastes like wood smoke going down. It’ll relax him for the next appointment, though he will have to remember to have a piece of gum on the way over to Franklin.

“Didn’t know that,” Rowley says. “Congratulations. Business must be good,” he adds. Rowley has the face of a man who hardly ever goes outside. He’s thin through the chest, Sexton sees, soft through the belly.

“Yes, it is, Mr. Rowley. I’m selling a lot of business machines.”

“Call me Ken.”

“Well, thank you, Ken. Actually, I’m here on a personal matter. What I wanted to talk to you about is the house. The one my wife and I just purchased. It needs a new roof and we have to upgrade all the plumbing. I’d like to get this taken care of as soon as possible.”

"The missus wants her plumbing," Rowley says with a slight leer.

"She does indeed, Mr. Rowley. Ken. I've got a contractor lined up who'll start on this right away, but he needs to see I've got the cash before he'll go ahead with the work."

Rowley nods slowly. "I can understand that," he says. "You need a loan, then, Mr. Beecher?"

"Yes, I do."

"How much?"

"I figure seven hundred will do it."

"You got a breakdown of costs with you there, Mr. Beecher?"

"Call me Sexton if you'd like. Yes, I do." Sexton reaches into the pocket of his jacket and takes out an envelope. "I think everything you need to know is right there," he says, slipping the envelope across Rowley's desk.

Rowley opens the envelope and reads. "It says here your mortgage is with the Franklin Institution for Savings?"

"That's right," Sexton says, his breath tight.

"They hold the deed?"

"Yes, they do."

"You know this man's work? This contractor?"

"Yes, I do. He's renovating a house about a mile and a half from us. Doing a terrific job." Sexton has seen the scaffolding on a house at the other end of the beach. He's copied the man's name and forged a signature on the estimate.

Rowley puts the paper down. He taps a pencil against the desk. "I don't think this will be too much of a problem," he says. "We can advance you the cash today and get the paperwork for a lien on the house sorted out next Monday or Tuesday." Rowley thinks a minute. "Well, probably not Monday or Tuesday," he adds. "Might not be until Wednesday or Thursday on account of the holiday."

No, thinks Sexton. With any luck, it won't be until next Wednesday or Thursday or even later. "Thank you very much, Mr. Rowley," Sexton says. "Ken. I can't tell you how much I appreciate this."

"Not at all," Rowley says, waving Sexton's gratitude away. "My girl will get you settled on your way out."

He refills Sexton's glass. He holds his own up. Sexton clinks Rowley's glass and smiles, but he's conscious now of only one thing. He has to get out of the room. He has his sale; if he lingers, Rowley might change his mind. "I think I'd like to get that money over to the contractor this afternoon before my wife and I leave for Taft," Sexton says. "He says he'll get a start on our project tomorrow if I can get the money to him."

"That so?" Rowley asks, furrowing his brow. "Over the weekend?"

Sexton blinks and instantly sees his mistake. He's moved too fast, and if he isn't careful, he'll lose the deal. He makes a show of relaxing. He crosses his legs, leans back in his chair, studies his drink. He lets the silence play itself out.

"Say, did you read about that French airman yesterday?" Sexton asks. "The one who was forced down into the sea halfway across the Atlantic?"

Sexton opens the door of the Buick so fast that Honora jumps. "Gosh," she says, sitting up straight on the navy mohair upholstery. "You startled me."

"Oh, baby," Sexton says. He kneels on

the driver's seat, leans over and kisses his wife so hard that he bends her neck back over the seat.

"Well," she says when she can breathe. "I take it your appointment went okay."

"Beautiful," he says, twisting into his seat.

"What did you sell?" she asks.

"A Copiograph and two Eights," he says.

"That's wonderful," she says.

Sexton puts the clutch in and adjusts the power lever. He pushes the starter button with his foot. Now if he can just make it to Franklin by four o'clock, he'll be set. Norton will be waiting with the paperwork for the mortgage, Sexton now has the cash for the down payment, and with any luck, by four-thirty, he and his wife will own their own house.

Honora

When Sexton is away, Honora practices cooking. She plans a spring garden and walks to the store with a dime in her pocket to buy a dozen eggs. She darns Sexton's socks and unravels a sweater she doesn't like and begins an argyle vest for him that she hopes to finish before it turns too cold. She takes up yard work because she knows that he doesn't enjoy it. She rakes years' worth of leaves out from under the hedges and trims the bushes with a pair of clippers she found in the cellar. She tries to cut the beach roses back, but some of the thicker stalks resist the dull blades. She weeds the walkway and mows the lawn with a machine Jack Hess has lent them. She likes the dune grass out front because it doesn't need tending. She studies the scarred patch at the side of the house. In its center is a marble bench. In the spring, she thinks, she might plant a rose garden there. The marble bench will make a pleasant place to sit.

In the afternoons and early evenings when the tide has drawn off, Honora looks for sea glass. She finds a slim sliver of amethyst and a jewel-like bit of cobalt. She picks up a thick chunk that looks like dirty ice after a long winter, ice that has been skated on and has gone cloudy with use. She fingers a piece the color of young dandelions and finds shards that look like flower petals: hyacinth and wisteria and lilac. She puts the pieces in her pocket and takes them home and lays them on a windowsill.

She finds a piece that once was a bottle neck. She picks up a delicate shell-like shape with scalloped edges. She touches a shard the color of mint sauce, another that is ice blue and reminds her of a waterfall frozen in winter. She finds an olive-green that resembles the state of New York, another shard that seems to be made of the salt film that once coated the windows of the house. She discovers whites that are not white at all, but rather blond and eggshell and ivory and pearl. One day she almost misses a piece because it so closely resembles sand. When she picks it up and holds it to the light, she sees that it is a translucent golden color, seemingly ancient.

She finds scraps of celadon and cucumber and jade, specks of pea and powder and aquamarine. Once she comes upon a chunk that reminds her of dishwater in a sink. She doesn't like the browns, but occasionally she collects a topaz or a tea. Sometimes all there is is brown, and she goes home slightly depressed. She never keeps a piece of sea glass if it hasn't gone cloudy or if it still retains its sharp edges. Those she buries deep in the sand.

The sea glass ranges in size from that of a broken cookie to slivered bits no bigger than a clipping from a fingernail. Sometimes there is writing. One says "OCHRANE," another says "eder." Another, simply, "to be." One piece says "DOLPH," as though part of a name. And is the 12-14 beneath it a date? Occasionally, the writing gives clues as to the origin of the shard of glass. The "WINE" is self-evident, the "LA" less so. But one day, when she takes down a jar of stewed tomatoes her mother gave her, she recognizes the letters *L* and *A* on the glass jar. She lays the piece of sea glass over the "ATLAS" of the jar and feels she's solved a mystery.

If she looks closely at the glass, she can sometimes see the infinitesimal nicks, the imprints of the sand and rocks that have buffeted it. There's a lump with bubbles in it; another piece, blue violet, in the shape of a bird in flight.

She prizes the oddities—a nugget of crystal threaded with rusted metal; a pale aqua rectangle the exact size and shape of a microscope slide; a shard that looks like ancient Roman glass, a lovely mottled green and gold. She finds a translucent ochre chip imprinted with a *W,* another bit that bears a thicket of white crosshatching, the paint still more or less intact. She finds larger pieces that are flat and guesses that they might once have been parts of windows, and that makes her think of shipwrecks. Once she finds a deformed bit of bottle, and that makes her think of Halifax. Is it too fanciful to imagine that a bottle melted in the aftermath of the explosion and then was swept out to sea on the tidal wave that followed? Was a whole city of shards made smooth by time and sand?

Eventually, Honora collects so much sea glass that she has to put it in a bowl. But in the bowl, the colors jumble together and take on the hues of the bits below and, on the whole, don't amount to much. She experiments by putting the shards on the bedsheet, spread apart, and discovers that their true colors emerge on a clean white background.

In her housedress, she walks to Jack Hess's store. When she arrives, she tells him she wants a white dish, good sized.

He thinks a minute and leaves the room. He is gone a long time, and she can hear him moving from room to room upstairs. He returns carrying a white platter with a flat rectangular center and a fine crack running out to a corner.

"My wife used it for roasts," he says. "I'm never going to cook a roast."

"I won't take something that belonged to your wife," she says.

"I'm selling it for fifteen cents," he says.

"You wouldn't be selling it if I hadn't asked you for it."

Jack Hess sets the platter down. "Fifteen cents," he says.

She smiles and relents and gives him the dime and the nickel. She holds the platter under her arm and walks home as fast as a schoolboy who has just bought a jar of marbles might. Once inside, she sets the platter on the kitchen table. She lays out her pieces of sea glass and studies them.

Some are sturdy and some are paper thin. A few tell stories, while others seem more secretive. Many are as beautiful as fine jewelry; others are blunt and ugly. Honora arranges the bits of glass, trying to form a satisfying whole. She puts a dot of cobalt in the center.

She tries to imagine where each piece has come from, who has used the glass and why. Is the blue-violet from a bottle of iodine that was once taken from a medicine cabinet and used for a scraped knee? Is the topaz from a bottle of whiskey tossed overboard by a rumrunner? How long does it take to make a piece of sea glass, anyway—a week, a year, ten years? Was the glass originally that lovely aquamarine color or has the ocean imparted its own stain, as if spewing out calcified bits of itself?

Sometimes she forces herself to remember that sea glass is only other people's garbage. It is useless, of no value whatsoever. Trash, Sexton once said. And yet, when Honora comes upon a piece of aquamarine or cerulean lying on the sand, she feels she's found a gem. She picks it up and puts it in her pocket, and on good days, she goes home with heavy pockets.

For a time, Honora thinks about making an object with the glass. A mosaic on a tray of sand. A frame for a mirror. A necklace for her mother. Perhaps she could fill a jar with sea glass and use it as the base of a lamp. But after a few minutes, these ideas always lose their appeal. It's the individual bits that interest her, the ability to pick them up and let them fall through her fingers and guess at the story behind each one.

Honora cannot find a red, and so the idea of red consumes her for whole days at a time. Logic tells her red is out there, but though she finds pinks and lavenders and yellows, she cannot find a red. Sometimes the sea glass reminds her of gumdrops—grape and lime and lemon. Sugarcoated bits of jelly.

"The only problem with looking for sea glass," Sexton says one day when he and Honora are walking along the beach, "is that you never look up. You never see the view. You never see the houses or the ocean because you're afraid you'll miss something in the sand."

Vivian

Fog smothers the horizon line, then the ocean, then the beach, until Vivian can hardly see beyond the railing of the porch. It moves as though racing and veers around the corner of the porch. Visiting ghosts, Vivian thinks as she reaches down and scratches Sandy's neck. With Dickie gone, Sandy hardly ever leaves her side.

Dickie fretted that Vivian would be bored, that she'd have nothing to do. Had to go, he said. Had to travel down to the city to restructure his holdings. The opportunities in the stock market were just too good to pass up right now.

Shoo, shoo, Vivian said to him, pushing him out the door.

A foghorn sounds, and Vivian sees a shape moving through the mist. A woman in a cloth coat.

Dickie needn't have worried, Vivian thinks. She has not been bored, not for one minute. When Dickie called her that first day to see how she was faring, she could hardly keep contentment from her voice. She hadn't seen a single soul socially, she told him, nor had she once put on a decent dress. She'd read, she said. And she'd actually cooked a meal. (*Not really,* Dickie said.) She'd walked down to the general store, met the proprietor, and walked back again with milk and coffee. She'd spent hours on the verandah watching the water. (*Are you squiffy?* Dickie asked.) Not at all, she wanted to say. (*Well, a bit,* she said on the phone.) Last night, she had to feign disappointment at his news that he would be gone another day. (*Oh, how boring,* she said. *Is that really necessary?*)

The woman in the fog seems to be searching for something in the sand. She moves in and out of visibility, and occasionally Vivian catches a glimpse of color, the faded loden of a cloth coat, a flash of blue in a head scarf. But then a mist surrounds the woman, and the colors subside, and it is as if the woman has never been there at all.

The light reminds Vivian of mornings in Venice: the sun overhead doing its best to burn off the fog and produce a luminescence. Funny how this same view with Dickie in tow would bore her, would make her feel compelled to complain about the fog. About how they couldn't go boating, couldn't play golf. But without Dickie with her on the porch, whining about the fog seems absurd. The light is marvelous, really.

The fog drifts a bit, revealing the woman in the cloth coat again. She still appears to be searching for something in the sand. Vivian stands up from the black wicker rocker and walks out onto the beach with Sandy following. "Hello there," she calls. "Have you lost something?"

The woman looks up and blinks, clearly startled by the apparition in front of her. "No," the woman says. "I haven't. I was just . . . I was just looking for sea glass."

Vivian is struck by the woman's thick dark eyelashes and her squarish chin. Though her coat is plain and dowdy, Vivian can see a beautifully knit pink lambswool sweater under it. She takes a step closer. The woman pulls her kerchief off, revealing lovely dark hair that immediately begins to unfurl in the humidity. The woman's skin is pale. She seems embarrassed, which produces a bit of pink in her cheeks.

"Sea glass?" Vivian asks.

"It's just something that washes up on the beach," the woman says. "I collect it. I'm not sure what for. It's pretty useless. I just like the shapes and the way it looks," she adds. She reaches into her pocket and pulls out a piece of glass. "Here," she says, handing it to Vivian. "This is a piece I found earlier."

Vivian looks at the object in her open palm. It is apple green, so thin it feels like mica. Its light seems to come from within, like the fog. When she was a child, she used to collect shells and sand dollars, but it never occurred to her to collect glass. In recent years, the staff of the Highland Hotel has taken to raking the beach out front so that there's no debris there at all. "It's very pretty," she says, returning the shard to the woman.

"It's trash, actually," the woman says, pocketing the piece of sea glass. "People throw things overboard or their trash gets dumped at sea. The glass breaks and then takes a beating from the ocean and the sand. This is what washes up."

"My name is Vivian Burton. I live just here." Vivian turns and points up to Dickie's cottage, invisible now in the fog. She laughs. "It *was* there," she says.

The woman smiles. "I'm Honora Beecher," she says. "My husband and I live at the end of the beach."

"Oh, really? Which house?" Vivian asks.

"It's white with black shutters. Three stories tall? They say it used to be a convent."

"Oh, yes," Vivian says. She has an impression of an absolutely derelict house.

"Do you live here year round?" the woman asks. "Cute dog."

Vivian wraps her cardigan across her chest. "No," she says. "We'll leave just before Thanksgiving."

"Oh," the woman says. "We're here for good now. We just bought the house."

"Congratulations," Vivian says.

"Thank you, but I'm a little nervous about winter storms. I've never lived on the coast before. They say the storms out of the northeast can be fierce. What's his name?"

"Sandy. Is your husband a fisherman?" Vivian asks.

The woman tucks a strand of hair behind her ear. She's hardly more than twenty, Vivian guesses. "He's a typewriter salesman," the woman says.

"Oh," Vivian says with some surprise.

"He travels a lot. He's away now."

"You don't mind being alone?"

"I miss him," Honora says with a slight flush. "But I keep myself busy. There's so much to do to get ready for winter."

"Where are you from?" Vivian asks.

"Taft. It's inland. How about you?"

"Boston," Vivian says.

"We went there once this summer," Honora says. "We had dinner at the Parker House."

"How nice," Vivian says politely.

"Well, I'd better get back," Honora says, looking at the fog.

"You're sure you can do it? I can't even see the water now," Vivian says.

"Oh, I'm fine," Honora says. "How lost can I get? The ocean is on one side, the seawall on the other. And if I walk too far,

I'll hit the rocks. I'm bound to find the house."

"Well," Vivian says. She wonders if she should invite the woman in. "I'm here until Thanksgiving," she says. "If you're ever at this end of the beach and feel the need for a cup of tea, just give a holler."

The woman smiles. "Thank you," she says. "I'll do that."

Honora disappears into the fog. Vivian feels, unusually, a sharp pang of disappointment. Beside her, Sandy is wrestling with a crab.

"Sandy, stop," she says.

The dog, sheepish and obedient, trots along with Vivian as she walks to the water's edge, guided more by sound than by sight. The tide is low, and it seems she has walked farther than she ought to when suddenly her feet are covered by an incoming wave. The shock of the cold immediately clears Vivian's head, and she laughs. And now even the hem of her dress is wet, but she doesn't care at all.

Honora

When the munitions boat caught fire, Honora was just eight years old and living with her family in her uncle Harold's house overlooking Halifax Harbor. Honora's three older brothers—Charles and Phillip and Alan—had already left the house for classes at the McKenzie Boys' School in Armsdale, some two miles away. Honora's cousin Emma, still a baby, was in bed. Honora's one remaining brother, Seth, who was four, rushed to the window with his uncle Harold to see the fire. Honora briefly went to the window herself, ignoring the calls of her mother in the basement to help carry up the laundry before she herself set off for school, the opening delayed because winter hours had already begun. The column of smoke rose higher and higher, and already Honora could see dozens of children, on their way to school, gathering in the streets to watch the aftermath of what Honora would later learn had been a collision between the *Mont Blanc* from France and the *Imo* out of Norway.

Uncle Harold knew, from the fiery smoke, that the *Mont Blanc* was burning fuel.

"Honora!" he bellowed sharply as he bent to pick up Seth. "Go help your mother."

Reluctantly, Honora left the broad windows of the dining room of the house perched high above the harbor in a neighborhood known as Richmond. The windows had been built to Harold's specifications so that he and his family might be able to watch the large ships come into port while eating breakfast. When his wife, Marguerite, died in childbirth, Harold had begged his sister—Honora's mother, Alice—to come north to live with him and help him take care of his infant daughter.

"Tell William there's plenty of work in the foundry," Harold had written. "There's a war on up here. Halifax is the busiest harbor in the British Empire."

Honora's mother had said to her husband, "It's a way to save for a house of our own."

Honora and her mother were still in the basement, holding wicker wash baskets of wet sheets and towels, when the *Mont Blanc* exploded with a force that blew apart her three thousand tons of steel. The shock was felt in Cape Breton, two hundred and seventy miles away.

A thick gravy smoke rose high above the city. The blast leveled three hundred and twenty-five acres, wounded nine thousand, and killed sixteen hundred, including Honora's father, who'd gone to the foundry earlier that morning to catch up on paperwork. As for Harold, he was blinded by shards of glass that blew inward from the window. The baby, Emma, was crushed by falling rafters. Four-year-old Seth simply vanished. No trace of him was ever found, and it was never known if he had been whisked away with the roof that had lifted from the house like a hat on a blustery day, or if he had crawled under the wreckage of a nearby house that had later burned in one of the hundreds of fires that moved through the city. Honora preferred to think that he had been obliterated into atoms, about which she was learning in school, and that one day he would reassemble and fall to earth, intact and unharmed, somewhere in her vicinity—not unlike Dorothy, say, in *The Wonderful Wizard of Oz.* In the interim, she believed, Seth was floating just beyond her reach. It was an idea that, when she was brave enough to voice it to her mother, produced a look of horror so precise in its features that Honora never mentioned it again. That the atomic-ghost Seth would have been able to emigrate back to Taft, New Hampshire, with what was left of the family shortly after the disaster was taken on faith—much as the miracle of the loaves and the fishes was, for example. Or the Resurrection.

Hundreds of people, Harold among them, were blinded by flying pieces of glass as sharp as knives. Had the *Mont Blanc* simply exploded outright and not sent up its enticing plume of flaming smoke, drawing half the city to its windows, many of the blinded might have been spared. But it was not, in general, a sparing disaster. Houses were picked up and smashed, and those left standing had bowed walls and rooms open to the sky. Many of the corpses were headless, making identification difficult; most of the bodies had inexplicably lost their clothing. A tidal wave of epic proportions swept over the city minutes after the blast, killing dozens of others. Later that night, a snowstorm began, blanketing the wreckage and the hidden corpses alike.

Honora and her mother were buried under a pile of wet sheets and towels, to which they owed their lives. Her mother's right leg was broken, and it was Honora who had to go for help. She found her uncle Harold on his back on the kitchen floor, alive and dazed and not yet feeling the pain of the glass in his face and neck. Honora yelled for Seth and ran out of the house, where an astonishing sight greeted her. Horses had died standing, trees were coated with ash, and the neighborhood known as Richmond had simply vanished.

The town that Honora returned to was so unlike the city that had been leveled that for years she thought of the Halifax disaster as a kind of childhood nightmare that had no relation to the present. Her mother never spoke of it, nor did her brothers ever mention it in their mother's presence. The small cape into which they moved in Taft, New Hampshire, had once belonged to Honora's grandmother. It had green shutters and sat at the end of a dirt lane. It was surrounded by lilacs in which the bees buzzed in summer. A picket fence swayed in the wind, the house had only three bedrooms, and the windows in the dining room were immediately painted shut by Honora's mother. But the smell of the earth under the porch was so evocative of a childhood that had vanished that even at eleven and twelve and thirteen years of age, Honora was unable to resist climbing under the porch, poking the earth there and inhaling its fresh scent.

There was insurance money from her father; Harold, forever chastising himself for having invited his sister's family up to Nova Scotia in the first place, gave his insurance money to Honora's mother. All of which lasted long enough to see the boys through high school and out of the house and off to Syracuse and Arkansas and San Francisco. From the age of fourteen until her wedding day, it was just

Honora and her mother and Harold in the cape at the end of the dirt road. Uncle Harold never complained about his injuries, although he had aged so quickly that no one ever believed he was Alice Willard's younger brother. As for Alice Willard herself, she effaced her memories with industry, selling produce from her garden in summer and making quilts in the winter to support the unlikely family of three. String was saved, bathwater was reused, and everything that ripened was preserved in glass jars that had been slowly emptied during the previous winter. Honora learned thrift and stoicism at an early age, though she was often baffled by her mother's need for silence.

Honora's fondest memories of her childhood home are of the nights when she and her family would all play Michigan poker using Diamond matches for chips. Some mornings, she would awaken and discover that a gentle fog had blanketed the mountain hamlet. Her mother would have left the bedroom already, and from the kitchen the sound of eggs sizzling in grease would be floating up the stairs. Honora would dress and leave the house and stand at the end of the lane near the swaying picket fence. She would look down through the tunnel of trees. The air would be soft and milky, and if the fog was just right, it would leave the lane visible but obliterate all the world beyond it.

Alphonse

Alphonse waits on the corner where he met the man in the blue shirt four weeks ago. Every Sunday he has stood here and hoped that McDermott would come and take him fishing. He waits on the corner because he thinks that if he stays in the apartment the man won't bother to come up the stairs. And besides, Alphonse doesn't want his mother or Marie-Thérèse to talk to McDermott because they will have a million questions and the man will naturally get sick and tired of answering them and then he will never ever come back for Alphonse and that will be that.

Probably the man won't come today anyway because it's too foggy to go fishing. The fog is so thick that he can't see the end of the block. It moves through the streets like smoke, and Alphonse pretends the Germans are right around the corner and that the smoke is from the guns and the bombs. *Pow. Pow,* he says. *Bam. Bam.* He raises his arms as if he had a rifle in them and goes into a crouch and swings the gun wide.

The man puts a hand to his chest and staggers a step or two and then goes down onto the sidewalk.

Oh, Jesus, Alphonse thinks.

"You got me," McDermott says.

Alphonse quickly lowers his arms. The man gets to his feet and says hello and Alphonse says hello back.

"You ready to go fishing?" McDermott asks.

"Sure," Alphonse says.

McDermott crouches down in front of his face. "Hey," McDermott says, tilting Alphonse's chin up. "Remember you have to look at me? Otherwise I might not know what you're saying."

Alphonse wonders how old McDermott is. Probably not as old as his mother.

"I would have come before," McDermott says, "but my sister Eileen has been sick, and I've had to take care of the kids. My brothers and sisters. They're a handful."

"So are mine," Alphonse says. And isn't that the truth.

"I've been down to the river to have a look," McDermott says. "I left my gear down there. You can't even see to the other side of the river, but, hey, the fish don't know that, do they?"

McDermott chuckles at his own joke, but Alphonse, even though he thinks the joke is kind of funny, can't quite manage a laugh. McDermott stands up and cocks his head in the direction of the river.

McDermott lights a cigarette as they walk. "Have you been waiting here every Sunday?" he asks.

"Yes," Alphonse says. "But I didn't mind." He has hardly thought of anything else since the man first mentioned fishing the Sunday that all the men went into Arnaud's father's house. Arnaud said that the men were planning a union and that it was a big secret, but if Arnaud knew a fact it couldn't possibly be secret anymore, could it?

"I should have sent one of the boys to tell you," McDermott says. "I'm sorry about that. It's been pretty chaotic for a few weeks."

Alphonse shrugs. He knows all about household chaos. He takes a quick look at his feet. He polished his shoes and stole the laces from Marie-Thérèse's boots and he's hoping she won't notice until he gets back.

"Have you always lived here in Ely Falls?" McDermott asks.

"No," Alphonse says. "We used to live on a farm in Quebec."

"What kind of farm?"

"Mostly blueberries. We had some chickens."

"You miss it?"

"Yes," Alphonse says. "But the farm went bad. That's why we had to come here."

Alphonse can remember the sick, hollow feeling inside his belly. All the kids crying for food—even, to his great shame, himself. His mother crying while she was nursing Camille. His father standing in the open doorway just staring out at dead fields.

But before that, before the farm went bad, Alphonse remembers being happy. He didn't know it was happiness and couldn't have put a name to it then—in fact he's pretty sure he never even thought about it—but now he knows that it was happiness. He would fish in the river with his father and collect eggs from the henhouse for his mother and hide with his dog in his fort under the front porch.

"My dad grew up on a farm," McDermott says. He lights another cigarette and stubs out the first on the sidewalk. They are at the bottom of Alfred Street now, away from the mills and the mill housing. Alphonse turns his head for a quick look. He can hardly see the clock tower because the fog is so thick. Without the mills and their thick smoke, the world looks almost beautiful.

"It was in Ireland. Do you know where Ireland is?"

Alphonse thinks he might know but he isn't too sure. He lifts his shoulders.

"It's on the other side of the Atlantic Ocean," McDermott says.

"Oh," says Alphonse. "What kind of farm?"

McDermott has on a beat-up leather jacket with stains on it and a gray sweater underneath. There's a hole in the sweater just below the neckline. He puts his hands in the pockets of his pants.

"Dairy farm," McDermott says. "They had cows. The farm was on the ocean. The fields were high above the water and, *Oh, wasn't that a beautiful sight!* my father used to say. You could walk across a field and just look out at the sky and the water, he said." McDermott looks down at Alphonse. "He was almost your age when he had to leave. His farm went bad too."

Alphonse nods. Almost everyone he knows came from a bad farm.

"When did you leave school?" McDermott asks.

"Last year."

"How old are you really?"

"Eleven."

"Thought so," McDermott says.

"I've just the one pole," McDermott says, putting a worm on the hook. "You start. When you get tired, I'll take over."

Alphonse takes the pole from McDermott's hand. It isn't too fancy a pole and it's more or less like the one his father used to have. He wonders what happened to that pole. Probably his mother sold it.

"There's a little hillock over there,"

McDermott says. "You could sit on that, lean against that stump."

Alphonse does as he's told, but he feels uncomfortable holding the fishing pole while McDermott sits empty-handed to one side of him. Truth be told, he'd be content just to watch McDermott fish. Alphonse struggles to think of something to say, something that won't make him seem stupid, but after a time he has to give up on that. McDermott hums occasionally or lies back and looks at the sky. He lights one cigarette and then another. The man smokes a lot.

"Your mother works the night shift, doesn't she?" McDermott asks finally.

"Yes," Alphonse says.

"I sometimes work the night shift myself. Not too often, though. Who takes care of all of you when she's away?"

"We all kind of take care of ourselves," Alphonse says, though that isn't quite true. Camille can't and of course Marie-Thérèse won't. A family of ducks swims out of the fog in a line and then goes back into the mist again.

"You ever think about what you're going

to be when you grow up?" McDermott asks.

Alphonse shrugs. He hates this question, he just hates it. Sister Mary Patrick used to ask it of him all the time, and he would try to think up something noble and worthy. One time he said a doctor and she nearly fainted with happiness, and then another time he said a priest and he could see he had gone too far and that she didn't believe him and because of that was probably having doubts about the doctor too. And then he had to be sure to remember, in confession, that he had lied about the doctor and the priest, neither of which was remotely within the realm of possibility.

"Probably a weaver like my mother is," Alphonse says. "She said she would teach me."

Right away Alphonse knows this is the wrong answer, because McDermott sits up. "You don't want to make the mill your life," he says. "You want to get more out of life than just standing at a loom all day. One of these days, you're going to have to try to go back to school."

Alphonse doesn't have the heart to tell McDermott that going back to school is pretty much out of the question now. "If I could do anything I wanted to," Alphonse says, revealing a fact he has never told anyone, not even his mother, "I would fly."

"Be a pilot, you mean."

"Yes."

"Well, that's a good idea. You have to go to school, though, to be a pilot. Did you know that?"

"Why?" Alphonse asks. He's shivering, but he doesn't want McDermott to know because the man might decide Alphonse should go home, and he would hate having to go home before he's even had a nibble. He wishes now that he'd worn something warmer than just his cloth jacket. He should have taken Marie-Thérèse's sweater, even if it does have a ruffle.

"You have to know all sorts of things like vectors and wind velocities and how to work the instruments," McDermott says. "You have to know a lot of math. Why do you want to be a pilot?"

Alphonse has an image of flying and struggles to describe it. "You'd be up in the sky all by yourself," he says. "And you could go where you wanted to and get there fast and when you got there you'd be a hero, like Charles Lindbergh."

McDermott thinks a moment. "Those are good reasons," he says.

Alphonse feels a distinct tug and his heart does a little skip of excitement. He yanks the pole like his father taught him to—not too much, just a bit, just enough to snag the fish. If you tug at it too hard, you'll tear the hook right out of the fish's mouth.

"Easy now," says McDermott, standing beside him.

The fish takes the line out so far that in the fog Alphonse can't see the end of it. It's a strange feeling, not being able to see the end of the line. Like having a ghost fish.

"Reel it in nice and slow," McDermott says. "And give a small hitch every once in a while just to let him know who's boss."

Alphonse wants McDermott to know that he can do this. He reels in slowly, and the fish springs out of the water.

"Jeez," says McDermott. "It's a big one."

Alphonse is excited now and reels in a bit faster. In the gray water he sees a flash of fin. In the distance the clock tower rings three bells.

McDermott takes off his shoes and socks and goes into the water to grab the line and the fish. He starts prancing with the cold. "Holy Joseph," he says, "it's *freezing* in here." He wraps his shirt cuff around his hand and catches the line. "It's a beauty."

McDermott brings the fish to shore. Alphonse thinks he might pass out with joy.

"You take the hook out," McDermott says. "If you catch a fish, you have to know how to take the hook out."

Alphonse takes hold of the bluefish, which is still wiggling. He always hates it when the fish is alive, and he wishes that this one would die soon. He pushes the barb all the way through the fish's cheek the way he has been told. The fish flops on the bank. It won't last too long now, Alphonse thinks.

"Thirty-two inches, anyway," McDermott says. "You want to take it home?"

Alphonse nods. He thinks of his mother's face when he walks in the door. Fresh bluefish for a Sunday-night supper. She will fry it in butter and make fish cakes for the rest of the week. Just thinking about it makes Alphonse hungry.

"You know how to clean a fish?"

Alphonse shakes his head. His father always cleaned the fish.

"Okay," McDermott says. "Watch me carefully."

Honora

Honora makes Sexton's favorite breakfast of tomatoes with cream and sugar. He has a trip and won't be back for eight days. As she always does before he goes away, she has a bath and washes her hair and puts on lipstick, so that when he is gone, he will remember her in a pretty dress and not in her apron. She has on the marcasite-and-pearl earrings.

Sexton shakes out the newspaper, and from across the table, Honora reads the headlines. *BLACKEST DAY ON WALL STREET IN MANY YEARS. Selling Orders Swamp New York Market. Billions Quoted. Values Fade.*

"Sexton?"

He cocks his head around the paper.

"What's happening with the stock market?" she asks.

He frowns slightly, as if reminded of a dentist appointment later that day. "A panic," he says. "It's nothing. It will pass. The stock market goes down, everybody sells, but they'll start trading today like crazy. You'll see."

"How much do we have in the bank?" she asks.

"About thirty-five dollars. I'm due to get my commission check tomorrow. It won't be too much, though. Not after the mortgage payment."

"Oh," she says.

He looks at her and seems only then to notice the lavender wool dress she has on. "Walk me to the car," he says.

Honora puts her coat on and follows Sexton to the Buick. It's a filthy day, just filthy. The wind is whipping so hard that she has to hold on to the fence posts as she makes her way to the car.

Sexton slides into the Buick. Honora leans on the door. He rolls down the window and tucks the tips of his fingers inside the top of her dress.

"You look like a wild woman," he says happily.

Vivian

Dickie goes sheet white on the telephone.

Vivian glances at the mantel clock, as if fixing the moment of disaster. Nine-fifteen in the morning. She was reading in the front room in her bed jacket and Dickie was about to leave the house for a lunch at a club in Rye when the phone rang. He spoke a phrase or two and then sat down hard at the telephone table. Dickie, a man who never sat for the phone, who couldn't bear the phone, actually.

Vivian, who can see Dickie through the open doorway, puts down her book and unfolds her legs from the divan. Sandy perks up his head.

In his wool tweed suit, Dickie sits huddled over his lap. He throws his head back and his knees fall open. She has never seen Dickie, who is nothing if not elegant, in such an ungraceful position. His hat tumbles from his hand.

"Everything?" he asks in an incredulous voice.

Vivian sits forward.

"Oh, God," Dickie says. He puts his hand to his forehead, as if shading his eyes. "For God's sakes," he says.

Vivian stands. The rain pings hard against the diamond-paned windows.

"I'm getting in the Packard," Dickie says. "I'll be there by tonight. Stay there. Don't leave."

Dickie puts the telephone back in its cradle.

"What is it?" Vivian asks from the doorway.

Dickie shakes his head back and forth. He seems oblivious to her presence. When he looks up at her, he blinks.

"Be a good girl, would you, and pack me a bag?"

Vivian sees Dickie out to the car and stands in the rain in her silk bed jacket. It seems the least she can do. Dickie tries to start the car, but his hands tremble so badly that he can't get a grip on the shift. Vivian has never seen a man so shaken before. She reaches into the car and puts her own fingers around his hand. "Steady now," she says, as one might to a horse.

She stands and wipes the rain out of her eyes. "It'll be all right," she says. "You'll see."

But she has no idea whether or not it will ever be all right, does she? She waves encouragingly as Dickie drives away. She walks back into the house and towels herself dry. She changes into her chartreuse-and-black-checked silk, as if she needed to be ready for the worst. As if she were awaiting news of a relative's death. She telephones her father.

"You're sure not?" she asks, in a voice equally as incredulous as Dickie's was.

With guilty relief, she puts the telephone back in its cradle. Never more grateful for her father's conservatism.

The rain stops late in the afternoon, and the sun makes a brief appearance. Vivian stands at the open doorway to the porch, aching to step out onto the beach and feel the sun on her face. But she doesn't dare be out of earshot of the telephone in case Dickie calls. She has calculated as best she can that even if he shot down to Boston, he can't have gotten there before four o'clock. Five o'clock if he hit traffic on Route 1.

The light is never the same, she thinks. Funny how she's lived most of her life within a mile or two of the ocean in Boston and never paid a minute's attention to the sea. Of course it's there, and of course ships come and go—and sometimes even friends come and go on those same ships—but the water has held no interest for her. Now, it seems, she can't get enough of it. As if she needed to make up for years of neglect.

When the telephone rings, Vivian braces herself, the image of Dickie in his Packard, his face white and his hands trembling, flitting across her vision. She leans against the wall by the telephone table and takes the phone off its cradle.

"Vivian," he says.

"Dickie," she says. "Darling, are you in Boston?"

"Vivian," Dickie repeats, his voice oddly calm. Frighteningly calm, really.

"Oh, Dickie, what is it? Is it very bad?"

"It's very, very bad," he says. "Worse than I ever thought possible."

"I'm so sorry," she says.

"Have you talked to your broker?" Dickie asks.

"I did," she says. "There's some damage," she lies. "But not too bad."

"The reason I ask is that I need you to do something for me," Dickie says.

"Anything," Vivian says. "Anything," she repeats with the guilt of the survivor. "I'll come right now. I'll get on the train. I can be there by noon tomorrow."

"No, don't come," he says. "I need you to stay there."

There's a silence over the wire.

"Dickie?" she asks after a time.

"I need you to buy the house," he says.

Vivian makes it onto the beach just before the sun is about to set. Sandy runs on ahead as if he too had been bursting to get outside. Vivian takes off her town welts and unrolls her stockings. She still has on the chartreuse-and-black-checked dress she put on in anticipation of some kind of bereavement. On the telephone, she was flustered and, for once in her life, speechless.

Think about it, Dickie said.

She turns to look back at the house, comfortably settled in its nest of dunes. Behind it, the sun is low on the horizon. The house has three gables, a screened porch in the central one. Behind the screen, there's a bedroom. On fair days, Vivian takes her tea on the porch instead of in bed.

She doesn't want to leave the house, and she can afford to buy it.

There, she thinks. *That's settled.*

She drifts north toward the lifesaving station, noticing that the storm has left more detritus on the beach than usual. She steps around the seaweed and the razor clams, the scallop shells and a piece of netting from a fishing boat, and she thinks of Dickie in Boston.

She will call him as soon as she gets back to the house. She will tell him that she will buy the house immediately, and then Dickie will come back up and they'll live together again just as if this horrible stock market thing had never occurred. Though even as she imagines this scenario, she knows that it will never happen like that. Dickie's pride would never allow him to live in the house if she owned it.

She tries to imagine what it would feel like to know that one had lost everything, that one had to sell all the dresses and the jewelry and the cars and the houses. That one could never go to Havana or throw a party at the Plaza Hotel. That one would have to get a job. She tries to picture what possible work she herself could find if it happened to her, and that thought frightens her. She had one year of finishing school at Mount Ida, near Boston, a year she used primarily to prepare for her coming out. She can't think of a single practical skill she learned. She isn't at all sure she could survive the sort of ruin Dickie is facing.

Vivian doesn't have to walk very far before she finds what she is looking for. It lies pressed upon the beach, its slightly curved edges digging into the sand. When she picks it up, the glass has a satisfying heft. It's a good-sized banana-colored chunk, not too unlike the shade of her

Maggy Rouff. She runs her thumb around the edges, which are smooth. She puts the bit of sea glass into the pocket of her dress.

McDermott

McDermott edges his way toward the notice that's tacked up on the wire fencing at the mill entrance. The men and women who have read the notice move away and stand with their hands in their pockets, as if uncertain about going through the gate.

McDermott shoulders his way toward the front. He can see that Ross, with a large wad of tobacco in his cheek, is standing by the notice board.

"What's going on?" McDermott asks when he reaches Ross's side.

"Read it," Ross says.

ANNOUNCEMENT

Operating costs at this mill have undergone such changes that we are confronted with a situation that is not only abnormal but extremely critical.

LOWER WAGES IN OTHER COMMUNITIES

In many of the cotton mills of New England, wage reductions have become effective. The operatives in the Ely Falls Mill now receive wages that are much higher than what is paid for the same class of work in competing mills elsewhere. Some of the mills can operate 54 hours a week.

ELY FALLS MILL HANDICAPPED

It should be obvious that the manufacturers of the Ely Falls Mill, paying by the old wage scale, and limited to a 48-hour week, must be doing business under a serious handicap.

RELUCTANT TO REDUCE WAGES

When, in other sections of New England, cotton manufacturers reduced wages, the Ely Falls Mill refrained from taking similar action. But owing to the competitive conditions which now exist, the Ely Falls Mill is forced to make a reduction in wages of 10 percent, effective Monday, November 24, and have posted notices accordingly. It is hoped this will relieve the situation sufficiently to enable the mill to take orders which would otherwise go to competitors.

"They've finally done it," McDermott says.

"Fuckin' owners," Ross says.

"They expect us to feel sorry for them?" McDermott watches the men and women gather in groups. Still no one has gone through the gates. "What will happen now?" he asks.

"We'll get the union."

"We didn't get the vote," McDermott says.

"We will now."

McDermott knows that the wage cut, on top of the speed-up, will change the minds of the loom fixers who've been reluctant to form a union. The wage rates are already below poverty level.

Ross spits on the ground. "It's beautiful the way the bosses do the organizing for you, isn't it?" he says.

Alphonse

All day and all night the men have been going in the front door of the apartment house and even milling around outside, and no one seems to be sneaking in the way they did the last time. Alphonse has counted nearly forty men who have gone through the door and he wonders how Arnaud Nadeau's front room will hold them all. Alphonse knows that all the activity is because of the wage cut and the talk about unions. His mother and his aunt are in the bedroom speaking in low tones all about unions and strikes and whatnot, and Alphonse thinks that a strike would be just fine with him because he hasn't had a day off except Sundays and Labor Day and Christmas since he started in the mill a year ago. He can't imagine what everyone would do on a Monday in the middle of November if they didn't go to work.

Sam Coyne, who moved up from New Bedford last year, told him all about what it's like to be on strike and Sam says that after a while it's no picnic and that everyone gets hungry but that it's mostly all right for the kids because the charities put soup in their pails and give them hunks of bread, although it's sometimes a bother to have to stand in line all morning just to get a meal. You have to eat the soup sitting on the sidewalk, he says, even if it's snowing out, because if you go home you have to share it with your sisters and your brothers and maybe even your mother and your father, and by that time there won't be anything left for you. Alphonse can't imagine trying to eat his soup on the sidewalk if he knew his mother was hungry. If Marie-Thérèse was hungry, well, that's another story.

Sam also told him about the scabs, who everybody hates. The strikers spit at the scabs and might even beat them up because the scabs go into the mills and work for the owners and take the strikers' jobs and that just makes the strikes last longer. Alphonse prays that no one in his family will be a scab, though Marie-Thérèse would be a perfect scab, and he thinks he wouldn't mind being allowed to spit at her one bit.

His mother would never be a scab. Tonight at dinner when they had the stew his mother said to eat up good because you never knew where your next meal was coming from.

Sam said that some of the grocery stores would let you run up really high bills and that a couple of the landlords would let you wait on the rent in case the strike was settled in a hurry, but if the strike went on for a long time the landlords would come and put your furniture outside, and if you didn't have any relatives who would take you in, you were pretty much stuck out on the street. Which is what happened to Sam Coyne and his family, and after that his mother and Sam and his two sisters moved to Ely Falls. Sam doesn't know where his father and his two older brothers are, and his mother said to stop asking her because she didn't want to hear his father's fucking name anymore. Alphonse sometimes says the word *fuck* in his head, especially when Marie-Thérèse is talking to him in that horrible taunting voice she has, and he says *fuck fuck fuck* in his mind just to make himself feel better. But Sam Coyne says the word aloud like he's been doing it since the day he was born.

Holy Joseph, McDermott said.

His mother didn't believe that Alphonse had caught the fish himself and he didn't want to tell her about McDermott because then she would ask a million questions, so Alphonse kept talking about how good the fish would taste in butter and after a while she stopped asking him where he got the thing.

When they came back from fishing, McDermott said it was probably getting too cold to fish anymore, but they would see in the spring.

Alphonse watches the men come out of Nadeau's apartment and light up cigarettes. Alphonse searches for McDermott and finds him standing off by himself under a streetlight. He has on his leather jacket and the same sweater he wore when he took Alphonse fishing. Alphonse wonders if anyone has fixed the hole. A fine mist has started and Alphonse can see it slanting in gusts under the light of the street lamp. He wishes McDermott would look up at his window, but before McDermott even has his matches out two men go over to him and say something that must be pretty funny because McDermott throws his head back and laughs.

And that's an odd thing, Alphonse thinks. Because nobody seems upset about the wage cut. Even though it's raining harder now, the men just put up the collars of their jackets and stand around in groups, chatting and laughing and smoking.

Honora

For Thanksgiving dinner, Honora prepares a turkey with a breaded stuffing and bowls of squash and turnip and potatoes. She sets out a relish tray while she and Sexton drink glasses of S.S. Pierce sherry from a bottle given to him by the owner of a paper mill in Somersworth. Having practiced her crust for weeks, Honora decides that her pies are suitably flaky. Sexton, however, hardly eats a bite of the turkey or the turnip or the mincemeat. Honora asks him if he is sick and he says no, but he works at his dinner as if it were a chore, dividing the food into sections and then rearranging them until Honora can bear it no longer. She stands and runs the water in the sink, and Sexton, with obvious relief, puts down his fork.

That afternoon, before it grows dark, they drive in the Buick to a school yard with the idea that on this cold, but not unbearably cold, holiday they will do something frivolous, such as roller-skating on the school's cement courtyard. They sit on a bench and bend to their skates, but Sexton cannot make his key work. After a time, he gives up and reaches into his pocket for a package of gumdrops. He hands them to his wife. She notices that he doesn't keep any for himself.

Through October and November, Sexton has grown thinner.

He thought the debacle with the stock market only temporary, but now, he says, he isn't so sure about that. Honora aches for his anxiety, for she has grown to love him despite the thing in his character that makes him tell small lies in order to make sales. And anxious, he isn't quite as handsome as he was—the small flaws somehow magnified, the crooked teeth more apparent, the eyes seemingly having edged closer together. She is learning in a way she might not have for years what it is to love someone who is changing, and not necessarily for the better.

"Have one," she says, sliding the packet of gumdrops across the bench. His eyes seem blue today. They change color every day, depending on his skin tone or what he is wearing that day or the color of the sky. Mini chameleons in his face. Blue, gray, blue gray, gray green, hazel.

"I'm not hungry."

"You hardly ate any dinner."

"It was a good dinner."

"Thank you."

"I went to Manchester," he says, pocketing the gumdrops. "I had an account at the Manchester Five Cents Savings Bank. They had an Eight I had sold them that had jammed. My plan was to pick up the machine, give them a replacement, and then sell them a new Copiograph machine as well." He pauses. "That was the plan."

"And what happened?"

"When I got to Manchester, I couldn't find the bank. At first I thought I'd forgotten the correct street, so I drove around and around. Then I consulted my address book. I had the right address." Sexton leans back against the bench. He opens his palms.

"There was nothing there," he says. "Just a building. No sign. Nothing. I tried to find out if the bank had moved and had notified the head office instead of me. But no—the bank had simply failed." Sexton puts his hands in the pockets of his overcoat. In the flat light of a late-November afternoon, Honora thinks he looks years older than he did just the week before.

"Overnight," he says.

For suppers, Honora serves baked macaroni and stewed tomatoes, or codfish cakes and white sauce. She watches the pennies closely and consults her recipe book for meals that are both filling and cheap. Sexton reads the paper almost incessantly, as if the words there might rearrange themselves into more palatable stories. He sits at the table with one of his adding machines, calculating and recalculating the sums, but no matter how many times he reconfigures the numbers, the end result is always the same: Sexton Beecher has risked everything he owned on the eve of the single biggest economic disaster in American history.

Honora finds a large rectangle of lavender glass. She discovers, half buried in the sand, a nugget of such vivid blue that she thinks at first it is a piece of cloth. When she holds it up to the light, the shard takes on an inner glow of smooth teal, a color unlike anything she has ever seen before at the beach. She hesitates over a round starburst in the sand, thinking, despite the season, that it might be a jellyfish. But when she dares to poke it with her finger, she discovers that it is the bottom of a crystal goblet, the stem snapped off at the base, the crystal battered and misshapen, but a treasure nevertheless.

She tells herself that Sexton will pull through this difficult patch, that marriage is about surviving the bad times as well as enjoying the good. She has imaginary conversations with her mother in which Alice Willard gives advice about how to live with a preoccupied husband in the same way she might tell Honora that a woman can make her own cake flour by combining regular flour and cornstarch, and that vinegar is best for windows.

Alice Willard

Dear Honora,

Harold and I missed you at Thanksgiving. I made my butter turkey and we had Richard and Estelle over. Estelle made me furious when she said she couldn't eat the stuffing because it had onions in it, you know how irritating Estelle can be. I stewed about that until we had the pies, and I wish you had been there to talk me out of it, which I know you would have done.

Try not to worry so much about Sexton and his work. You could always take up sewing. I used to do custom work for the mill in Waterboro back when the boys were still in school and we needed the extra money. There is no shame in custom work, and you are a very good seamstress. You could see if one of the mills near you needed someone to make drapes and slip-

covers and that sort of thing. I always liked the work because I could bring it home and lay the pieces out on the living room floor and do the cutting and pinning and sewing when you children were in bed. You have such a big house I am sure you could find a room in which to lay out the material. Some of it gets pretty long, you know, especially the drapes.

Speaking of the mill in Waterboro, the workers there started a run on the bank in town. There was a story going around that there was a shortage in the bank's funds, and so everyone went to the bank to get their money out. They had to call the police force to keep everyone in line. The newspaper said the bank was $1000 short, but Muriel, who used to work there, says the shortage was much bigger. The newspaper also said there was no danger that the bank would go out of business, but no one believes that either. Truthfully, it all comes down to a matter of belief, doesn't it? If you think the bank is sound, you won't panic, and then the bank will be sound. I have our savings in the Five Cents Savings here in town, but it isn't so much that I *would keel over if it wasn't there. We mostly make do from week to week.*

I am sending the recipes you asked for. The tomato rarebit is good because you only need Campbell's tomato soup and a bit of Kraft cheese, and if you are hard up, you can have it on Saltines, like we used to do when you and the boys were at home. The other one, the Spanish rice, only takes the one can of tomato soup as well. And rice is not expensive. You only need one or two slices of bacon to give it flavor. Have you made the tapioca yet?

Look in the mail for a package. Along with your Christmas presents, I am sending some jars that I canned this summer. Harold and I worked one whole afternoon to pack the box so the contents wouldn't break. Harold is very knowledgeable about packing. We have too much to eat here as you well know and I hate to see it go to waste. I think you will like the blackberry jam the best.

It wasn't the same not having you here at Thanksgiving. And of course we are all sad about May. I hope I go quick when it's my time.

Tell Sexton not to get discouraged. Life is full of ups and downs.

Love,
Mother

P.S. If you find that the winter weather is making your skin harsh, you could try the Frostilla Skin Tonic. I have always trusted it.

Vivian

This has to be the house, Vivian decides. It's three stories tall, painted white with black shutters—not quite as bad as she has remembered. Work has been done on the front door, and a trellis surrounding it has fresh white paint. She steps from the four-year-old beach wagon and draws her coat around her. Snow started falling in the morning, lightly at first, and then more heavily. She is glad that she had her fur-lined boots and coat sent north from Boston, despite her father's protests.

Her father has nearly given up calling. He refuses to be dissuaded from the notion that Vivian has taken up with a married man (and who started that wicked rumor? Vivian would dearly like to know), when nothing could be farther from the truth. She hasn't even been out to dinner with a man since Dickie left. Periodically, she hears from Dickie, who is staying with Johnny Merrill on Marlborough Street. Short bulletins that suggest a kind of panic. Holding a finger against one leak while another starts at the other end of the boat.

Vivian knocks against a windowpane inside a Christmas wreath. When the door opens, Vivian watches the woman's features rearrange themselves—dipping in a flash from expectant to disappointed and then rising immediately to pleased.

"Hello," Honora says when pleased has been reached.

Vivian notes the shell-pale satin blouse and the brown wool skirt. Marcasite-and-pearl earrings. Ordinary brown pumps.

"Come in," Honora says. "What a surprise."

"I don't want to bother you. I was just on my way to the airfield. I'm leaving, and I wanted you to have these." Vivian opens the antelope-and-sardonyx bag Dickie gave her for her twenty-ninth birthday in September and takes out a small tissue-wrapped packet tied with string.

"When does your plane leave?" the woman asks.

"I have a few minutes. It might not even go at all because of the bad weather."

"I'll make us some tea."

Vivian wipes her feet on a doormat and follows Honora into the kitchen. The woman is as slim as a wand, Vivian sees from behind. She has beautiful shoulders as well—a swimmer's build.

Honora sets the tissue-wrapped packet on a kitchen table covered with a linen cloth. An apron has clearly just been tossed aside. Vivian removes her chamois gloves and unbuttons her coat.

"May I take those?" Honora asks.

"I can't stay long enough for a proper visit, though I should have come by ages ago. I'm off to New York—having Christmas with an aunt—and . . . well . . . open the packet."

Honora sits at the remaining kitchen chair and unties the string. Spread out upon the tissue paper are two dozen pieces of sea glass. "Oh," Honora says, clearly moved.

"After I met you that time, I started looking for sea glass," Vivian says. "It gets addictive, doesn't it?"

"Thank you. They're very beautiful."

"I thought you could add them to your collection," Vivian says. Her own favorite is the meringue disk that seems to have melted and bubbled as if it had been cooked. Honora holds up a shard of white milk glass. "I wasn't sure if milk glass counted," Vivian says.

"Oh, yes," Honora says and then laughs. "Well, how would I know? I just make up the rules as I go along. These are lovely. It's rare to find these colors. Most sea glass is white or brown."

"Look at us," Vivian says. "We're like two diamond merchants exclaiming over a shipment."

Honora rises to fill a kettle with water. Vivian notices the mismatched cups hanging from hooks under an oilcloth-covered shelf, the two pies (they smell like mincemeat) on a table next to the stove, the cleanliness of every surface, even the floor. Mrs. Ellis, who comes twice a week to Vivian's house, doesn't do half as good a job. A copy of *Woman's Home Companion* is on the kitchen table next to the apron.

Honora lays a tea cloth on a tray and sets upon it two mugs and a pink glass sugar and creamer set. She is unapologetic about the mismatched crockery, a trait Vivian immediately admires.

"Can I tempt you with a piece of mincemeat pie?" Honora asks.

"I don't want you to cut into your pies. You're obviously expecting someone."

"I'm expecting my husband," Honora says. "I'm not sure when he's coming. He said he'd be here for lunch, but he didn't make it. He and I can't eat both pies anyway. I didn't realize you were still here. I thought just about everybody had gone home."

"We had an unexpected turn of events," Vivian says. "My friend Dickie Peets, the fellow who owned the house, had to sell it rather quickly. And so I bought it. I'm not sure why, other than that I've loved being here."

Honora opens her mouth to ask a question, but then closes it. Instead she fetches the kettle from the stove. The water must have been near a boil already, Vivian thinks. Yet another indication of the way in which the woman has prepared for the arrival of her husband. For a moment, Vivian envies that sense of expectancy.

"Dickie and I were *living in sin,*" Vivian says lightly. "I hope you're not shocked."

"Oh," Honora says, flustered.

"He's gone now," Vivian says, taking a sip of tea. "I've never been on my own. What do I taste?"

"Cinnamon. And cloves."

"I'm sure your husband is tied up in a department store. With all the other husbands picking out last-minute gifts for their wives."

"You don't want any milk with that?"

"No, no. This is perfectly fine."

Honora cuts two slices of pie and sets them on the table with forks. Vivian wonders briefly about the snow. She has no idea how a Ford wagon will fare in bad weather. Mrs. Ellis's husband taught Vivian how to drive shortly after she purchased the beach wagon from Archie Swetnam, a man in straits not dissimilar to Dickie's. At first, Vivian thought the idea of profiting from someone else's losses distinctly immoral, but now she has decided that it is much the other way around: she is simply helping her friends out of tight spots. "Lovely pie," she says.

"Your plane," Honora says, glancing at the clock on the wall.

"I've still a minute or two," Vivian says.

"My husband has had a lot of worries lately," Honora says. "Business isn't going well."

"He sells typewriters."

"And other business machines."

"This can't last forever."

"No, but you see we'd just bought the house."

Vivian nods, once again experiencing the guilt of the survivor. The fiasco with the stock market has ruined a good number of her friends: the Nyes, the brothers Chadbourne, Dorothy Trafton. She finds it hard to muster sympathy for Dorothy Trafton. "What are you giving your husband for Christmas?" she asks.

"It's called a Multi-Vider pen. It multiplies, divides, works percentages and proportions."

"Sounds clever."

"It's crimson and black, gold filled," Honora says with a flush of pride.

"I'm sure he'll love it," Vivian says. "Men love gadgets." Vivian has bought her father a movie camera for Christmas. She'll be up all night wrapping presents; she has seven parties to go to in the next ten days. The stock market thing will be all the talk—who is destroyed, who is not, quaint economies one has heard of.

"I'd show it to you, but it's wrapped," Honora says.

Another pang of something like regret passes through Vivian, regret that she hasn't a lover to whom to give a Christmas gift. Of course she will give Dickie a present—a small painting by the artist Claude Legny—but it isn't the same. Their meeting will almost certainly be strained and tense.

"I'd better go," Vivian says.

"Where's the airfield?" Honora asks.

"The other side of Ely Falls."

"How are you getting your car back to your house?"

"I've a fellow who'll take the trolley to the airfield the day after tomorrow and drive it back," Vivian says.

"I was just going to suggest I drive it for you."

"You know how to drive?" Vivian asks with more incredulity than she has intended.

"I do indeed," Honora says. "My husband taught me this summer. I'll just get my coat."

Vivian sits a moment and then politely finishes her tea and pie. She puts her dishes in the sink and slips on her coat. She moves into the hallway and follows a corridor that leads to what appears to be a front room with floor-to-ceiling windows looking out onto the beach. The sky seems to be brightening, and Vivian notices a sliver of blue to the east. A grand piano is in one corner, a decorated Christmas tree in the other. Several carefully wrapped packages have been set upon a tree skirt. A small settee near the tree is covered in a white crocheted throw, doubtless meant to hide a stain. Vivian has a sudden and powerful need of cheer—of fireplaces and highballs and brittle chatter and women covered with velvet and pearls.

Sexton

Sexton leans against the lamppost as if drunk already. He wants only to be drunk. Men and women brush past him, some with heads bent, letting the brims of their hats catch the snow, others with their faces tilted back, laughing. It seems that the entire city is on the streets this afternoon, ducking into doorways and balancing packages, everyone expectant and purposeful. He fingers the summons, now crumpled in the pocket of his coat.

Dear Mr. Beecher,

Would you be kind enough to come to my office at nine o'clock on the morning of December 24th. There is a matter of the utmost importance I should like to discuss with you. We have been unable to reach you by telephone.

Sincerely yours,
Kenneth A. Rowley

The summons is typed on a Fosdick No. 7 that Sexton sold the bank. The note was Copiographed for the files on a machine Sexton himself carried into the building just weeks earlier.

Sexton moves with the crowd, scarcely knowing where he is headed, too tired even to light a cigarette. After he has gone a block, he finds his path obstructed by a group of men and women waiting their turn to enter the revolving door of Simmons Department Store, and this reminds him again that he has to buy a Christmas present for Honora. He cannot go home empty-handed—no, of course he can't. He has ten dollars saved from his last paycheck. He sincerely doubts there will be another. Last night he slept in the Buick and shaved in the lavatory of a Flying A filling station in Lyndeboro. He can still feel the mantle of a bad night's sleep all about his face and eyes.

He enters through the revolving door

and is deposited at a perfume counter just inside the entrance. Men stand in a cluster, trying to attract the attention of a blond woman in a smart red dress who is spraying an atomizer onto their inner wrists, flirting a bit as she does so. Sexton longs to be among those men, lighthearted with the holiday, spending slightly too much on an easy gift for the wife. He doesn't even know what kind of perfume Honora prefers. She always smells like soap.

He wanders through the millinery department and then passes by the glove counter. He is pushed aside ("Excuse me, sir, I didn't see you") and finds himself in the hosiery department. He is fairly certain Honora would like hose. Once he walked into the bedroom when she was mending a stocking with a tiny hook that was all but invisible. She hadn't wanted him to see her doing that, and so she very quietly let the sewing fall into her lap while she spoke to him. He can't remember the conversation now. He can recall only the image of Honora in her white slip on the bed, the slip not even reaching her knees, her legs bare and beautifully formed.

He imagines her at home waiting for

him. She will be sitting on a chair in the kitchen, flipping through the pages of a magazine, looking out the window from time to time, worrying about him driving in the snow.

The image is unbearable.

"You can appreciate," Rowley said, his voice cold, not a hint of drink upon him. No sign of the affable and lazy bank president who had wanted to talk cars and baseball scores and leave the decision-making to the girl out front. No, this was a different Rowley altogether, and, sitting across from the man (not having been invited to remove his coat), Sexton had an image of Rowley's shoulders strung up like a puppet's. "You can appreciate, Mr. Beecher, that in this current economic climate, this bank, and indeed most of the banks that I am familiar with, are taking a very close look at the loans that have been issued. And, frankly, in so doing, we have discovered an irregularity with your particular loan. Now that we have all the paperwork in front of us."

"I'm sorry?" Sexton asked, attempting a smile.

Rowley smiled thinly back at him. "As you recall, Mr. Beecher, you came in on Friday, September fourth, requesting a loan of seven hundred dollars for the purpose of home improvement."

He's enjoying this, Sexton thought. *Of course he is. Man bites dog bites cat.* The bank would have tremendous shortages now, for which Rowley would be held responsible.

"At that time, you told us that you owned your home on, let me see, Fortune's Rocks Road. Isn't that correct, Mr. Beecher?"

A bead of sweat angled across Sexton's temple. With an effort at the nonchalance of innocence, he shook his head. "I'm not sure what you mean, Ken."

A small flinch, like a tic, passed across Rowley's features, and Sexton realized that the *Ken* had been a mistake. The paneled walls that once seemed the very epitome of graciousness now felt oppressive, the windowsills too high, the room taking on the punitive menace of a classroom. "I'm sure there's been an error of some sort in the paperwork," Sexton added.

"There's a very simple way to settle this.

I can pick up the telephone and call Albert Norton over at the Franklin bank. I've been reluctant to do that, Mr. Beecher, as you can appreciate, for it would almost certainly precipitate an investigation into your loan with them." No need to play the innocent now, Sexton thought: Rowley had him in his sights. "However, I am afraid that we *shall* have to call in the loan this bank gave to you. The loan of seven hundred dollars for home improvements to a house you did not, in fact, own."

Sexton sat forward. "But in essence I did. Really, what does a day or two matter—particularly since it was over a holiday weekend and business was suspended for three days?"

"There can be no debate on this matter," Rowley said. "As a banker, I cannot tolerate any irregularities. Seriously, Mr. Beecher, can you imagine a depositor not minding the irregularity, say, of a miscalculated sum in his passbook?" Rowley waited a moment for an answer to his rhetorical question. "No, I think not," he answered himself.

Is the bottle in that right-hand drawer an irregularity? Sexton wanted to ask. "Could we talk about restructuring the loan?" he asked instead.

"No, that will not be possible."

The trickle of sweat pooled on Sexton's cheek.

"And I am afraid, Mr. Beecher, that while I have refrained from notifying the Franklin bank in hopes that you and I might reach an easy settlement here, I did have to speak with the head office of your company. We were unable to reach you by telephone, you see."

Sexton briefly closed his eyes and watched his life tumble away from him. His job. His car. His house.

"You spoke to whom?" Sexton asked.

"I have it in my notes here. Mr. Fosdick himself, I believe. Yes, that's right."

Sexton took his handkerchief out of his pocket and wiped the sweat from his face. Rowley too was sweating, Sexton noticed. His collar was limp and—was it possible?—dirty.

"Mr. Fosdick has asked me to have you call him at your earliest convenience. I do encourage you in future, Mr. Beecher, if you are to continue in business of some sort, to install a telephone at your residence."

In business of some sort.

"So then. Not to prolong this unpleasant matter. We should like repayment in full of the loan in question no later than Wednesday of next week."

"But I can't raise that kind of money by next week," Sexton said, stifling a note of rising panic that had crept into his voice.

"No, I thought not. But, as I recall, Mr. Beecher, you mentioned you drove a Buick? What do you imagine it's worth now?"

Sexton was silent.

"I'm trying to find a way for you to keep your house, Mr. Beecher. Frankly, I consider this an awfully generous gesture on my part. If your automobile is worth what I think it is, then it could go a fair distance toward repaying this loan we're speaking of."

Sexton thought frantically.

"So you'd say it's worth how much, Mr. Beecher?"

"Four hundred and seventy-five dollars," Sexton said. "That's what I paid for it."

"Well then, Mr. Beecher. If you would be so kind as to deliver the Buick to the address I have written on this piece of paper next Wednesday, we would be most grateful. As you will see, the address is that of an auction house. I can't guarantee the four hundred seventy-five. Indeed, I should think not in this economic climate. But with commission we might net four hundred."

Panic blossomed in Sexton's voice. "Without the car, Mr. Rowley, I can't make a living."

Rowley winced as surely as if Sexton had begun to cry. "I hope we're not going to have a problem here," Rowley said quietly.

With a supreme effort, Sexton stood.

"Well then," said Rowley, relief evident in his voice. And without a trace of irony added, "Good luck to you."

"May I help you, sir?"

A lithe, diminutive woman, beige of hair and of face, who suddenly seems so precisely the color of the product she is selling that Sexton wonders if she has sprung to life from behind the counter, tilts her head to catch his attention.

"Can I show you anything in particular?

Are you looking for a gift for your wife? Your girlfriend? Is she tall or is she short?"

"She's . . . long," Sexton says. "She's very long."

The beige woman looks sharply up at him, as if she might be dealing with a fruitcake. Or a man who's celebrated just a bit too heartily at an office party around the corner. Sexton struggles to attention. The task seems monumentally difficult, but he cannot go home to Honora empty-handed.

"I have some marvelous chiffon hose I could show you," the salesgirl says. "Some lovely pairs. Dressy. Quite smart. Chiffon is all the rage now. But serviceable as well. A woman must have durability, don't you agree?"

Yes, he does agree. Honora has durability.

The salesgirl holds a slim pair of delicate stockings between her outstretched fingers. The chiffon flows like liquid from hand to hand. Briefly, Sexton imagines the silky feel of the stockings on Honora's legs.

"Sir?" the salesgirl asks.

Above him, the chandelier seems to be burning too brightly and, for a moment, to spin. Around him there are voices, animated and brisk, rising to a crescendo. He thinks again of Honora at the house waiting for him. He cannot bear the thought of going back to her. How can he ever explain to her what he has done?

"Get a move on," a man behind Sexton calls out. "Haven't got all day."

"I'd like two pair," Sexton says quickly. He takes from his pocket a thin roll of bills secured by an elastic band and gives the salesgirl a two-dollar bill and a one.

Behind him, someone cheers.

McDermott

It seems to McDermott that he has been waiting an age behind the man in the long brown overcoat. The customer has been staring at a pair of hose for minutes now, and McDermott can see that the salesgirl is growing impatient and slightly frantic. The line behind McDermott is five or six deep, and already someone has called out to get a move on. He himself would get out of the line if he could, but Eileen was specific: two pairs of Blue Moon silk stockings in Mirage, she said, and at the time, McDermott was happy to have instructions. Eamon and Michael were specific as well: they said they wanted jackknives. McDermott suspects that his brothers belong to one of the gangs that periodically terrorize the younger girls from the mills and steal their pay packets. McDermott has asked around for information, and if he ever gets proof or catches them at it, he'll beat them to a bloody pulp. Just a half hour ago, McDermott bought them hockey skates in the sporting-goods department. Take it or leave it, is what he thinks.

McDermott wishes he had twenty people to buy Christmas presents for. He would like an excuse to visit every section of the department store—men's shirts, household appliances, children's toys, even ladies' hats. He admires the gaiety of the displays, the color and the glitter, the world that the mannequins, in their dressing gowns and dinner suits, offer. McDermott lets the din settle around his ears and he doesn't strain to hear the words. It's enough that the voices sound happy—happy mostly for the early closing, he thinks.

The man in front of him finally makes a purchase, and someone behind McDermott cheers. The salesgirl wraps the stockings in tissue paper and then in brown paper and ties the packet closed with a string. When the man collects his package and turns, McDermott sees a face not unlike those he has seen often in the mill—a face gray with exhaustion and waxy with resignation. *Poor bastard,* McDermott thinks as he considers flirting with the salesgirl—though flirting is difficult for him. A fellow has to be able to hear the words that slide out of the side of a woman's mouth, and McDermott can't do that. He gives the girl Eileen's instructions, and she seems relieved not to have to demonstrate her product. McDermott watches her tie his package with a string.

"Do you have any ribbon?" he asks.

"Ribbon in Notions on Three," she says automatically. "Gift wrapping on Four."

McDermott lifts the thin package from the glass counter. It flops in his hand. He folds it in two and sticks it in the pocket of his leather jacket.

"What they're doing to Mironson stinks," Ross says, shaking his head. He picks his teeth, his breath as foul as a rotten fish.

The speak is packed because of the half day and the Christmas pay packet: an extra buck, a cartwheel, they call it. McDermott did his shopping before he allowed himself a drink; he has seen too many men who have drunk their pay packets and then sobbed at closing time because they had no Christmas to take home to their wives and children.

Ross means the stories the *Ely Falls Gazette* has published about Mironson's involvement with the Communist Party, about his belief in free love, and about the fact that he's been married three times. They followed up with an article accusing Mironson of stealing union funds in North Carolina. The bit about being a Communist is probably true, McDermott thinks, but he's prepared to bet the rest are lies.

"We get the weavers and the carders," Ross says, "we're set."

"But what about the others?" McDermott asks. "You can't have a successful strike without the nonunion workers. They're ninety percent right now."

"They look to the unions," Ross says. "It happened in Gastonia. It happened in New Bedford."

"Beal wouldn't picket."

"Mironson won't either," Ross says. "You read about how they stripped that woman who was a scab? Stripped her naked right on the street."

A movement catches McDermott's eye. A man in a now-familiar brown overcoat takes a table by himself. In the heat of the basement speak, he shakes the coat off and yanks his tie through its knot. He puts his hat on the table, runs his fingers through his hair, and then pats it down. His face is no less waxy than it was at the hosiery counter.

"The Francos don't trust Mironson anyway," McDermott says.

"They don't trust anyone who isn't Franco," Ross says. "If we strike, we'll go to our own. The church, the Ladies' Aid Society, St. Vincent de Paul. When the strike is under way, we'll call for help from the TWU. They'll want to move in and take over, and by that time everyone will be more than happy to let them."

The English girl, without her glasses today, slips into the empty seat at the table with the waxy-faced man. McDermott watches the man order and then drink in quick succession three shots of whiskey, the next as soon as he puts down the first. The English girl has on the orange lipstick, and when she smiles, McDermott can see a bit of it on her eyetooth.

"The thing we need," says Ross, "is propaganda of our own. We have no way to get information to the workers. It's all rumor."

The English girl and the man are laughing. The English girl isn't stupid: a woman can jack up the price for a stranger in a gabardine coat and silk tie who downs three straight shots.

"We need a press. For leaflets and posters," Ross says.

McDermott gazes over Ross's shoulder at the shoes passing by the basement window. He likes to imagine the people inhabiting those shoes, particularly the women, and particularly the women in the pumps or the pretty fur-lined boots. It's a fleeting pleasure: one minute the ankle and calf are visible, the next they're gone; McDermott has only a second to imagine a face. He watches a pair of impractical high heels mince along and imagines a blonde in pink lipstick. He sees a pair of serviceable brogues cross the window and thinks of Eileen.

"What are you doing for Christmas?" McDermott asks.

"Go to church," Ross says. "Eat a meal. We'll go to my brother's for the meal. I got Rosemary a watch. Six bucks at Simmons."

"Nice," McDermott says.

The man whose face now has a bit more color stands with the English girl and lifts his coat off the back of his chair. McDermott watches the man walk away, only then noticing a slim packet on the floor. He dips his eyes for just a second to catch a light from Ross and when he looks over at the table, thinking to call to the man with the English girl, McDermott sees that the package has already been snatched. He quickly scans the faces of the men sitting nearest to the table, but not a one gives away his sleight of hand. He hopes the man realizes he has lost the package before the stores close.

McDermott glances up at the window, thinking he might see the man pass by, though what McDermott could do by then he has no idea. Beyond the passing feet, he can see a newsstand, and occasionally, he can read the day's headline. *New*

England Business Outlook Good. A slight figure moves in front of the headline. Spindly legs stick out below a pair of pants that are too short and into boots with no laces. Boots McDermott would know anywhere. He tosses a few coins onto the table.

"Merry Christmas, Ross," he says.

The boy has the sleeves of his jacket pulled down over his fists for warmth, and his nose is running in the cold.

"Hello there," McDermott says.

The boy looks up. He wipes his nose on his sleeve.

"What are you doing?" McDermott asks.

"I'm supposed to go to Tsomides Market for my mother."

"And what happened? You lost the money?"

The boy opens his fist. McDermott counts the coins. "Then what's the matter?"

"She told me five things to buy, but I wasn't paying attention and now I can only remember four. If I go home with only four she'll be mad and give me another chore to do or she'll send me to church to say the rosary."

McDermott knows that Franco parents send their children to church when they misbehave. Sometimes, when McDermott passes by St. André's in the summer and the doors are open, he sees a dozen kids just sitting in the pews, holding their beads. Not such a bad deal, McDermott thinks. Sit in a quiet church for an hour, maybe even say a rosary if you have to. It beat the belt any day.

"Well, let's see," McDermott says. "What's your mother making for Christmas dinner?"

"The pork-and-fish supper."

"Is it the fish? Is it the pork?"

The boy shakes his head. He sticks his hands in the pockets of his pants.

"The coffee? . . . The flour? . . . The milk? . . . The bread?"

Still the boy shakes his head.

"Cream? . . . Lard?"

Alphonse brightens. "Sugar," he says and seems to gain an inch of height.

"How could you forget sugar?"

Alphonse shrugs.

"You'd better run to the market."

"Thank you," Alphonse says.

"No need to thank me. After you take the food back to your mother, how would you like to take a trolley ride?"

"Where?" the boy asks.

"It's a secret," McDermott says.

Alphonse

They have good seats on the trolley, and Alphonse thinks the snow is beautiful in the sudden sunlight. It isn't the first snowfall of the year but it's the one that has stuck the best and already the streets are white with only trolley marks to ruin them. McDermott sits beside Alphonse and smokes a cigarette, and from time to time Alphonse sneaks a look at his face. They boarded the trolley going west, which confused Alphonse because there's nothing in that direction from the city but pitiful farms. Maybe McDermott has a relative on a farm, Alphonse decides, and they are going visiting. That would be all right with him.

When they set out, McDermott asked Alphonse if he had a sweater because it might be cold where they were headed. Alphonse sprinted away and was back at the corner inside of four minutes with a sweater that belongs to Marie-Thérèse, who is closest to him in size, Alphonse being large for his age and Marie-Thérèse being small for hers. The sweater is light green and has a frill down the front, but if Alphonse holds his jacket closed no one can tell it's a girl's. Sometimes Arnaud Nadeau wears a flannel shirt to the mill that has a ruffle around the collar. It's red plaid, and Arnaud pretends it's a hand-me-down from his brother, but anyone can see that the shirt once belonged to his mother.

Tomorrow Alphonse's family will go to church and have the pork-and-fish dinner, and his mother's cousin will come to visit with her seven children and if Alphonse doesn't get out pretty quick after the meal, he'll be stuck inside until ten o'clock or so at night keeping his eye on his younger cousins and that will be the end of his holiday. It isn't going to be too much of a holiday anyway, his mother said, because of the pay cut. It's hard enough just to put food on the table, she said, and they shouldn't think about Christmas presents this year, and she didn't want anyone complaining. Marie-Thérèse whimpered and said that she had wanted a velvet dress so bad, and everyone else was silent thinking about the thing that they had wanted so bad too. Well, it was no use crying about it, his mother said, for once looking at Marie-Thérèse, who normally got away with murder. Everyone else was feeling the pinch, his mother said. It was going to be a slim Christmas all over town.

McDermott and Alphonse ride in silence and Alphonse watches the people getting on and off the trolley, more getting off than on as they travel farther and farther west. McDermott has a word with the conductor and offers him a cigarette and when he turns to look back at Alphonse, he points out the window. Alphonse sees a large flat field with a building and a tower and, lifting from the snow, an airplane. Suddenly the day, which until that moment has not felt one bit like a holiday, turns as sparkling as the snow.

“I sometimes come out here and watch the planes take off and land,” McDermott says. “They have a little waiting room inside that building there where you can get a cup of hot chocolate. I bet you'd really like a cup of hot chocolate right now."

Alphonse has counted seven planes already. He doesn't know all their names, but McDermott identifies them as they walk in from the trolley stop.

"See that one there with the Texaco star?" McDermott says, pointing to a bright red plane. "That's a Lockheed monoplane just like the one Frank Hawkes piloted from New York to Los Angeles and back again last summer. Nineteen hours ten minutes going west. Seventeen hours thirty-eight minutes going east. West to east is faster."

"Why?"

"The winds, I think. That big red one there? That's a Fokker Thirty-two. Wingspan ninety-nine feet. It has four rooms, a kitchen, two lavatories, and sleeps sixteen. That one there—taking off?—that's a Travel Air open cockpit. One hundred and twenty-two miles per hour. That'll be headed out to New York. Most of these planes, they go to New York or to Boston, and then the passengers make a connection to another plane and go off to Miami or Saint Louis or Havana. There should be a crowd of people in the waiting room today, all trying to get home for Christmas. That one there? Coming in? That's a Boeing mail plane. Pretty plane, isn't it? It'll be loaded with cards and packages today."

Alphonse and McDermott walk through the snow, and even though it goes in the sides of his boots and sometimes reaches above his sock line, Alphonse doesn't care. He can see a man in the tower with a microphone in his hands. To think that the airfield has been here all this time at the end of the trolley line and Alphonse hasn't known it! Even if he was too shy to go all the way to the building he could have stood at the end of the field and watched the planes taking off and landing.

McDermott steers Alphonse into the waiting room. The warmth is a surprise, though everyone still has a coat on. In the corner there's a woman in a fur coat talking to a woman in a cloth coat and when Alphonse looks at them again he notices that the woman in the cloth coat is the same woman who was in the brown bathing suit at the beach that day, the one who dug her hands and knees into the sand.

Alphonse worries that someone will

come over and ask McDermott and him to leave, because everyone in the room is so beautifully dressed and there he is in shoes without laces and his pants not even reaching his socks, and McDermott—well, McDermott looks better than Alphonse does, but not as good as the people standing around drinking coffee and chatting as if they did this every day. And then Alphonse glances down and spots the light green sweater with a frill, which everyone can see now because he's opened his jacket in the warmth, and he freezes the way a dog does when it knows it has done something bad.

"I'll get you a cup of hot chocolate," McDermott says.

Alphonse wraps his jacket tight across his chest and nods. He should have let his mother fix the zipper. McDermott goes to the counter and comes back again with a white china cup that has a blue line and an airplane on it, and Alphonse takes a long drink of the hot brew and thinks that it is just about the best thing he has ever had to drink in his whole long life.

The schedule is printed in chalk on a blackboard beside the ticket agent's window. The 2:15 flight to New York has been crossed out twice and now reads 3:35, which is only ten minutes away. The woman in the fur coat says something to the woman beside her, and when they laugh, Alphonse imagines bits of beautiful glass falling through the air.

Honora

Honora has never been to an airfield before and is glad she thought to ask Vivian if she needed someone to ferry her automobile back to the beach. At first the Ford wagon felt stiff and unfamiliar (*Don't ever buy a Ford,* Sexton said that first day at the bank), and Honora wasn't at all sure she could manage it. But before they passed through the marshes, she had adjusted her driving to suit the quirks and oddities of Vivian's automobile, and after that, the journey was simply fun. It strikes Honora that it has been quite some time since she has experienced anything like fun, surely not since the summer, before she and Sexton learned that the house was for sale. She left Sexton a note on the kitchen table. *Gone to take a neighbor to the airfield in the neighbor's car. Will explain later. Should be back about 5:00.*

Happy Christmas. Love, Honora. Of course she will forgive her husband for having missed the promised Christmas lunch, but it won't hurt Sexton Beecher one little bit to be the one left waiting for a change.

The trip to the airfield took Honora and Vivian through Ely Falls, where they drove slowly past the displays in the windows of Simmons Department Store, exclaiming over the dioramas of old-fashioned Christmases with mannequins in high-necked dresses and long dressing gowns sitting around trees decorated with ribbons and cranberry chains and candles (though surely those cannot really have been lighted candles, Honora thinks now). Vivian and she played a game in which they tried to guess, by the demeanor and the dress of the shoppers darting in and out between traffic, what was in their packages. Vivian saw a dapper little man in a tweed coat and a bow tie and guessed a Charis foundation garment with an adjustable belt (for his mistress, of course). Honora saw a plump middle-aged woman and guessed a Hormel ham. Vivian hooted beside her.

Honora and Sexton had talked about

traveling to Taft for the holiday, but Sexton said he was reluctant to take too much time away from his clients. Honora wrote her mother asking if she and Uncle Harold might get on a bus to Ely Falls and spend the holiday with them at Fortune's Rocks (Honora anxious to show the house off), but her mother replied that Harold was still too feeble to travel (no surprise) and that they would have to make do this year with packages and letters.

"Are you afraid to fly?" Honora asks.

"Gosh, yes," Vivian says, drawing a mother-of-pearl compact from her purse. "White knuckles all the way."

"Where's your luggage?"

"I had the trunks sent on ahead. Useless stuff. What on earth did I imagine I was going to do with a white ermine wrap?"

"And you'll take Sandy with you on the plane?" The dog, in a small wooden basket, looks nearly as apprehensive as Vivian.

"He'll be fine. Most people find flying is quite lovely, actually, and I'll admit the service is miraculous, and the gin is first-rate. The cabin has six rooms. The ceiling is painted with stars, the toilets are modern, and the club chairs pivot so you can play cards. I'll hardly have time for a rubber before we land."

"I envy you."

"They say it's safer than driving a car, but don't believe it for a minute."

Wooden chairs line a spare but freshly painted room. A woman in a flying suit disappears behind a door marked "Operations" and emerges carrying a map, and when she crosses the room on her way to the landing strip, everyone pauses to gape, especially the half dozen men who are waiting for their planes. The face of a small boy next to the window can only be called rapt. Honora wonders if the boy is getting on a plane himself, but then decides not; he is poorly dressed and pitifully thin. She's surprised that his father, who is standing next to the boy, would let him out in such bad weather in boots that have no laces and in pants so short they don't reach his socks. As Honora watches, the father takes an empty china cup out of the boy's hands. The boy turns and presses his face against the glass.

"That will be my plane," Vivian says.

"Where do you want me to put the car?" Honora asks.

"Right out in front of the house," Vivian says as she reapplies her lipstick. "I've a man who'll take care of it."

Vivian's hair is ridged like sands after a storm. Honora studies the woman's fur-trimmed afternoon coat and the tweed sport suit she has on underneath. The suit is beautifully cut and fits her too well not to have been made especially for her. Honora envies the woman's fur-lined ankle boots as well—much smarter than her own shower boots, which she neglected to put on in their haste to leave the house. Her brown pumps are wet and cold and will have to be dried out by the stove when she gets home.

"You needn't wait for me," Vivian says, snapping the compact shut. "You have a bit of a drive."

"I'd like to see you take off. If something happens and your plane doesn't go, you'll be stranded here."

"I'd find a ride back somehow. It's almost dark already. You should get a start."

"When will you be back?" Honora asks.

"Not till May, I think."

"Oh," Honora says, suddenly minding

that her newfound friend is leaving her. "Such a long time."

Vivian nudges Honora and tilts her head in the direction of a man in a smart fedora and a Harris Tweed overcoat. He is carrying a flat rectangular package wrapped in red paper with a gold bow.

"Mint green silk charmeuse nightgown, cut on the bias," Vivian says, and the two women laugh.

Despite the gathering darkness, Honora cannot bring herself to leave the waiting room. She watches the passengers climb up the steep steps of the plane and duck under the low door. When Honora glances around, she sees that only she and the small boy remain inside, and she wonders where the father has gone. "It's pretty exciting, isn't it?" Honora says to the boy.

The boy turns, leaving a nose-and-lip print on the glass. The plane outside starts its engine. Honora puts her hands up around her face to shade her eyes so that she can see into the lighted windows of the plane. If she spots Vivian, she will wave. But though she can make out figures in the small circles, she can't identify anyone who might be her new friend. The plane makes a turn and rolls away.

"If we hurry," says a voice behind Honora, "we can catch the last trolley. I just asked the maintenance fellow outside."

Honora turns, drawing on her gloves. She has a brief impression of dark curly hair and vivid blue eyes. And seeing the man close to, she realizes that of course he can't be the father of the boy—he's too young. Perhaps he's the boy's brother, though the two don't look much alike.

When Honora pushes the door open, the wind fills the spaces of her coat. She prays the beach wagon will start. Will there be a trolley to Ely at this late hour? Beside her, the boy and the man hunch their shoulders against the weather and start out on the long road to the trolley stop. The boy must be terribly cold, Honora thinks.

"Excuse me," she calls. "Can I give you a lift?"

The man and the boy stop. Honora moves closer to the figures so that she can see their faces. "Where are you headed?" she asks.

"Back to town," the man says after a brief hesitation.

"I have to go through town to get to my house, so why don't I give you a ride? It's too cold to have to wait for a trolley."

The man puts his hand on the boy's shoulder. "Thank you," he says simply.

McDermott

McDermott and the boy follow the woman to her car. He wouldn't have accepted the ride for his own sake. The woman's hat tilts in the wind, and she has to hold it with her hand. Her shoes make precise imprints on the snow as she lifts each foot up and places it down.

McDermott hasn't ridden in a vehicle, discounting the trolley, since Mahon took them all to a speak in Rye in his bread truck in November. McDermott and Ross and Tom Magill sat on the floor in the back, the smell of yeast and waxed paper all about them, his ass sore as hell afterward from all the hard bumping on the road. A breeze, gusty and erratic, makes glittery snow showers from the tops of the half dozen automobiles parked just beyond the airfield tower. McDermott glances at the boy and sees that he is nearly as excited as he was when he first spotted the airplane taking off, and he wonders if the boy has ever ridden in an automobile.

The woman turns abruptly, and McDermott nearly walks into her.

"It's not mine," she says. "I hope I can get it to start."

Her eyes are watering some in the cold. He judges her to be about his age, perhaps a year younger. Under her hat, there is just a fringe of hair. Dark like her eyes.

"I'm sure that between us we can manage something," McDermott says.

"Are you good with engines?" she asks.

"I'm good with machines," he says and holds out his hand. "I'm Quillen McDermott."

The boy flashes him a dubious look. "He's just called McDermott," the boy says.

"My name is Honora. Honora Beecher. What's your name?"

"Alphonse," the boy says. "I saw you at the beach one time."

"Really?"

"You had on a brown bathing suit."

"So I did," she says, sounding mildly

surprised. "Are you brothers?" she asks, gesturing from McDermott to Alphonse. McDermott notes that Alphonse hesitates a moment before he shakes his head.

"I think we can all easily fit in front," the woman says.

The Ford's seat is taut and springy. The floorboards are covered with sand and wet snow. The woman's coat falls open, and her skirt rides up over her knee. McDermott watches her slim leg move back and forth. Between them, the boy stares bug-eyed out the window. Every time McDermott catches sight of the green sweater under the boy's jacket, he has to turn away and smile.

The car glides along the icy road. He wants to tell the woman to take it easy because they might skid on such a slippery surface, but he doesn't know her well enough to give advice. The three bodies, wedged together, are producing a sort of warmth.

The woman asks him a question, but with the rumble of the car, McDermott can't quite make out what she has said.

"He's almost deaf," the boy says protectively. "You have to look right at him so that he can see what you are saying."

The woman smiles. "Well then, I won't say anything at all," she says lightly. "My husband taught me to drive only recently and I don't dare take my eyes off the road."

"I'll just lean forward," McDermott says. "Like this."

He has a good view now of the woman's face. There's a neat furrow of concentration between her eyebrows. She drives hunched forward over the steering wheel, a slight smile on her lips. "Were you born deaf?" she asks.

"The mills did it," he says. "The looms. The sound of all those looms in one room. Almost everyone gets a bit deaf. Mine is just worse."

"We both work in the mills," the boy says.

The woman looks surprised. "Aren't you too young to be working?" she asks.

Lights have been lit in farmhouses, and smoke rises from intermittent chimneys. McDermott has nearly lost the feeling in his feet. He wants to wrap the boy's wet boots in his jacket and dry them. He wonders where the woman lives. He tries to imagine what sort of house she is going back to, but all he can picture are the displays in the Simmons Department Store windows of the impossibly fake old-fashioned Christmases. No one really lives like that, do they? In the distance, he can see the silhouettes of chimneys against the night sky. The mills are silent now—no plumes of smoke spreading across the city—and already this afternoon he noticed that the air was cleaner. Men and women are joining the unions in droves now, and when the weather is warmer, McDermott is certain there will be a strike. You have to have a strike in summer, Mironson said, so that the workers who get evicted from their apartments won't freeze to death in the tent cities.

Fucking bosses, McDermott thinks.

He gives the woman directions to the boy's house, though, truthfully, he wishes they could just keep driving. He imagines them all stopping for dinner at a roadhouse. It wouldn't be too crowded because everyone would be home for Christmas Eve, but it would be warm. The three of them would sit in a booth and McDermott would say things that would make the woman laugh.

When they reach the corner of Alfred and Rose, McDermott and the boy get out of the car. He hands the boy a small package wrapped in brown paper. He puts his hand on the boy's shoulder. "You have a good Christmas," he says and watches as Alphonse sprints around the corner.

McDermott walks back to the car and leans on the driver's-side door.

"He's happy," McDermott says.

"What did you give him?"

"A pocketknife. It's for fishing. For cleaning fish."

"You take him on outings?"

"Once in a while. I feel kind of sorry for the kid." He pauses. "Hey, thanks for the ride. How long is your trip home?"

"Not far," she says. "Only to the beach."

"So you live on the beach."

"I do."

"Lucky you."

"I don't know. Not this time of year."

"Still, though."

"Still, though," she says, smiling.

"How will you spend Christmas?" he asks.

"We'll get up late," she says. "Then we'll wander into the living room and open our presents. What about you?"

"I'll go to my sister's. It'll be chaos. My brothers won't like their presents. The usual." He pauses. "What do you want for Christmas?"

"A baby," she says without hesitation. "And you?" she asks.

"Peace and quiet," he says.

She laughs and he tries to laugh with her, but his mouth is nearly frozen. Jesus God, he feels happy. It's Christmas Eve and he doesn't have to work tomorrow and the city is almost beautiful and when the weather gets warmer there will be a strike, and in a gesture that shakes him right down to his socks, the woman reaches over and touches his hand briefly where it rests on the window.

"I'm sure you'll get what you want," she says.

With effort, McDermott pushes himself from the beach wagon and watches as the woman pulls away from the curb and turns the corner. He raises the collar of his leather jacket and looks up at the stars. He says a quick prayer—for Eileen, for the boy, for the woman in the car, and even for his brothers, who are a handful—and then he shakes his head and laughs. He hasn't said a real prayer—a hopeful prayer, a message direct from himself to God—since he was a kid.

Honora

Honora drives through the marshes, shaking her head. She can't imagine why she told that man that she wanted a baby, nor why she touched his hand. It's because of Christmas, she decides; it makes you do impulsive things—like telling Vivian she'd drive her to the airport. She's glad she did; it was good to get out of the house. She thinks about the boy, his possessiveness, his pride. The rapt expression on his face at the airport. His grin when the man gave him the present. The way the man had to look at her, to watch her speak her words.

She hopes now that Sexton isn't too upset that she wasn't there to greet him. She will explain, and she is certain that he will understand. She steers the beach wagon around a corner, waiting for the sight of the house and the Buick parked out front, but when she completes the turn, she is so startled by what she sees—or, rather, by what she doesn't see—that she inadvertently takes her foot off the clutch and stalls the automobile.

There are no lights on in the house, and the Buick isn't there.

She tells herself that Sexton has gone out to the store to buy coffee. That he has run out of gas and has had to walk to a filling station. That there were too many cars on Route 1, and he had no way to get in touch with her. That he left her present on a counter in a department store and had to go back to find it.

She doesn't believe a word of it.

She puts the car in gear and completes the turn. She parks in front of the house, where normally the Buick would be. She steps up onto the granite slab. The door is shiny in the moonlight. She moves into the hallway and thinks of the first time she and Sexton ever entered this house. The hallway is brighter now, the peeling wallpaper with the liveried servants gone, replaced by lemon paint. The electric sconces on the wall now work with the flick of a switch. The house no longer smells of mildew, and she doesn't think as often about the other people who lived here before her. She puts her coat over a hook and enters the kitchen. The windows are clean, the indoor shutters painted, the grime of years long removed. The oven door opens without the screech and bang now, and the water flows smoothly from the tap.

The sound of surf inside her head makes it hard to think. She sits at the table and runs her hands over the embroidered linen. The tea things are still in the sink; nothing has been touched. Sexton did not come home and then go out again for a pint of milk. He did not come home at all.

She glances up at the cuckoo clock on the wall. Ten past six. She runs the water and begins to rinse out the cups. She has planned a Christmas Eve dinner of roast goose with raisin stuffing, scalloped potatoes, brussels sprouts, and a dish called Spanish Onion Supreme. She has the pies for dessert. Neither she nor Sexton is particularly religious, so they will not be going out again to midnight services—nor even, she thinks, to church in the morning. No, tomorrow they will sleep late, and then they will get up and have their coffee and wander into the front room to admire the tree.

He has had an accident, she thinks now. The Buick is disabled and is lying in a ditch at the side of the road. Sexton is hurt, writhing on a stretcher.

She puts her wet hands to her face. No, no, she won't think like that.

Turning, she sees that Vivian has left behind a neatly folded newspaper on a chair. Her new friend must have had it in her hand or under her arm when she knocked on the door. Perhaps she was planning to read it in the waiting room at the airfield. Honora dries her hands, picks the paper up and unfolds it. *New England Business Outlook Good,* she reads on the front page, but then her eye travels to another headline on the same page: *Fifteen Banks Fail to Open for Business.* Honora sits down and turns the pages of the newspaper, looking at the advertisements to take her mind off the thought of the Buick lying in a ditch. *Cudahy's lunch tongue, 21 cents,* she reads. Sardines are 13 cents. Silk dresses are $4.89. There are ads for waxed rolls, chiffon hose, and picoted underwear. For Camay and Ivory soap. Rayon bloomers are 49 cents. *Legal Ruling Guards Purse of Husband,* she reads. *Head of House Made Immune for Purchase of Fur Coat.* Again she glances up at the clock, which is moving at an agonizingly slow speed. She studies the want ads. *Woman who can cook. Middle-aged woman wanted. Young girl. Girl for office work. Waitress. Salesgirl. Housekeeper.*

She puts the newspaper aside and reaches for the packet of sea glass Vivian gave her. She picks up each shard and inspects it. The electric light changes the colors—makes the lavender pink and puts a sheen on the watery blue. She stands and walks into the front room to fetch her platter of sea glass. Under the tree are several wrapped gifts, presents from the large box that her mother sent, as well as the pen she told Vivian about and a vest that she knit for Sexton. She lifts the platter, carries it into the kitchen, and sets it on the table. She sifts through the pieces, several layers thick now on the china, and lets them fall through her fingers like water. She empties Vivian's collection of sea glass onto the dish. The pieces jumble together, so that Honora can no longer tell whose are whose.

She hears the sound of a car on gravel, something between a purr and a rumble—a sound she would know anywhere. She runs into the hallway and opens the door and calls her husband's name.

Sexton emerges unsteadily from the Buick. He turns and puts a hand on the top of the car, as if for balance, and for a moment he seems not to know that she is there. She calls to him again and, hearing his name this time, he straightens.

She takes a step forward, but he holds up a hand to stop her.

"Sexton, what's wrong?" she asks.

"I'm fine," he says.

He makes his way around the Buick. He has his suitcase in one hand. When he reaches her, he puts his free arm around his wife, pulling her to him in a halfhearted embrace. The smell of him is foul, that of an unwashed body, of stale liquor on the breath.

Perhaps she recoils. He lets his arm drop from her shoulder. He walks toward the house, and it is as though he has already forgotten she is there. His posture is different—a slight hunch, the shoulders more rounded than she has remembered. He stumbles on a flagstone. He hesitates a moment on the doorstep, as if taken aback by the wreath.

Honora follows Sexton into the house. In the brighter light of the kitchen, she can see the uneven stubble on his chin, the deep bluish circles under his eyes, which are red rimmed.

He's been crying, she thinks.

"I was worried when you didn't come," she says.

"I'm sorry for that."

"What happened to you?"

"What happened to me?"

She waits for his answer, but he seems unable, or unwilling, to fill the silence. After a time, she puts the kettle under the tap. But then she has to put the kettle down because her hands are shaking so badly.

"I've lost my job," he says.

She presses her fingers hard against the lip of the sink.

"I'm going to lose the car," he says. "The bank is calling in the loan."

"Why?" she asks, turning.

He sits abruptly in the chair, as if his

legs have simply given out. He rests his elbows on his knees and puts his head in his hands. "Banks are calling in loans all over the place," he says. "It's the same everywhere."

"They can't do that," Honora says. "I don't understand. They made that loan in good faith."

"They can do anything they want."

Honora wishes her husband would look at her. She can see only the top of his hat. There's a smear of something like slush on the crown, as if he'd dropped it. "Have we lost the house?" she asks.

"Not yet."

Not yet.

"What happened?" she asks. "You got a letter?"

"I got a letter. I went to the bank this morning."

"Why didn't you tell me?"

Still he won't look at her. Even when he glances up in her direction, his eyes slide sideways off her face.

"And that was it?" she asks. She can hear the rising note of panic in her own voice. "They just said, 'Well, we made this loan and now we're taking it back'?"

"Something like that."

She moves to the icebox and removes the tray beneath the ice. It's full of water and sloshes as she draws it out. Carrying it carefully, she walks with it to the back door, opens the door, and tosses the water out. She puts the tray back in the icebox.

"What are you doing?"

"I'm emptying the ice tray."

"For God's sakes, Honora."

"I'll heat up something for dinner. There's no time to cook the goose now."

"I'm not hungry."

She moves slowly to the kitchen table and sits in the only other chair. He turns and puts his arm on the linen cloth, but he doesn't reach far enough to touch her. He still hasn't taken off his coat, and she can smell his whiskey breath across the table.

"I took a gamble," he says. "I did something that wasn't exactly wrong but wasn't exactly by the book either. Wasn't strictly on the up-and-up."

"What was it?"

"You don't need to know."

"I don't need to know?"

"For crying out loud, Honora."

She draws the platter of sea glass toward her. She thinks of her Christmas Eve dinner—the goose, the onions, the brussels sprouts, the pies. She fingers a piece of milk glass and holds it up to the light. How dare he take this tone with her? Isn't it her car, her house, her life too? She lifts a shard of bubbled glass from the platter and examines the edges. She thinks of the presents in the front room: the Multi-Vider pen that she paid for by scrimping from the household money, the argyle vest she spent hours knitting. She sifts the sea glass through her fingers. She minds most of all that he has taken from her the pristine jewel of what might have been.

I've married a man who isn't entirely honest, she thinks.

"You and your goddamned sea glass," Sexton mutters.

She wants her husband to leave the room. To go upstairs and have a bath and go to bed and not speak one more word to her tonight.

"Go upstairs and have a bath," she says. "I'll heat up some dinner."

She pushes her chair back. Sexton stands, leans across the tablecloth, and takes hold of the platter of sea glass. He flips the pieces of glass hard into the air, the way one might toss a person in a taut blanket, or a flapjack in a pan. The glass flies up and hits the ceiling and the windows and the walls and the cuckoo clock and the stove and the icebox and the shelves, and for a moment it seems that all the world is raining bits of color. Honora raises her arms over her head to shield herself.

Sexton drops the platter onto the table. He spins around, his coattails snapping behind him. She hears the front door shut, the engine of the Buick start up.

Honora brings her arms away from her head.

The silence in the kitchen is worse than the shards of glass falling from the sky.

A piece of sea glass slips from her lap onto the floor with a tiny ping. She bends to pick it up. It is the jewel-like bit of cobalt. Turning, she sees that there is sea glass everywhere.

She stands and collects the glass from the windowsills and from the top of the stove. From the shelves and from beneath the icebox. From the chair that her husband has so recently sat upon and from the waxed paper she has put over the mince pies. She collects all the bits that she can find and puts them back on the white platter.

She sits again at the table and studies the shards of glass.

It's a miracle, she thinks. Sea glass doesn't break.

Honora

It is always more than she has imagined it to be, even after the three hundred–odd days that she has lived in this house and walked out the porch door and looked at the wet beach. The tide is dead low—so low it seems as if it will never make its way up the long shallow grade, glistening until the last fifteen feet, when it hits the drop-off.

The year is 1930. A June day. Not quite an ordinary day.

The cottages are mostly still empty, though some, seemingly boarded up, are surreptitiously inhabited by drifters, men and women without a place to live. She sees them when she walks the beach—a face in a window, a figure quickly rounding a corner, smoke from a house that appears to be abandoned—and occasionally these same people come to her back door looking for food. Even if Honora has next to nothing, it is understood that she will not turn them away. In Taft, her mother keeps soup simmering and bakes an extra loaf of bread each morning. Honora does the same, though she will have to give bread, and cheese when she can get it, as an alternative to hot soup through the summer.

Her feet sink slightly into a patch of soft, wet sand. When she reaches the road, she will brush them off and put on her shoes and walk the short distance down to the store. It will be a faster walk home because she won't want to linger. With the lobster bodies, eight cents a pound this week at the fish shack, she will make a stew. Not enough money this week for meat.

Sexton did not reappear until Christmas night, by which time the marriage Honora and he had enjoyed for six months—that ordinary and innocent universe of checked oilcloth and women's magazines, of erotic baths and gumdrop packets, of trust and hope and modest dreams—was gone. What replaced it was still a marriage, she thinks now, as a play will still be called a play, though the characters and the dialogue and even the tone of the drama may be so radically altered as to be almost unrecognizable. Theatergoers would be alarmed, unnerved, by such a change.

That night, Sexton was hungry and demoralized and dirty and wept like a nearly grown child—with harsh gestures and hiccupping sounds that frightened her—and sometimes she thinks she agreed to forgive him for the dishonesty and the Christmas debacle and the hideous incident with the sea glass simply to get him to stop. Three days later, when the auctioneer came for the Buick (her husband having refused to drive it to the address he had been given), Sexton waited on the porch, facing the sea, so that he would not have to witness the ordeal. It was Honora who stood at the end of the front walk and who watched the auctioneer's assistant stall the unfamiliar automobile as he drove it from its parking place.

For weeks afterward, Sexton and Honora scarcely spoke, he lost in a kind of stunned reverie, as if he could not believe in his own disaster, Honora so frayed and raw that she could not bear to be touched, nor could she summon the wherewithal to converse, even about the mundane. Each day Sexton left the house in search of work—first seeking a job in sales, and then, when it became apparent no one was hiring, a position in one of the offices of the eleven mills in the city. Finally, desperately, he took a job as a ring spinner in the Ely Falls Mill. Every day he sees to it that two strands of slightly twisted roving are transformed into one strand of tightly spun yarn that is wound onto a bobbin. Honora doesn't know much more than this because Sexton never talks about his job. He works from 6:30 in the morning until noon, and then from 12:30 until 5:15. For this work, he is paid twenty-two dollars a week, eight of which go for room and meals at a boardinghouse entirely inhabited by other men who work in the mills as well.

After Sexton lost the one job and finally found another (far lesser) one, Honora tried to tell her husband to let the house go. It drained them of every extra cent, she said. There was precious little left over for food—often nothing at all for clothes. She could move into Ely Falls and share an apartment with him. It wouldn't be so bad, she said (though privately she knew that she would hate that outcome), but Sexton wouldn't hear of giving up the house. He worked, he said, so that they could have a proper place to live, far from the filth of the city. He worked, he said, to hold on to the one thing that hadn't yet been taken from him. And Honora understood finally, in a way she had not at first, that Sexton's manhood was more wedded to the house than it was to her. That something inside him would be irretrievably lost if he failed to keep the house that he had ruined himself to buy.

When Honora meets Sexton's trolley on Friday evenings, he kisses her as he alights. He is the last passenger at the last stop, and for a time, Honora imagines that his descending the steps and kissing his wife will erase the past or make it inconsequential, so that whatever happens *from that moment on* will be the true marriage, will be the thing they were meant to have. Husband and wife will walk home, and though Sexton is covered with bits of lint—in his hair and on his neck and even in his nostrils—so that she cannot entirely forget where he has come from, and though they are so guarded in their conversation as to be almost mute, she keeps alive the notion of a fresh start. When they arrive home, Sexton bathes in the tub, and sometimes Honora is just shocked at the filth that is left behind. She scrubs the grime from his neck and his face and his hair and his ears, and he enters a kind of trance as she does this. In the early weeks, when he first went into the mill, he could not raise his right arm to wash himself. He couldn't reach his back or lift his hand to hold a pitcher of water.

But at some point between the bath and the meal, perhaps even during the meal itself, Honora will catch the first evasive glance on her husband's face, the first glimpse of the set jaw. Resentment will begin to well up inside of her so that when she washes the dishes, her nerves will already have begun to sound a taut note just below the silence. And then she and Sexton will meet in the bedroom, her husband undressed and waiting for her between the sheets (ironed just that day, because two days in the sea air puts the wrinkles back in), and the notion of a fresh start will have vanished like a song. Honora's limbs will be stiff as she undresses, her own sliding into the sheets more hurried than she has intended. And though her husband will appear to come alive, she knows that it is lust—too quickly ignited and too quickly extinguished—that animates him.

Walking to the store would be easier on the sandy pavement of the road, she knows, but because of the contours of the landscape, the journey is only half as long on the beach. The soles of her feet (tender after the long winter) hurt on the sand and shells, and so she moves along the shoreline, letting the waves lap over her toes. After a time, Honora sees a familiar shape and glisten, washed up by a wave from the incoming tide. But when she runs and reaches for the piece of sea glass, another wave snatches it away.

She has never lost her love of sea glass, nor the excitement of the hunt, despite that terrible moment on Christmas Eve when the kitchen rained glass. She waits for the roll of water to subside. Where the sea glass was, there is nothing now—only a smooth surface of wet sand awaiting yet another deposit, yet another erasure. The beach is made and remade this way hundreds of times a day, its entire geography instantly effaced, redrawn. Sometimes when she looks out the window of her bedroom, there are hills and gullies that weren't there just the day before. Occasionally the sand is covered by rocks—thick fists of gray and brown and black. At other times, the beach is so filthy with seaweed that she can hardly see the sand. The surreptitious people from the empty cottages scurry onto the beach and collect the seaweed, as if it were a treasure. She imagines that they cook and eat it.

And once in a while, especially during the winter, Honora will look out the window of her bedroom and the sand will be *gone.* Against the seawall, the beach will be five or six feet below the previous day's level. It is as though the sand has simply been scooped away from the beach, the residue neatly smoothed, like icing. No sign of cataclysm, no melee, a sight defined only by absence. In the spring, the sand will mysteriously return. Overnight. As if it had been borrowed.

She picks up a pottery shard with rounded edges and a red-and-brown flower painted on the glaze. She puts her shoes on behind the abandoned Highland Hotel—bankrupt now, scheduled for demolition in the fall.

One day a man has a job, and life is full of possibilities. The next day the job and the car are gone, and the man cannot look his wife in the eye. There is no paycheck, no way to earn money for food and clothing. Life is taken up with trying to survive.

It takes all the time there is, this trying to survive.

There have been days when all they have had to eat is cornmeal: cornmeal porridge for breakfast and then fried up for lunch, and then because there simply isn't anything else to eat, and no money left from the pay packet, Honora will warm up those fritters for supper. Once, after they had already sold the radio and the clock and the Multi-Vider pen (never used), and there wasn't anything else in the house to sell, they had only dried berries and peanut butter sandwiches to eat for days. Today, when she goes to buy the lobster bodies, the fish house will stink and Honora will have to tie her kerchief around her nose. There will be no tails or claws to speak of—those will all have been shipped to Boston. When she gets home, she will painstakingly remove the meat with a pick, and then she will make her stew. Night after night, sometimes that's all there is to eat: lobster bodies.

Once, when Sexton was away, she put bread in water and tried to make a kind of porridge. The next day, she walked to Jack Hess's store, and that was the first time she ever asked for credit. That Friday, when Sexton brought home his pay packet (the four silver dollars—*cartwheels,* the workers call them—and the ten paper dollars), Honora walked to Hess's store and paid the man back. House or no house, she said to Sexton, they would not owe money to Jack Hess.

Poverty, her mother has written, makes you clever, and Honora knows that this is true. If you don't have ingenuity, you don't eat, and so you have to be smart. You take the lace collar and cuffs off a dress to make it appear as if you had a new dress. You get old coats at the church and carefully rip out all the seams and turn the material inside out and make new coats and jackets. You find old sweaters with holes in them and unravel the wool and wash it and reknit the yarn into new sweaters. You put fresh cardboard into your husband's shoes every Sunday to keep the soles from wearing out. You turn his shirt collars, and you make your own laundry soap out of grease and lye and borax and ammonia. Such economies are embarrassing to Honora. She never speaks of them to anyone. She hides this effort in the way she hides the douche powder and the rubber hose and bag. High on a shelf so no one will ever see them.

And yet. And yet. If asked—if pressed—Honora would have to say she is strangely content. It's an odd feeling that she cannot describe to anyone—not to her mother and certainly not to Sexton, whose unhappiness seems to have no bounds, whose unhappiness is defined now by what he does not have, which is almost everything. He will always, in his mind, be the salesman who no longer has anything to sell. A man who longs for the open road but who cannot ever take it.

Whereas Honora, oddly, now has more purpose than she ever did before. She is a dutiful wife who tends to her husband in spite of his weaknesses. She is a woman with ingenuity. She is a woman without illusions. She is a woman who, above all, is too busy trying to make a go of it to fret about her marriage.

Honora has hired herself out as a caretaker to five of the cottages on the beach, one job leading to the other, the first the result of a recommendation from Jack Hess. Most of the time, Honora's duties consist of making sure there are no burst pipes in the basement or animals in the cupboards or glass panes cracked in a storm. On good days, she opens all the windows to dry out a house, to rid the place of the smell of mildew. In the best of the five cottages, she will take the sheets off the furniture if she knows that the owners are arriving for a visit. When there is an emergency (bats in a bedroom, a shutter blown off in the wind), Sexton comes with her on the weekends and helps to make the repairs. For this work, Honora makes fifteen dollars a month, all of which goes to meet the mortgage payment.

Every time Honora visits Jack Hess's store she is struck by how much barer the shelves are now than they used to be, and she wonders how it is that Jack feeds as many people as he does when he appears to have less and less to offer. It is a conjurer's trick, and Honora has sometimes imagined a kind of alchemy in the back room, a modern-day reworking of the loaves and fishes. Today she would dearly love two pats of butter, but she won't be able to get them home in the heat. She hasn't ridden in an automobile since she drove Vivian's beach wagon to her house on Christmas Day and then walked back to her own empty house. Honora needs rice and beans and flour and greens of some sort, though a quick perusal of the store tells her Mr. Hess has little in that line. And today she will splurge on strawberries and sugar. She wants to make a strawberry-rhubarb pie with the rhubarb that grows wild near the street. Today is her wedding anniversary.

One year ago today, Honora and Sexton were married and they were happy. Why not celebrate that event, she has been asking herself all week, even if the marriage that followed is complicated and cloudy? She cannot imagine a life in which the day of her wedding is never acknowledged, never honored.

"Good mornin', Mrs. Beecher."

"Good morning, Mr. Hess."

Jack Hess's back is so stooped she cannot figure out how it is he stocks the shelves himself, how it is he sleeps. He has on, as usual, his bow tie and hat. A fresh shirt.

"You were lost a bit there," he says.

"Yes, I was."

"How are you?"

"Just fine, thank you."

"And Mr. Beecher?"

"He'll be home tonight. It's our anniversary." She hadn't planned on saying that aloud; it isn't like Honora to discuss something personal. But she cannot deny that she has wanted to tell someone.

"I remember clear as day when your

husband first came in here," Hess says. "Dapper young gent, I thought to myself. All crowed up about being married."

Jack Hess stands behind the counter with the grabber he uses for the items on the high shelves. As Honora selects a product, he puts it on the counter and then writes the price in pencil on a paper bag into which he'll later put the groceries. Then he'll add the figures, and the sum will always be five or ten cents below an accurate total. At first Honora felt obliged to point this out (once walking all the way back to the store), but now she knows better. It is Hess's way of helping. A cynic, she thinks, might say it was his way of making sure a customer returned to the store, and that his shortages represented little more than advertising specials, but Honora knows that Hess's contribution to the community consists of far more than just creative mathematics.

"By the way, Mrs. Beecher, I just wanted you to know that for the next couple of weeks, or however long this durned thing lasts, I'm not taking cash from mill families."

Honora looks up.

"Till it's over," he says, explaining.

Honora, baffled, shakes her head.

"The strike," Hess says.

Honora's grocery list vanishes from her thoughts.

"I thought you knew," Hess says.

"No, I didn't."

"Well, I expect your husband didn't want to worry you until it actually happened. I'm sorry to have been the one to tell you."

Honora approaches the counter.

"The day the new pay cut takes effect," Jack Hess says. "Monday. All the mills are involved. They say the tension is so thick over to Ely Falls that the air is just cracklin'."

No, Honora has not heard about the impending strike. She knows only what her husband tells her. And when he is home, he never mentions his job. In the beginning, she would ask him about his work, ask him if he had friends, if he had met anyone he liked in the boardinghouse—the same way a well-meaning mother might query an awkward son who didn't quite fit in at school. But shortly it became clear that Sexton didn't welcome the questions, and she gave up. When he comes home weekends now, he never speaks of where he's been, and if it weren't for the lint in the laundry and the grime in the tub, she is certain they would simply pretend that he had been "on a trip."

"I don't like to see any family go without," Hess says. "But conditions over to Ely Falls are inhuman. I go in there every once in a while to visit my sister and her family. Arlene married a Franco, don't you know. And I tell you I never saw anything like that mill housing. No one can make do on the wages them mills pay. My sister's kids are unsupervised most of the time because there's no one at home to watch them. They've never had such a problem with gangs as they do now." Hess pauses. "I'm sorry I put my foot where it wasn't wanted," he says, "but I expect your husband was going to tell you this weekend—after your celebration, that is."

Honora pays for her groceries. She puts the paper bag in her satchel.

"We'll manage," she says.

"Course you will," Hess says.

* * *

Her pace is furious as she walks along the beach, the surf competing with the noise in her head.

Why didn't you tell me?

She is tired of the withholding, sick of the deception. How is she to trust the man? The unfairness, the injustice of it, fills her with rage. She will tell Sexton so tonight. Tonight they will have it out as they should have done months ago. She will scream at him if need be. She cannot be silent any longer. What is the point of scrimping and saving? They will lose the house anyway. They can't survive even a two-week strike. All their savings have been poured into the house, their entire marriage ruined by a mortgage.

She stops abruptly on the beach. The lobster bodies stink today. They just stink. She reaches into her satchel and takes out the waxed bag with the shellfish carcasses in it. She walks to the water's edge and hurls them into the sea.

McDermott

The machines might be organs or violins or pianos, the men and women at them as fluid as musicians. Their movements are precise: this note and then that note and then this note, moving toward a furious crescendo, sounding a particular beat as the music reaches a fever pitch and then warbles down to a simple melody. The music is always demanding and repetitive; there is no time for the musicians to catch their breath. They must raise their instruments immediately and begin again. And then again. And then so many times that they know every measure, every nuance, every note by heart. More than by heart, they know it in their blood and in their bones. They can carry on whole conversations with their minds while their bodies complete this virtuoso performance with the spools and the creels, the shuttles and the bobbins.

There's only a minute left until the dinner horn sounds. McDermott doesn't need a watch; he knows this with his inner clock. Sean Rasley, a weaver, looks over at him, and it is just a look—steady, no smile, no nod—but it says everything McDermott needs to know.

I'm ready, it says.

Rasley means the strike. He means Monday. Today could well be their last day at the looms for weeks.

McDermott nods his head. There are only ten, fifteen seconds until the horn. One by one, the weavers around him stop their machines. Lunch break. Thirty minutes. The first chance they've had to sit since they entered the mill at 6:30 this morning.

The air is soft and hits McDermott full in the face as he steps out of the mill door. Summer, he thinks; it's officially summer now. The air has a hint of the sea beyond the city, and the sky above him is an almost unnatural blue. He puts his hands in his pockets and sets out for the boardinghouse.

He searches in his pocket for a piece of gum and finds instead a crumpled piece of paper—one of the leaflets that he and Ross and Tsomides were putting out just before the raid. Thinking about the raid makes McDermott's stomach clench, even though it's been three weeks since the men in masks that looked eerily like those of the Ku Klux Klan broke into the abandoned warehouse where McDermott and five others were printing up posters for the coming strike. For a moment McDermott froze, too astonished to move when the men smashed doors and windows and entered the building. Swinging sledgehammers, they shattered the press that had been sent up from New York and hit Paul Tsomides a glancing blow on the head that put him in the hospital. McDermott, crouching behind a barrel, watched the rout before fleeing through a side entrance.

Eighteen months of owner-ordered layoffs and wage cuts have left most workers nearly disastrously destitute, he reads as he walks.

> A half dozen craft unions have been made operational and have joined forces for a strike that will commence on Monday. Twenty-five hundred union men and women, who boldy speak for ten times that many non-unionized workers, have already voted unanimously and in a heart-felt manner to strike. Union members will be paid twenty percent of their hard-earned wages during the strike. Non-union members will receive necessary relief in the form of contributions from their comrades in other trades. The Citizen Welfare Committee, the Catholic Relief Bureau and the Soldiers and Sailors Relief Fund will be making soup kitchens available starting on Monday. Throw off the shackles of oppression and join forces with the international brotherhood of workers!

Telling the mill families where they can get relief is essential, McDermott has been told, since New England workers are notorious for not accepting relief of any kind in the belief that assistance goes against the grain of their own (or their inherited) Yankee culture. Thus they starve more quickly and give in more rapidly to management's demands. In order for the strike to succeed, Mironson has stressed, strikers have to be persuaded of the necessity to accept relief.

Management has pared wages down to next to nothing, McDermott reads, and he thinks of fingernails scraping a cement wall as they go down. *The bosses live in high style on the other side of the river.* McDermott can see the massive houses from the mill yard—poor planning on someone's part, he thinks. No hint of an economic depression over there. Not with all their power lawn mowers and swimming pools and fancy automobiles. In fact, it's possible the bosses are doing better than ever now. Money goes farther these days: gardeners and cooks and chauffeurs come dirt cheap. At lunch, McDermott knows, as he hops up the steps of the boardinghouse, the strike will be all the talk. If it doesn't happen Monday, McDermott thinks, the entire city will self-combust simply from pent-up energy.

* * *

McDermott washes his hands and finds a place at the table with men not shy about showing their appetites. They eat as if they might not eat tomorrow, and it seldom matters how bad the food is, how mysterious the ingredients in the stews that fill their bowls. Today it is fish, and McDermott doesn't want to think about what kind. Madame Derocher has an impenetrable face, one that doesn't invite conversation or questions. If sufficiently annoyed, she will answer in a French patois that McDermott thinks a Parisian wouldn't understand. She has been known to snatch a bowl of stew from a complaining boarder's hands, leaving the man with nothing to eat at all. A boarder usually makes that mistake only once.

Sometimes the lunch break is strangely silent, the men too focused on their food to talk, too quickly sated and then stunned at meal's end to think coherently. Talk requires energy, and the men are careful, McDermott has observed, not to squander too much of that. There are still four and a half hours at the mill to go that day.

But today the talk is brisk, though McDermott can make out only some of the words, men with full mouths being difficult to understand under the best of circumstances. The boardinghouses are transient places, the men always coming and going, constantly shifting lodging when one or another of the houses changes ownership or loses its lease or is foreclosed upon; and lately there has been more turnover than usual. McDermott has spoken personally to only a handful of the twenty or so men at the long table. Still, though, he likes to listen and strains to follow what is being said. He needs to know the mood of the men, the way they speak and what's important to them.

He puts a pill in his mouth and takes a bite of stew, his ulcer worse now than it's been in weeks. Sometimes he can't eat Madame Derocher's food at all and has to go to Eileen's for a meal. She makes him a bowl of bread soaked in milk to keep him from starving. There has been talk of an operation, but McDermott can't afford either the time or the money for such a drastic step right now.

It is strangely quiet when he visits Eileen these days. Eamon has gone off to Texas, and McDermott doesn't know where Michael is. His sister Mary is married, which leaves only Rosie and Patricia and Bridget, all of whom seem too tired at night to make much of a fuss. McDermott feels sorry for Eileen and gives her the same amount of money he did when all the kids were in the house. He encourages her to buy pretty things for herself, and sometimes he brings her gifts: bonbons from Harley's chocolate factory, an Italian Morain brooch he found in a thrift shop, once a Toastmaster from Simmons.

Last winter McDermott had a girl of his own—Evangeline, a weaver on his floor. She had violent red hair and the clearest skin he has ever seen. He met her when he had to repair her drawing frame. A week later, the frame was broken again, and he suspects now that she probably did it deliberately so that they could meet a second time. He didn't guess in all the time he knew her that she was the scheming type. Their relationship was innocent enough, and he thought about asking her to marry him. On Saturday nights, they went dancing or to the movies. In April he bought her a watch he'd seen in a jeweler's window. But on Easter Sunday, when he went to her house to give it to her, she cried and told him that she was pregnant. She was leaving Ely Falls to marry the father, a bricklayer from Exeter. McDermott can still remember the shock of that betrayal: he hadn't even once touched her breast.

Beside him a carder belches from having eaten his stew too fast. McDermott reaches for a pitcher of milk. He can't get the stew down, but if he has some bread and milk, he'll be fine. The men are squeezed around the table, more of them it seems than there were just the day before. Madame Derocher must be packing them in like rats, he thinks. Anything to make a buck.

McDermott hears the words *business* and *machines.*

He sets the milk pitcher down and searches for the speaker. A man who looks vaguely familiar to him gestures with his hand and says the word *salesman.* McDermott's seen this man before, but where? He bends forward and cups his ear, turning it so that it might catch the entire sentence. The man has dark blond hair, parted in the middle, and bloodshot eyes. He gestures with a kind of military precision.

The weaver on the other side of McDermott starts to laugh at what must have been a good joke. Mule spinners and slasher tenders are knocking spoons against bowls, glasses against wood, hitching chairs forward, shouting to be heard. Someone demands more food and says that if he is paying eight dollars a week for room and board, he wants more bread. Madame Derocher sits in her chair in the corner as if she hasn't heard a word. In the din, three words float the length of the wooden table, and McDermott strains to catch them. Three mundane words of no apparent interest to anyone except McDermott. McDermott, whose heart lifts as he takes them in.

Typewriter, he hears.

And *Copiograph machine.*

Alphonse

Across from him, McDermott is ripping open a waxed packet of bread. The packages are stacked by the hundreds on wire shelves, with Alphonse wedged between them like an oversized loaf. McDermott and Ross and Rasley and another guy take three slices apiece and when they are done, Alphonse will get the heels. That's the way it goes, and Alphonse doesn't mind one bit. He has never eaten as well as he has the last couple of months, ever since McDermott told him to walk off the job, he had work for him to do, and he would pay him the same wage he was being paid in the mill. Alphonse almost fainted with happiness because there practically isn't anything worse than having to do bobbins.

All he does all day now is run. He runs

with the leaflets and gives them to mill workers as they're leaving the mills. He has to be quick enough to get away before any of the bosses can nab him. He puts posters on telephone poles and he is so fast it is as if the posters blossomed on the poles all by themselves. He takes messages to men in the mills and in rooms he has sworn never to talk about, and he fetches food and cigarettes and newspapers and lifts boxes and practically never leaves McDermott's side after hours except when he is doing an errand. Shopkeepers give McDermott and his friends food, and sometimes Alphonse just cannot believe his good luck.

Ross hands him the two heels. Alphonse wishes they would break open the cupcakes, though he knows better than to ask. The secret to keeping his job, he has learned, is to say absolutely nothing. He never speaks unless it is really important, like the time he told McDermott that Father Riley came out of St. André's and tore a poster down. Once McDermott asked Alphonse if he wouldn't rather go back into the mill because the work wouldn't be as dangerous and he would at least know people his own age, and Alphonse was so shocked by the question that he couldn't even answer. He just shook his head back and forth until McDermott laughed and put a hand on his shoulder.

Alphonse wonders who the new guy is, because he looks kind of familiar. Nobody introduced him, and nobody will, Alphonse knows. In fact, hardly anybody is talking at all because it's so noisy in the truck. A guy named Mahon is driving. Alphonse has ridden in the truck four or five times now. He loves the smell of the bread that leaks out of the waxed wrappers. He's always hungry, even though he is eating better than ever before, and McDermott says it's because he is getting his growth spurt.

Before Alphonse quit the mill, McDermott asked to "have a word" with Alphonse's mother. Alphonse stood outside on the porch while they talked, and when he was allowed to come back in, his mother looked at him in a whole new way that made him feel, well, terrific, even if he was a little scared. And that's when he stopped having to do the floors and the lunch pails and the sheets. Marie-

Thérèse would do that now, his mother said, and Augustin would help her. Alphonse had other business to attend to. Alphonse will never forget the look on Marie-Thérèse's face, and it almost doesn't matter what happens to him on this job because just that look was worth anything he ever gets asked to do. Sometimes he sticks pieces of cheese or apples or bits of chocolate in his pocket and brings them home to his mother. He never talks to her about what he is doing, though she seems to know, and sometimes she gives him a quick hug when he leaves the house, as if she might not ever see him again, as if he might just take off like Sam Coyne's father did.

And Alphonse can hardly believe it, but across from him, Ross is opening a box of cupcakes. Alphonse quickly counts how many there are in the box and thinks that if every man, including Mahon, takes only one then he will get the last one, and he has to swallow because they look so good. But then Ross passes the box to McDermott and McDermott does a wonderful thing. He holds the box out to Alphonse. Just then Mahon brakes the truck hard as if he had hit a pole, and before Alphonse can even bite into the chocolate, the back door swings open and he has to put an arm up to shield his eyes from the light.

Vivian

She sets the dog, who is trying to run in midair, onto the parquet floor.

"I took the sheets off, miss, like you said."

"Thank you, Mrs. Ellis."

"And I put milk and eggs and a nice leg of lamb and a chicken and whatnot in the Frigidaire."

"Marvelous," Vivian says.

"Your change is on the counter."

"Terrific."

"And Mr. Ellis got the beach wagon all tuned up. He took it to the battery station just this morning."

"Many thanks," Vivian says, taking a five-dollar bill from her purse. If she doesn't tip the woman soon, she'll have to listen to an entire litany of chores completed.

"Thank you, miss. The water and the electric are up and running."

Vivian nods and moves into the front room. The ocean is flat and Lido blue, reflecting a cloudless sky.

"So if there's nothing else . . ."

Vivian turns. "Oh, no, I'm fine. Absolutely fine."

"I couldn't help noticing you only have the one trunk this time."

"Yes."

"There was eight last time."

"So there were," Vivian says. "I don't need much here, do I?"

"Well, that's up to you. You'll be wanting me to do the laundry, I expect."

"As always."

"Well, that's settled, then. Glad you're back."

Vivian listens for the click of the latch at the back door. She sighs and unhooks the cape from her daffodil suit. She slips off her shoes and pads to the front door to let Sandy out. After five months in New York, the dog nearly levitates with happiness at being able to walk on a substance that is not concrete—seagulls! crabs! dead fish! paradise!—and something inside

Vivian begins to levitate as well. The day is marvelous, the light scintillating and crisp. Tomorrow, perhaps, she will go to work, but not today. Gerald has said that if she writes every day except Sundays, she can just about complete the revision before September—a prediction Vivian thinks is wildly optimistic.

"Strengthen Roger's character," Gerald said. "Use fewer stage directions."

He wanted to go into production by the beginning of December, he said, and Vivian held her breath, astonished at promising so much. Her play, *Ticker,* about the disintegration of a family after the stock market fiasco, pleased Gerald, but he had reservations. "This doesn't want to be a tragedy," he said when he had read the first draft. "It's neither fish nor fowl right now. There's a comedy in here trying to get out."

Vivian had met Gerald at the Plaza Hotel in Havana one night in January. They'd been drinking highballs with the Gibsons, and Gerald had told funny stories all night. Vivian really hadn't noticed the time until he had fallen asleep fully clothed across her bed at six in the morning. She hadn't actually slept with the man, and she'd more or less worked out that he was queer, which had been an enormous relief. Two nights later at dinner, Gerald said suddenly, "Tell me a play." Vivian asked him what he meant. "Give me an idea," he said. "You're clever. Tell me a play." Thinking fast, she suggested the idea for *Ticker* to Gerald, who everyone knew had just had a success with a mystery spoof on Broadway. The idea came to Vivian only as she was speaking, and of course she didn't really intend it as something anyone might want to develop, never mind with her in tow.

"Good," he said.

"Good?" she said.

"Write it," he said. "You've practically written it just talking to me."

"I can't write plays," Vivian said.

"Why not?"

"I can't even write a decent letter."

"I'll teach you," he said. "We'll go to the theater. You'll read plays. You can do it."

After Havana, Vivian moved to New York, mostly for the promise of the theater every night and the parties to follow, and, really, she did love the Plaza Hotel. But then, one evening in March at dinner, Gerald said he wouldn't take her to the theater anymore unless she showed him a page. The next morning, at her desk at the Plaza, Vivian began to write.

As she surveys the beach, Vivian ponders Gerald's advice about the first draft. She agrees with him that something dark is lurking beneath the surface of *Ticker,* something that threatens to drag it down, give it a whiny note. She can excise it if she tries. And of course she wants to write a comedy. Truthfully, she distrusts tragedy and often finds it stilted and false: all that wailing and gnashing of teeth! Give her a razor wit any day, dialogue that crackles, characters who don't take themselves too seriously, and the ones who do deliciously skewered. Two pages a day, Gerald said. That's all it would take.

She stands at the water's edge and squints back at the cottages, wondering if any of the old crowd will reappear this summer. The Nyes certainly won't, nor will Dorothy Trafton, and Vivian thinks she might actually miss Dorothy Trafton, if only as someone to dislike. It could be terribly lonely here without the usual crowd. Dickie is in Indianapolis now, working for the Arrow shirt company. She tried to persuade him to come east for a visit, but he said he couldn't do that, he was new to the job and had to wait at least six months before he could take a vacation. Vivian was appalled. Neither of them mentioned the house.

As she searches each cottage for signs of life, her eyes continue on to the end of the crescent, where she sees the house of the woman who collects sea glass. She sent Honora a postcard from Havana, but of course the woman had no address to reply to. Perhaps Vivian will take the beach wagon out later this afternoon, see if it's running all right, and stop in at Honora's house. Maybe she'll meet the husband—the elusive typewriter salesman who was late for Christmas Eve lunch.

Vivian digs her toes into the sand. "Sandy, come here," she calls.

The dog trots obediently to Vivian's feet. She picks him up and walks with him into the water until her ankles are so cold they ache.

Alice Willard

Dear Honora,

I thought I would just write you a couple of lines. Seems hardly time enough even to do that these days. Harold isn't at all well. He has lost a great deal of weight and as you know there wasn't much there to begin with. He said to me last week that he has not truly felt like a man since Halifax. This morning he said, "Life is a long ladder, Alice, and I'm not afraid of the top rung."

If you should get a chance to send him a note I know that he would appreciate it very much.

Are you eating well? I worry about this most of all, because I know how tight money is for you. I don't know what we'd have done without the produce from last year's garden. If there is any way you can make a garden for yourselves, even by the sea, you might want to try. Get Sexton to dig it for you.

We all have been hard hit around this area. The mill in Waterboro closed its doors and so did the bank, and here in Taft the bank is paying depositors 50 cents on the dollar and will close July 1. Bernice Radcliffe said the other day that she never wanted to see another raisin again, and I know just how she feels. In May, you could get raisins and honey for a good price, and that's all anybody ate for weeks.

Richard told us a funny story last night about how when his brother Jack was visiting and they were headed back to the house, they didn't think they had enough gas to make it, so Jack turned his Model T around and backed it up the hill since the gas tank is under the front seat. Gas is 19 cents a gallon now.

Vinegar is cheap, so make sure you have some handy. It keeps apples from turning brown, as you know, and it is a good meat tenderizer. A dash of it in breads and rolls will make them crusty. Also, a tablespoon in place of cream of tartar in meringue makes it beautifully high.

Here is a good recipe for English Monkey that I clipped out of Estelle's Ladies' Home Journal that doesn't need too many ingredients. Soak one cup of bread crumbs in one cup of milk. Melt one tablespoon of fat. Add one-half cup mild cheese, grated. Add it to the crumb mixture. Beat one egg and add to the above with salt and pepper. Cook three minutes. Pour over toast and serve.

Love,
Mother

Honora

Honora lets the letter fall onto the kitchen table and thinks of Harold. Harold, who stood in as best he could for her father in life as well as in the church. Harold, who has not felt like a man since Halifax. Harold, who has character, who can be trusted.

She puts her handkerchief back into her sleeve. She thinks for a moment about making the pie. She has already prepared the rhubarb; she has only to fix the strawberries and roll out the dough. She stands and removes the covered dish of rhubarb from the icebox, the fruit looking like a slimy sea creature in the shallow white bowl. But she is just too hungry and too tired to make a pie. She finds the box of Saltines in the cupboard, spreads some rhubarb between two crackers, and eats it. She chews experimentally and then with more enthusiasm. The stewed-fruit sandwich is delicious. She stands at the window, looking out at the pink beach roses, which have just come into bloom, and she has an idea. A very good idea, she thinks.

She finds the butter yellow wedding suit in a shallow closet in an empty room upstairs. She has the paper bag the dry goods came in from Jack Hess's store. In her bedroom, she cuts the bag to make wrapping paper, puts the suit inside, and writes a note.

Dear Bette,

I am sorry to have kept this suit so long. It is still in pretty good condition. I don't want my money back. I hope everything is going well at the store.

Sincerely,
Honora Willard Beecher

She ties the package with string and sets it on her night table.

There, she thinks. *That's done.*

She turns and looks into the mirror. Her face is narrower, more hollow cheeked than it normally is, and her skin is still winter white despite several long walks along the beach. And there is something else, something that wasn't there a year ago—a tension in the muscles, a niggling unease.

When were you going to tell me about the strike, Sexton?

She will not meet her husband's trolley tonight; indeed, she has probably already missed it. That might alarm him some, at least make him wonder. She doesn't have a dinner planned either. Let him eat boiled rhubarb and Saltines like she just did.

She walks to the window, the one that overlooks the ocean. The sea is flat tonight, a blue suffused with pink. She watches a fisherman on a lobster boat drawing in his pots. Usually, she sees the lobstermen when she wakes at daybreak. She likes the way they are always intent upon their methodical work, and she wonders if they hate lobsters as much as she does.

Oh, it is just too bad, she decides, moving to the bed and sitting at its edge. She loves this house, she loves it, and now they will lose it, and who knows what the future will bring? What if the strike drags on for months and all the mills close as a result? She has heard of strikes that have exhausted, decimated, whole communities. She supposes she and Sexton could always go to Taft and live with her mother, find work there. No disgrace in that. Not really.

She hears a deep rumble and grind, as if from a truck changing gears, then a short screech of tires. Honora heads toward the hallway. She hears the slam of a metal door, voices through an open window. She realizes that there are men in her house, downstairs.

"Honora," Sexton calls up to her, his voice more buoyant than she has heard in months. "Honora."

Three syllables. A lilt.

She walks to the railing at the top of the stairs. She has an impression of dark coats and caps, a restless moving about in a confined space. She sees Sexton peering up at her, and for a moment, he seems not to remember what it is he wants to say. She thinks his face will lapse into its former shape, the shape that has greeted her since Christmas, and that she will see, as always, the evasive glance, the set jaw. But he holds her eyes, balancing on a tightrope somewhere between *fresh start* and perhaps despair.

"There are people here," he says.

She descends the stairs, holding on to the railing. A figure steps out from behind Sexton. The word *you* is on her lips, and perhaps it is on his as well. It seems another life in which she met this man, gave him a ride into the city. Near the bottom of the steps, she notices the boy, who is looking at her with his mouth open.

"Honora, these are men from the mill. This is . . . ." Sexton appears to have forgotten the man's name already.

"McDermott," the man says, stepping forward. "Quillen McDermott."

"Hello," Honora says, and looks to see if the boy will remind them that they have already met.

"And this here is Alphonse," Sexton is saying. "And, well, everybody, this is my wife, Honora."

Honora nods in the direction of the others, who have removed their caps and are looking down at the floor.

"They're from an organizing committee," Sexton says quickly. "There's going to be a strike, and these men need to get out leaflets, and they're interested in seeing the typewriter and the Copiograph machine."

Typewriter? she thinks. *Copiograph machine?*

"In the attic," he says, glancing away.

She finishes her descent so that she is in the hallway with the others.

"I'm going to take them up to the attic," Sexton says. "To see the machines." He seems like a boy with a treasure in his bedroom that he wants his new friends to admire. Shyly, a man steps forward with a box of chocolate cupcakes in his hands. "These are for you, ma'am," he says.

And, oh God, what will she feed these men? she thinks, for surely they have not yet had their dinners.

Sexton reaches across the space between them and kisses her on the side of her mouth. "Happy anniversary," he says.

McDermott stands to one side, holding his cap behind his back. The boy scuffles his feet against the wooden floor. And then, through the open door that nobody thought to close, the figure of a woman, impossibly sleek and shiny, emerges into the crowd of gray and brown men.

"Yoo-hoo," Vivian calls brightly. "Anybody home?"

McDermott

He sits in a wooden chair in the kitchen and smokes a cigarette. Over by the sink, the woman is peeling potatoes. She peels slowly and methodically with a small paring knife, leaving as little potato on the peel as possible. The kitchen has an icebox and shelves with oilcloth on them, and every surface, as far as he can tell, is clean. Through the window, the June air is darkening.

He can see only the back of the woman at the sink, the pink blouse tucked into a gray skirt that falls just below the knees. She has on ankle socks and brown pumps, and the skin between her socks and skirt is bare. Maybe he should offer to help, but he senses that she would say no. Just a minute earlier, Ross and the new fellow, whose name is Sexton, and the other woman, Vivian, were in the room, and the space seemed crowded and noisy. But then Sexton said he was going to oil up the Copiograph machine and the woman and Alphonse went to her house to get food and drink, and Ross, well, he has no idea where Ross is, but now the room is quiet and empty. Too quiet. Too empty. He wonders if he should leave, if he is making the woman uncomfortable.

"I guess you didn't get your wish," he says.

She turns, her hands still over the sink. "I'm sorry?"

He takes a quick pull on his cigarette and blows the smoke out the side of his mouth. It pauses at the window and then coils back into the room, as if with a life of its own. "At Christmas," he says, flicking his ashes into a glass ashtray on the table. "You said you wanted a baby."

She smiles. "Oh," she says. "I guess not."

She has the sleeves of her pink blouse pushed up to her elbows. The skin on her forearms has delicate dark hairs. "How about you?" she asks. "You wanted peace and quiet."

He shrugs. "Still looking for it," he says.

She has to turn back to the sink to finish her task, and he can see that carrying on a conversation is going to be impossible if he sits at the table. He crosses the room and leans against the wall near the sink, one hand in his trouser pocket, the other still holding the cigarette. "You're a good sport," he says. "All of us barging in on you like this."

"It did take me by surprise," she says. "I'm just worried I won't have enough food."

"That woman, what's her name, Vivian, she's gone back to her house to get some stuff."

"Yes."

"She's a friend of yours?"

"Sort of. A new friend. She was there that day, at the airport."

"Really?" He doesn't remember her. He remembers the woman pilot in her flight suit, the boy looking pitiful but happy.

Honora rinses a potato. "I was kind of surprised when I saw you just now," she says.

He nods, though actually he was more than surprised—he was stunned. He had just worked out minutes earlier where he'd seen the new guy who was riding with them in the bread truck: he'd had an image of the man downing the three shots in the speak, leaving with the English girl. He'd recalled the package the man had left on the floor—all of which had meant nothing to McDermott in the bread truck. He was just glad he'd managed to remember, because something like that could drive you nuts all day—a face you couldn't place, a song you couldn't quite get the name of. But then when they all stood in the hallway and the woman walked down the stairs—and he knew right away she was the woman in the airport; how could he ever forget that?—and the guy went over to the woman and kissed her on the mouth and said *Happy anniversary,* McDermott felt the word *no* shoot through him, right up from his feet.

"And the boy," she says. "How is he?"

"He's fine, I think," he says. "I've got him working for me. Well, for us. I think he's better off than in the mill. He's happier, anyway."

"Is it safe, what you're doing?"

McDermott pauses. He stubs out his cigarette. He has a quick flash of the sledgehammer to Tsomides's head. "More or less," he says.

"Do you mind my asking you *what* you are doing?"

"No, I don't mind," he says. "You have every right, us using your house and all." Though he cannot for the moment think of how to phrase exactly what they are doing. He watches her rinse her hands under the tap, give them a quick shake, and dry them on a dish towel. She takes a pan from a shelf and fills it with water. "You know about the strike on Monday," he says.

"I do now," she says, putting the potatoes into the water.

"We're trying to get out leaflets and a newsletter. The unions have voted to strike, but they represent only ten percent of the mill workers in the city. We're trying to form an industrial union of the unorganized workers. The Ely Falls Independent Textile Union, we're calling it."

"You're striking because of the wage cut?"

He takes the heavy pot from her and carries it to the stove. "The wages in Ely Falls are the worst in New England. Well, you must know that."

"I knew they were bad. I didn't know they were the worst," she says, lighting the burner with a match.

"How long has your husband been in the mill?"

"Since February."

"He used to be a salesman, he said."

"Yes."

"Got laid off?"

"Something like that." He watches her take lard and flour from the cabinet. She measures them and sifts the flour into a bowl and then drops a teaspoon of ice water into the mixture.

"What are you making?" he asks.

"A pie. Strawberry-rhubarb."

"Sounds good."

"What do you do at the mill?" she asks, mixing the dough.

"I'm a loom fixer," he says, leaning against the lip of the sink so that he can see her face.

"What's that?"

"I fix looms."

She laughs, tilting her head back a bit. She has a long white neck, a squarish jaw.

"Can I help?" he asks.

She thinks a minute. "Would you mind cutting some strawberries?"

"Not at all."

"They're in the icebox," she says. "Just slice them."

He feels somewhat better having a task, though now it is more difficult to talk to the woman, and so for a while he just washes the strawberries and cuts them, and he feels all thumbs at this simple task. "You didn't know about that Copiograph machine and the typewriter, did you?" he asks after a time.

For a moment, she doesn't answer.

"No," she says finally.

"I could see it on your face." He puts the sliced strawberries back into their little wooden box.

"You must be good at reading faces," she says.

"Have to be," he says, looking at hers. He turns away and dries his hands on the dish towel.

"I think I'll go give your husband a hand," he says.

Honora

The front room hums with the sort of activity it has not seen in years, not, perhaps, since the unwed mothers sat in lively groups, drinking tea (Honora imagines them knitting baby garments) and occasionally glancing out to sea.

Prevent Hunger in Ely Falls, she types. Her fingers are a blur over the familiar keys, the enamel ovals in their silver rings. She has not lost her dexterity, not since the days when she was recording Sexton's sales pitch in the paneled rooms of banks. In the corner, her husband's arm is making repetitive round pumps at the Copiograph machine. As each copy is shunted out, he inspects the sheet and then sets it aside on a makeshift table fashioned the night before from a door he took off its hinges and laid over two sawhorses he found in the cellar. He has dressed in his best gabardine trousers (his Sunday-go-to-meeting trousers, Harold might have said) and a shirt kept for special occasions (though there have been precious few special occasions since Christmas). Honora, when she glances up, thinks that it has been some time since she has seen her husband with this much *snap.*

Dread poverty threatens thousands of Ely Falls workers, she types as the man named Mironson dictates the words from a sheet of paper in his hands. He brushes a long hank of hair from his forehead. He is a small, almost delicate man, his mouth, with its pronounced bow, nearly that of a woman, and so at odds, Honora thinks, with his professed calling as a union organizer—as if a priest had come calling in overalls, or an artist had on a clerical collar. At the opposite end of the room, Quillen McDermott, in blue shirt-sleeves, is collating and stapling a newsletter. The boy, Alphonse, is bundling batches of leaflets together with string. Vivian, in crisp white linen pants and a blouse, is holding a copy of the newsletter and pacing.

"You can't be serious," Vivian says to no one in particular, exhaling a long plume of blue smoke. "You can't print this drivel."

McDermott and Mironson glance up at her.

"Listen to this," she says, hooting to the room at large. *"In the industrial depression you did take a noble part / And ungrumbling shared the leanness of the floundering textile mart."*

McDermott gives a small chuckle, and even Mironson seems abashed. "It was a strike song in New Bedford," he says.

"I can't even say the words, never mind sing them," Vivian says. "And *textile mart?"*

Mironson brushes his hair off his face again. "The idea is to print politically inspiring poetry or songs. It doesn't really matter if they scan," he says.

"I think it matters if one can actually say them without gagging," she says, taking another delicate pull on her cigarette and holding the offensive doggerel away from her.

"Hear, hear," says Ross from the corner.

"Do you think you can do better?" Mironson asks Vivian.

Vivian appraises him coolly, and Honora

wonders if Mironson means this as a reprimand or a challenge.

"I could try," Vivian says.

"It's yours, then," Mironson says—a leader used to delegating.

As if there were nothing at all out of the ordinary in the previous exchange, Vivian sits near the makeshift table with the newsletter on her lap. She searches in her purse and removes a golf pencil. "When was the industrial depression?" she asks innocently.

"The mills have been in a depression since twenty-four," Mironson says.

"Oh," Vivian says, pursing her lips. Honora watches her write a word on the piece of paper in her lap.

"Employment and sources of livelihood are as of today eliminated by the shutdown of eleven Ely Falls mills," Mironson dictates just behind Honora's shoulder. Almost simultaneously she types the words, thinking as she does so that perhaps Vivian might want to take a look at this particular leaflet as well. *"It is no answer to say that this condition is a situation of their own making,"* Mironson dictates.

"Who is this going to?" Honora asks.

"It's an appeal for funds. It will be distributed in mills, union halls, sporting events, and working-class neighborhoods in this and surrounding towns."

"Wouldn't you want an appeal for funds to go to people who have money?"

"Yes, of course," Mironson says. "But this is more of an appeal for solidarity."

"I see," says Honora, though she is not entirely sure that she does see. If the objective is to relieve hunger, she thinks, leaflets directed at the owners of shops and grocery stores and churches and social clubs might make more sense. But she doesn't quite have enough of Vivian's gumption to object.

"It is a self-evident fact that a continuation of this lack of means of earning a living will reduce Ely Falls textile workers to a state of absolute destitution," Mironson reads.

"Suffering Jesus," Ross says from the corner.

Seven men and the boy spent the night sleeping in bedrolls in the previously empty bedrooms upstairs. Shortly after Sexton arrived with the other men in the bread truck, and McDermott and the fellow named Ross saw the typewriter and the Fosdick Copiograph machine, and, more important, Honora guesses, the empty house far from town—a house at which no one would ever think to look for strike leaders—Ross and the man named Mahon went back to the city and returned with Mironson and three others. By then Vivian had come from her house with a beach wagon full of provisions: a leg of lamb, a roast chicken, vegetables, butter and bread, milk, several bottles of wine, and all the silver and glassware and china from her own house—real silver, real crystal, and delicate porcelain plates ("I never eat anyway," Vivian said). Honora cooked the dinner and baked another pie. Sexton set up the sawhorses and the door in the front room, and Honora put her mother's tablecloth over it to make a dining table. The meal seemed more like a feast than the simple feeding of mill workers and strike leaders, and the wine disappeared as if it were water. Sexton, who had by then already quickly bathed and changed his clothes, sat at the middle of the table and, with his salesman's charm and affability dusted off, began to shed his aura of failure and despair—so much so that when Honora finally was alone with him in their bedroom after midnight (both of them exhausted and, for the first time in weeks, overfed), she found it impossible to summon the anger of earlier in the day. Chastising her husband for not having told her about the strike seemed absurd in the face of the astonishing arrival of the strike leaders themselves. Besides, having words with Sexton would have required whispering, since both were acutely aware of not being alone together in their own house for the first time since they had entered it. Sexton did not move to touch her, and she thought that he was perhaps too self-conscious about the other men. In any event, Honora was relieved.

The men had their own bedrolls, though Honora had had to find extra towels and soap. She worried for the boy, who was sleeping among so many men, but then she saw that McDermott was looking out for his young charge. As she lay in her bed, unable to sleep, she could hear the men snoring, even over the sound of the surf outside.

Vivian had gone back to her own house,

and briefly Louis Mironson had gone with her, needing to use the telephone there. Honora, who found sleep impossible, slipped downstairs to cut the precious grapefruit that Vivian had brought, to get a head start on breakfast. She was in the kitchen when Mironson came back into the house through the porch, his feet still bearing traces of wet sand; and for a few moments they sat together in the kitchen, each with a glass of milk. He'd walked back along the beach, carrying his shoes but still in his coat and tie, guided by the moonlight, he said, adding that it had been some time since he had spent any length of time near the ocean. He was grateful to her, he said, for letting them use the house. She asked him if he was married, if he had a family, and he said no, that he'd been traveling up and down the east coast for several years now and that he hadn't found anyone with whom to settle down. The work was too important and too urgent, he said, and she noted that he nearly added *too dangerous* but stopped himself. He looked away and thanked her and said that there might be more people coming from time to time and would that be all right, and Honora said it didn't seem to be her decision to make. He would see to it, he said, that she and Sexton were given money as compensation. If she would help with the cooking, he said, he would be most grateful, but he would arrange for provisions. It did not escape Honora's notice that it was she and not Sexton with whom Mironson seemed to be making the deal.

A woman named Sadie, a "comrade from New York," might be joining them at some point, he said, assessing Honora's response to the charged word.

"You're a Communist," Honora said.

"Yes," Mironson said. "I am. The others are not, though."

"Why are you and they working together?"

"This country has a long history of spontaneous strikes becoming interchangeable with the frankly revolutionary."

"In other words," Honora said, "you're using each other."

"In a nutshell, yes," Mironson said.

He added that Honora shouldn't expect much help from Sadie in the kitchen; she wasn't that sort of woman. Honora stood and took the empty milk glasses to the sink and washed them.

"Well, good night," he said, standing as well, and Honora was surprised to see how short he was. He unrolled his trousers, leaving a dusting of sand on the floorboards. He tried to pick the sand up with his fingers. "Oh, don't worry about that," she said. "I've got a broom."

"This is important, you know," he said.

"I can't pretend to understand this," she said.

"There's not a lot to understand," he said. "The workers and their families are living like dogs."

And Honora thought that Louis Mironson might be surprised at how much she knew about living like a dog.

In the morning, Vivian returned early, looking polished and nearly luminous in a peach linen ensemble, while behind her a man named Ellis brought in carton after carton of food that challenged Honora's organizational skills in the kitchen, though it was a lovely task to have to put it all away on her shelves and in her icebox. Vivian credited

Jack Hess with supplying the food, though it was perfectly obvious that Vivian was funding the provisioning. In her dressing gown, Honora fixed a breakfast of eggs and bacon and ham and toast and coffee—along with the precious grapefruit—as one by one the men and the boy came downstairs, looking a bit shy and sleepy. They once again ate in the front room, the sun from the east bathing the incongruous scene in a light that made them all squint. The boy, Honora noted with satisfaction, had four eggs, a toast-and-bacon sandwich of his own making, and a delicate porcelain cupful of milky coffee. After the meal, McDermott sent Alphonse into the kitchen to help with the dishes, and though Honora intended to ask him only to dry them, she noted that he had finished washing them almost before she'd had time to put the food away.

"You're good at this," she said.

"Yes, ma'am," he said.

"You've had a lot of practice, then."

"I have," he said. "But . . ." He paused.

"But what?" she asked gently.

"Well, this is easy, isn't it?" he blurted. "The water coming hot from the tap."

"You don't have hot water?" she said.

"No, ma'am."

Honora nodded and thought maybe she didn't know what it was to live like a dog after all.

"Don't tell me you're going to print this *workers of the world unite* guff," Vivian is saying as she reads a fresh copy of the first pages of the newsletter.

"Miss Burton," Mironson says quietly, turning in her direction, "though the immediate issue to hand is the wage cut and the appalling conditions of the workers in Ely Falls, the underlying problems are far graver."

"Maybe so," Vivian says, "but I don't believe for one minute that the men and women who show up on your picket line on Monday give a toss about the . . ." Vivian checks the wording in the newsletter, *"the sharp struggle furnishing irrefutable proof of the process by which the inner contradictions of capitalism in the imperialist period bring on economic struggles which speedily take on a political character."*

"Jesus Christ," Ross says from a corner of the room, where he is placing bound packets of leaflets into boxes. Mironson shoots him a quick look, as if to say, *Who asked you?*

"What I imagine the workers will be concerned about on Monday," Vivian says, "—this is going out on Monday, correct?"

Mironson nods.

"Is food for their families, how they're going to pay the rent, why are they striking—that is to say, what's the immediate reason for the strike—how long is it going to last, where are they supposed to go, and what are they supposed to do. And I imagine they're going to want to know something about the consequences of what they're doing as well. You know, will they lose their jobs ultimately, even if the bosses capitulate? That sort of thing."

Honora looks over at McDermott, who raises an eyebrow and smiles.

"I believe the workers will want to know in what way they are being exploited," Mironson says, "and how they are united with workers all over the world, not just in Ely Falls and not just in America, but internationally. By going out on strike on Monday, they become part of an international brotherhood."

"I sincerely doubt whether anyone who strikes on Monday will give a fig for international brotherhood," Vivian says, "or—shall we call a spade a spade, Mr. Mironson—the Communist Party." Vivian fishes in her purse for her silver cigarette case. "Possibly later, when everyone is fantastically bored because the strike has gone on for weeks and weeks and they've had nothing to do for days on end, then you can give them this *internationale* and Marxist rot, and *maybe,* just maybe, they'll read it. But if you hand them this now, it will end up underfoot on the street." Vivian lights one cigarette with the end of another. She offers the open case to Mironson.

"I don't smoke," Mironson says, and somehow his refusal, though justified, sounds boorish to Honora's ear.

"My advice," Vivian says, snapping the case shut, "though of course my advice is perfectly useless, is to put the newsletter in the form of questions and answers. Start with the most important question that's going to be on the minds of the strikers Monday morning and then go from there."

Vivian's suggestion is so simple and yet so insightful, Honora thinks, that Mironson cannot fail to see its brilliance. There is a long silence in the front room, during which hardly anyone moves—apart from Vivian, who continues to smoke as though completely unconcerned. Mironson brushes away his pesky forelock. Honora sees that Sexton has stopped the Copiograph machine in midrotation.

"There may be some merit in that," Mironson says quietly.

"Marvelous," Vivian says, as though this small victory held no personal significance whatsoever. "Then should we just put our heads together for a few minutes, you and I, and come up with a series of questions and answers? Or do you want to do it yourself?"

But Mironson isn't quite through yet. "What is at stake here, Miss Burton . . ."

"Oh, do call me Vivian," she says.

Mironson crosses his arms over his chest, the paper he was dictating from dangling from a hand. ". . . is nothing less than a way of life and the future of this country. I don't expect you to be able to see the importance of such a critical *over-*

turning of this way of life, being so mired in the capitalist class yourself. By definition, you *cannot* see. And while one can admire your charity and generosity, and it goes without saying how grateful we are, I cannot possibly expect you to understand the underlying significance of what is happening here and all over the country."

McDermott looks sharply over at Mironson and opens his mouth as if to speak, but Vivian puts up a hand to signal she can handle this on her own. "I do see what you're saying, Mr. Mironson. May I call you Louis? It sounds so, I don't know, not-*comradely* not to be on a first-name basis," she says.

"Yes, of course," he says.

"You have a wonderful way of putting things, Louis. And, really, I was just wondering, where did you go to school? You're obviously marvelously educated."

"I don't think where I was educated is at all the point here."

"Oh, but it's precisely my point," says Vivian, decorously crossing her legs.

Honora thinks that Mironson cannot refuse to answer the question. "I went to Yale," he says finally.

"Ah," Vivian says. "On scholarship?"

"No," he says.

Vivian nods, her penny-colored hair aglow in the morning sunlight. "Is it too personal a question to ask what your father does? Or did?"

Mironson hesitates. "He was a shoe manufacturer."

"He actually made the shoes himself, or he owned the company?"

"My grandfather started the company in Brockton, Massachusetts. He made the shoes himself."

"But your father?"

Mironson straightens his tie. "He owned the company."

"Never made a shoe."

"I can't say never."

"Would it be fair to say, then, that you grew up 'mired in the capitalist class'?"

Mironson removes a handkerchief from his pocket. "I'm a Jew, Miss Burton," he says. "My class-consciousness is very different from yours."

"Oh, did I miss something here?" Vivian asks sweetly. "Jews can't be capitalists?"

"I've been studying this for years," Mironson says, wiping his brow. "I've been working at this all my adult life. I've been to Moscow. I've worked with Eugene Debs."

"Of course," says Vivian. "And I cannot say how much I admire your dedication. We all admire your dedication. And without you, I imagine that the men in this room would be hopelessly lost. But as to being able to understand *what's at stake . . .*" She pauses. "Let's see if I've got this right. Capitalist owns textile company and makes huge amount of money and lives across the river in big house with Frigidaire and GE washing machine and Packard and Chris-Craft motor yacht while employing hundreds of workers to whom he pays pitiful wages, all the while thinking it perfectly normal that they should live in hideously filthy tenements with no running water and no indoor plumbing and not enough money to feed their children. How am I doing so far?"

The tension in the room reminds Honora of the aftermath of a thunderclap: full of sound and yet intensely silent.

"And then said capitalist decides for whatever reason," Vivian continues, "—perhaps his business is not doing well, perhaps he wants a trip to Havana—to cut his workers' pay ten percent so as to increase profits for himself. And, mirabile dictu, the workers mind!"

Mironson says nothing, but Honora can see a small twitch at the side of his mouth.

"Uppity workers," Vivian says, exhaling a long plume of blue smoke.

Mironson shakes his head and smiles.

"Of course, it's more complicated than I can understand," Vivian says graciously. "I think that goes without saying. Quite frankly, I don't even know who Eugene Debs is. My point is to keep it simple. One need tell the strikers only what they have to know in order to survive until Tuesday. And then until Wednesday. And then until Thursday. And so on. And if later someone actually asks you, what does this all mean?—well, then I suppose you can give them all the Marxist rhetoric you think they can stand."

"I hope you were on the debating team wherever you went to school," Mironson says.

"Oh, well, no," Vivian says. "Actually, I'm not sure my school even had a debating team. I took classes in table etiquette and deportment."

McDermott laughs, and even Ross is grinning.

"What shall we call it?" Mironson asks, looking at Vivian. "This *practical* newsletter of ours."

Vivian exhales a long curl of smoke. She stubs her cigarette out in an ashtray on the makeshift table. Beside the ashtray is a crumpled package of cigarettes.

"Lucky Strike," she says without a moment's hesitation.

Alphonse

All day yesterday they worked on the newsletter, which now Alphonse can just about read and which is a thousand times better than the one they were starting to pack up before Miss Burton spoke her mind and then went into a huddle with Mironson while they all kind of sat around eating a second breakfast, which Alphonse thought was frankly terrific. And then the other woman, Mrs. Beecher, saw Alphonse putting rolls with cheese in them in his pockets and asked him if he wouldn't rather wrap them in waxed paper, and Alphonse nearly died of embarrassment and then confessed that he took them for his mother, and Mrs. Beecher said well maybe it wasn't such a good idea to carry rolls and cheese in your pockets because of all the crumbs and wouldn't it be better if she just made up some sandwiches for his mother when it was time for Alphonse to go back to the city, and all day yesterday he was furious with himself for not even being able to say a proper *thank you.*

In the late afternoon, Ross and McDermott and Alphonse went back into the city with some of the newsletters and leaflets tied into bundles, and Alphonse thought Mr. Beecher's arm must be near to falling off with all the pumping he was doing on that nifty machine that printed the copies. After they delivered the leaflets to Nadeau's apartment, McDermott asked Alphonse if he wouldn't like to visit his mother for a while, after which he would pick him up in an hour and take him back to the house on the beach. Alphonse knew that McDermott and Mahon and Ross wanted to go to the speakeasy and drink, but he was glad anyway for the chance to see his mother and Augustin and Grard, and even, he had to admit, Marie-Thérèse, who seemed to have calmed down considerably. And also it was a chance to check to see if he was taller than Marie-Thérsèe yet—an exercise he liked to do weekly—though she wouldn't agree to a back-to-back.

And then McDermott picked him up as he said he would and for the first time ever Alphonse didn't want to eat any of the leftover bread or cupcakes in the truck because he knew that he and the men were headed for a good meal. Mrs. Beecher made excellent pies and potatoes and eggs and coffee, and just this morning, the smell of bacon was again so wonderful that Alphonse nearly tripped over himself trying to get down the stairs to breakfast.

Last night, the woman with the penny-colored hair brought more food and the men had a lot to drink and Alphonse noted that even Miss Burton had quite a lot to drink herself. She was teaching Mironson how to make something called a sidecar in a beautiful silver shaker and after he got the hang of it, everybody got more drunk, even Miss Burton. Mrs. Beecher didn't drink too much, though, and you could just tell by the look of her that she probably wasn't much of a drinker anyway.

After dinner Alphonse helped Mrs.

Beecher with the dishes, and McDermott, who was pretty drunk but not as drunk as Ross and Mahon and Mr. Beecher, who were just roaring drunk on the porch, sat at the table and smoked while Mrs. Beecher and Alphonse washed and dried. Alphonse didn't mind the job one bit because the hot water came from the tap and just putting his hands under it was a kind of treat. He couldn't help but think how much easier it would be to mop the floor and do the clothes and all the rest of it if they had hot water from a tap on Rose Street. But they didn't, and that was that.

All weekend, Alphonse had to remind himself that the strike was going to happen on Monday, because just looking at the men and Miss Burton getting drunk and laughing so much, and even Mrs. Beecher giggling at dinner, no one would ever have the idea that tough times were ahead.

This morning—his second morning in the house—Alphonse was the first one down to breakfast because Miss Burton had gone home and all the men were sleeping late and would probably wake up with terrific headaches. Mrs. Beecher sat with Alphonse at the table and asked him all the usual questions, and Alphonse considered telling her about wanting to be a doctor, because he knew she was going to be disappointed about the weaver, but when the time came, he just couldn't bring himself to lie to her and so he kind of shrugged and hoped she wouldn't ask him again what he wanted to be when he grew up.

Now they are all on the beach on blankets that Miss Burton brought from her house, and Alphonse thinks it is kind of amazing how lively she is considering how much he personally saw her drink last night. In fact, she's a lot more lively than some of the men, like Ross, who couldn't even eat his breakfast, and Alphonse imagines she must have some sort of vitamin tonic at her house for times like this. Mrs. Beecher and Vivian packed up sandwiches and made salads and deviled eggs, and even though they are all only sitting in front of the house and could go right inside and eat at a table if they wanted to, they are having a picnic as if it were a day at the beach, which he supposes it is. Mr.

Beecher has on his bathing suit and the other men have their pants rolled, and Ross was pretty funny when he stood up and walked into the ocean in his clothes and then hopped around like he'd been electrocuted. But when he came out he looked so much better than when he'd gone in that Mahon and McDermott and Mironson went into the ocean in their clothes too. Mr. Beecher ran to the water's edge and dived in and that was when Alphonse worked out where he'd seen the new guy before—at the beach that day last summer, swimming through the water like a shark. McDermott and Ross came out and got Alphonse and carried him kicking and screaming into the water and then just dumped him in too. And holy Joseph, it was so cold that Alphonse couldn't breathe and when he came up and got the water out of his eyes, Ross, McDermott, and Mahon and even Mironson were dripping like wet ducks and laughing like they'd never seen anything so funny in their whole long lives, and Alphonse thinks that if this is what it means to go on strike he wishes that the strike would go on forever.

Vivian

"They're little boys, aren't they?" Vivian says, watching the men throw Alphonse into the water. And indeed, though she means *Aren't they silly?* she does think they are all so very, very young. Honora and McDermott are only twenty-one, Louis twenty-five.

"In their way," Honora says.

"Poor Alphonse. Do you think he knows how to swim?"

"Doesn't look like it," Honora says.

"I've hardly been outside in months," Vivian says, stroking Sandy's fur.

"You've been in Boston?"

"No, in New York," Vivian says, slightly envying the men in the water. She wishes she had brought her bathing suit so that she could take a dip herself. "I'm trying to write a play."

"For the theater?"

"Well, it's the most remarkable bit of good luck—or bad luck, I'm not sure which. I met this fellow in Havana who's a producer in New York, and one night at dinner I was telling him about an idea for a play that more or less came to me as I was talking to him, and he said—mainly because he was drunk, I think—write it yourself. And as I didn't seem to have any other useful occupation, I decided to give it a try. It's great fun, though I've a lot to learn."

"That's very exciting. What's it about?"

"The stock market crash. The aftermath."

"Oh," Honora says, pulling her dress up over her knees.

"I worry about making light of other people's tragedy," Vivian says quickly.

"It's a comedy?"

"Not yet, though I think it wants to be. Not sure if I can write comedy, actually. It's a bit of a mess right now." And likely to remain a mess if she doesn't settle down to work, she thinks. "You've had it somewhat rough," Vivian says boldly, and Honora looks quickly over at her.

"Yes," Honora says truthfully.

"Your husband lost his job?"

"He did. The day I last saw you, as a matter of fact. Christmas Eve."

"Oh, I *am* sorry," Vivian says. She remembers the tree with its presents neatly arranged beneath it, the mincemeat pies on the counter.

"It was dreadful," Honora says, sighing, and Vivian wonders if this is the first time she's spoken about it.

"What happened?"

"He was . . . laid off, I guess you could say. He was, I don't know the right word, crushed. It took weeks for him to recover, even partially. He tried to find a job in sales, but no one was hiring. And then he went to the mills and tried to get a job in one of the offices, but they weren't hiring men in the offices either, and then he had to go into the mill itself. He's a ring spinner."

"Oh," Vivian says, letting Sandy drink from her cup of water. "But you've managed to keep the house."

"Just."

"And now this strike," Vivian says. "I hope it doesn't last long."

"No," Honora says.

"If ever you should need . . . ," Vivian begins.

"Oh God, no," Honora says quickly. "Don't even think about it."

Vivian wants to ask Honora about her marriage, but senses that now is perhaps not the time. Though she can never make out what couples see in each other, she is particularly puzzled by Honora and Sexton. Of course, he is a handsome man, but there is something a bit . . . well . . . *oily* about him that is somewhat off-putting, at least to Vivian. He seems too eager to please, yet hardly to notice when Honora is in the room.

"Are you bothered about all the men in your house?" Vivian asks after a time.

"I'm not sure I understand what the consequences are. I have a feeling that they're all keeping something from me. I felt it when Quillen . . . well, I can't call him Quillen, can I, he hates the name, McDermott then, when he was talking. And then again when Louis . . ." She pauses. "You really gave Louis what-for yesterday," Honora says.

"Oh, I was only half serious," Vivian says. "He's adorable. A saint, really. I've no experience with selfless men. They're remarkably unsexy, don't you think?"

"Vivian, you know that he's a Communist."

"Well, yes, I more or less worked that out."

"Why are you doing this?" Honora asks. "You of all people?"

"Well, I don't take this whole thing too seriously. It's a lark, isn't it?"

"But it's your class they're after."

"Well, Louis is. And in a rather abstract way, I think. He's more like me than you might think. As for me, well, last year I nearly died of boredom. Besides," she adds, leaning closer to Honora, "I just adore you and Alphonse."

Honora smiles. "I worry for Alphonse," she says. "He seems so young."

"He's devoted to McDermott," Vivian says.

"For good reason, I think."

"And your husband doesn't mind all the men here either?" Vivian asks tentatively, thinking that one's husband might have every reason to mind.

"No," Honora says. "He doesn't. To be perfectly honest, he seems happier than I've seen him in months. Since the late fall, really."

"We had quite a party last night."

"I counted eight bottles this morning," Honora says, lying back on the blanket and shading her face with her hat. "What happened to that man?" she asks. "The one who owned your house?"

"Dickie? Oh, poor Dickie," Vivian says. She thinks of Dickie the last time she saw him, in January. Dickie with his pasty complexion, his waxed mustache, his malacca cane, and his Haskell-and-Haskell tie with a spill of what looked to be tomato sauce on it. "He was ruined, really. He's working for the Arrow shirt company in Indianapolis now. As a salesman, I think. A friend of a friend got him the job." And then immediately Vivian realizes the insensitivity of referring to a man who has a job as a salesman as ruined. "I didn't mean . . . ," she says.

Honora waves away her concerns. "It's all . . . I don't know . . . relative, I think."

"I suppose it is," Vivian says, looking down at Sandy. "This poor dog is just panting."

"Why don't we throw him in?"

"He hates the water."

"Do him good," Honora says.

Honora

The beach is flat, stripped clean but for curved white shells, smooth oval pebbles. She walks north and east along the crescent, the sun behind her, her shadow growing to one side. At the ridge of the beach, where the soft sand begins before it hits the dunes, there are groups of people here and there, summer residents, newly arrived, looking white and overdressed and slightly shell-shocked in their canvas chairs. Honora hugs her arms, trying to ward off an east wind that has just come up and is blowing the tips off the waves. She has on only a rayon skirt she made herself and a cotton sleeveless blouse. She left her shoes on the blanket after most of the men, Sexton included, fell asleep on the beach and Vivian went back to her own cottage with her wet dog. Honora walks slowly with her head bent, glancing up from time to time, always surprised, no matter how many times she sees it, by the navy of the water—a blue that appears to be alive. A sailboat, leaning into the wind, zips along the shoreline. Tomorrow the strike will begin. It seems hardly possible.

Honora has been into Ely Falls only a few times since Christmas. It is, she thinks, an undistinguished city, dominated by its mills, long flat buildings with enormous windows and smoke billowing from their chimneys. The tenements, brick and wood, are built into the hills surrounding the city center—charmless houses with no yards, the wash hung on lines over what look to be perilous wooden porches. She has never been inside Sexton's boardinghouse, though she has seen it from the outside: a brick building, one of many similar structures built in terraced rows. She couldn't go inside, he said, because only men were allowed.

A chunk of bottle green glass snags Honora's attention, and she bends to retrieve it in the wet sand. She rubs it between her palms to clean it. It is a satisfying shard, nearly half an inch thick.

She tries to imagine what it might once have been. Though it looks like a bottle, it's too chunky. Can't be a window either. A jar of some sort? Perhaps a kind of dishware? The casing of a lantern? Something from a ship? She picks up a large white shell and lays the shard inside, cradling the shell in her palm.

"What have you got there?"

Honora flinches, startled by the voice. McDermott is slightly winded and bends for a moment to catch his breath. His hair, stiff with seawater, has dried into a comical shape. He has on a blue shirt, the sleeves rolled well above the elbows.

"Sea glass," she says.

"What's that?" he asks.

"It's glass that's been weathered by the sea and washed up on a beach. I collect it." She holds out the shell with the piece of bottle green glass inside it. He studies it in her palm.

"Where'd it come from?" he asks, touching the shard.

"A shipwreck, maybe? Something that someone tossed overboard? A fire along the shore? Sometimes I find pieces that have melted and have charred bits inside.

That's the mystery of it, isn't it?—the not knowing where it's from."

"A secret it won't tell," he says. His skin has pinkened from the sun. He squints in the bright reflected light from the water.

"Something like that," she says, lowering her hand. "You were all sleeping."

"We're leaving now," he says. "I came to say goodbye."

"You're going?" she asks, surprised.

"We have to be in place early in the morning when the strike begins. To make sure no one goes into the mills. To distribute the leaflets."

"Oh," she says, mildly disturbed that Sexton didn't tell her they were leaving before dinner. She wouldn't have made the lemon meringue pies if she'd known. To be fair, Sexton may not have known either. "I'll walk back with you, then," she says.

"Thanks for putting us up," he says as they set out. "Especially last night. We were all kind of wild."

"Everyone was having a good time," she says.

"I'm sorry?"

She remembers that she has to look right at McDermott when she speaks to him. The muted roar of the surf makes conversation difficult even under the best of circumstances.

"Here," he says, stepping ahead of her and turning. "I'll just walk backward like this."

"Are you sure?" she asks.

"I do it all the time."

His shirt is stiff and wrinkled with salt as well, she notes. His trousers are rolled to midcalf. It is awkward going, McDermott walking backward and Honora stepping forward, and it is slightly uncomfortable as well—having her face so closely looked at to make sure that her words are seen.

"I was just saying that it seemed like everyone was enjoying themselves," she says, aware that she is overenunciating each syllable. She tries to relax her mouth.

He shrugs. "We drank too much."

"Yes."

"You want some gum?" he asks, holding out a pack.

"Sure," she says.

He unwraps two pieces and gives her one. "That was nice back there," he says. "The way you were trying to teach Alphonse to swim."

Honora tied her skirt up and waded out with Alphonse and told him to lie as flat as a board. She would hold him up, she said, and she wouldn't let him go until he was ready. But every time he nodded and she removed her hands, his feet sank immediately to the bottom. "He needs a bathing suit," she said. "His trousers were dragging him down."

"He needs a lot of things."

"You care for him, don't you?"

McDermott shrugs. "I suppose I do."

"He was terrified of the water," Honora says.

"Is this it?" he asks, bending to pick up a speck of grass-green lying in the sand. She inspects the shard between his thumb and forefinger. "Yes," she says. "That's a beautiful color. Not very common."

"Well, here," he says, handing it to her. "Keep it for your collection."

"Thank you," she says.

"Actually, I came to find you because I wanted to tell you something," he says. "Friday night, when we first got to your house and you and I were talking in the kitchen, you asked me if it was safe, what we were doing, and I told you, *more or less.*"

Honora nods.

"Yeah, well." He looks away. "It's not," he says.

Honora slows her pace.

"It's dangerous," McDermott says. "I thought you should know that."

"Oh," she says.

"We're using you."

For a moment, she is taken aback by the bluntness of his statement. "I understood that," she says. "Just like Louis is using you."

"But we're using Mironson, don't forget."

"Are you a Communist?" she asks.

"Hell, no," he says. "A good Irish Catholic like me? No, I'm loyal to the union, not the Reds."

A man and a woman, both in straw hats and walking at a normal pace, draw up alongside Honora and McDermott. He waits for them to pass by before he speaks again. "It's perfect for us, a house far from town. Your husband says he's never told the mill where he lives and that the only address they have for him is the boardinghouse. So if we can keep this place a secret . . ."

Honora nods.

"The organization Mironson works for is sending up a press from New York, and we'll probably bring it over sometime this week," he says. "Obviously the Copiograph machine can't keep up with the volume we need."

"No," she says, brushing her hair off her face. She has goose bumps on her arms from the east wind. She rubs them to warm them up.

"The reason I say it's dangerous," McDermott says, "is that we had a press set up at a warehouse in the city, and one night some men in masks came in and destroyed the press and all the other equipment with sledgehammers. One of our men was hit as well. He's still in the hospital."

Honora stops in the sand.

"Look," he says, "if you tell me now that you don't want us here, I'll make sure none of us ever comes back and bothers you again."

"Who were the men?"

"We don't know," McDermott says. "They were sent by the bosses who own the mills. Vigilantes. I think one of them was the chief of police, though it was dark and it was hard to tell."

"You were there?"

He nods.

"And you weren't hurt?"

"I got out."

"Oh, I'm very surprised by this," she says, putting a hand to her chest. "Though I don't know why I should be."

McDermott is silent, watching her.

"It's really my husband's decision," Honora says.

"If we use your house," he says, "you're involved as well."

Honora and McDermott walk on again, this time side by side, Honora silent, imagining a raid on her own house. They pass three small girls making a sand castle and have to walk around it. Then Honora pivots, facing McDermott. "What will happen tomorrow?" she asks, walking backward.

"If New Bedford and Gastonia are anything to go by," he says after a minute, "there will be a mass rally and then picketers will march to the mills. The strike leaders will make sure no one goes in."

"Scabs, you mean," she says.

"Yes. We know already there will be armed guards, and the picketers could get belligerent. There's a lot of anger floating around the city. Mironson's speeches will get increasingly Marxist—"

"Not if Vivian has anything to do with it," Honora says.

McDermott laughs. "A lot of the strikers will look for work elsewhere. There will be evictions. The mill owners might use it as a weapon. Evict all the picketers from mill housing. The unions will set up tent cities. And possibly . . ." He stops.

"Possibly what?"

He looks away. "Possibly it will be over."

"That's not what you were going to say."

"No one can predict."

"What happened in Gastonia?"

"Some violence," McDermott says. "There were pistols and rifles. Bayonets. Tear gas, vomit gas."

"How will I know?" she asks. "How will I know what's happened?"

"We'll get word to you if there's trouble," he says. "But don't worry about your husband. He'll be on the picket line for the next several days like everybody else.

More than likely, the worst thing that will happen to him is that he'll get bored."

"And what about you?" she asks.

"I doubt I'll get bored," he says.

She walks with her arms held slightly away from her sides for balance. This walking backward is tricky, particularly in the sand and with all the shells underfoot. "How likely is it that the strike will be over soon?" she asks.

"Not very," he says. "The mills have a surplus of goods. In some ways, they must welcome the strike so they can get rid of the surplus without having to pay wages or keep the mill running. After a few weeks, though, when they run out of goods to sell, that's when the strike will make a difference."

"A few weeks?" she asks.

"The New Bedford strike lasted six months."

"Oh, Lord," she says, stopping suddenly. McDermott, unable to halt his forward progress, walks into her. He puts his arms out to brace himself. For a moment, he holds her arms while her palms are pressed against his chest. Both instantly move away.

Sandpipers hop like fleas all around them. "I don't want to worry you for no good reason," he says.

"We'll lose the house," she says. "We're barely making the mortgage payments as it is."

"Mironson won't let that happen."

"Well," she says. "I suppose that's one good thing." She looks for the house in the distance. "Why are you doing this?" she asks.

"Got roped into it," McDermott says, smiling. "Been hanging out with a bad crowd."

Sexton

"We really have to go," Sexton is telling Honora in the kitchen. He is watching her wrap up a half dozen sandwiches and a couple of pies in waxed paper. He wants to tell her to speed it up. Mironson and Ross and McDermott are waiting to take off.

"You'll be on the picket line tomorrow," she says.

"I guess," he says. "I'll do whatever they tell me to do."

"Be careful," she says.

"I will. Don't worry about me."

"The laundry is in the hallway," she says.

"Yeah. I saw that."

"Are you going to need forks?"

"They give us forks in the boarding-house," he says impatiently, although he doesn't know if this is true. Madame Derocher is a harpy. She keeps the forks locked up. Anyway, they'll eat the pie in the truck with their fingers is his guess.

"I can't use all this food," she says. "You might as well take it with you."

She puts the sandwiches into a paper bag. He hasn't much liked the way the other guys have been ogling Honora this weekend when they think he isn't looking. Though he can't deny that he is proud of her. In a way, he would have to say that Vivian is a prettier gal—she is certainly sleeker and better dressed (and definitely funnier)—but, oddly, not as sexy, not even for all her brassy talk. And of course she's much older—nearly thirty, he would have to guess. No, Honora is the more alluring of the two. And if he hadn't been so drunk these last two nights, he might have done something about it.

Jesus, these guys can really put the booze away. It was all he could do to keep up with them. Ross, especially. Sexton is actually glad they're going back to the city now, even if he hates the boardinghouse. Just to have a night off.

This strike thing is a miracle, he thinks. Just a miracle. Mironson is now taking care of the mortgage—and what a load off Sexton's mind that is—and he and Honora are eating better than they have since October. And all because of the Copiograph and the Eight he'd squirreled away in the attic. He knew he'd made his sale even at lunch that first day at the boardinghouse. He'd seen it on McDermott's face. Not a cash sale, but as good as. Better, in fact.

Funny about the way the guy can't hear unless you look right at him. A little spooky, actually.

"When were you going to tell me about the strike?" Honora says, turning and speaking so that only he can hear.

"What?"

"The strike," she says close to his face. "When were you going to tell me?"

For a moment Sexton is so surprised by the question and the tone in her voice that he can't think of how to answer her. "What does it matter when I was going to tell you about the strike?" he says.

"I need to know what you know," she says.

"It would have upset you," he says.

"You'd keep something from me if you thought it would upset me?" she asks.

He darts a quick look into the hallway,

but he can't see the men. They must be outside by the truck. "I have to go," he says.

"If you had a girlfriend," Honora is saying, "and thought that telling me would upset me, would you keep that from me too?"

"Jesus, Honora, what is this?"

"I need to know what you know, Sexton. That's what a marriage is all about. It's about trust, and you've made me not trust you."

"Why are you bringing this up now?" he says.

"Because I haven't seen you alone and awake in a room since you got here," she says.

Jesus Christ, why is she doing this? Doesn't she see that it's the first time he hasn't felt like a bum since Christmas? He hasn't felt this good, this *useful,* since the late fall, nearly a year ago. And she wants to pick this particular moment to have this fight? Has she forgotten what it was like all winter and all through the spring, when he was so tired and depressed and . . . *ashamed* . . . that he could hardly look at her?

"If it weren't for Louis and McDermott and Jack Hess," Honora says, "I wouldn't have the faintest idea what's going on." She folds the dish towel in her hands.

"I tell you what you need to know," he says.

"Like the fact that you had a Number Eight and the Copiograph in the attic? Machines we could have sold instead of starving ourselves and burning the mantel when we didn't have money for coal?"

"That's none of your business," he says, though truthfully he has felt guilty about that ever since he took the machines out of the Buick before the auctioneer came. Nonexistent deliveries to a nonexistent bank from a soon-to-be (though Sexton didn't know that then) nonexistent business machine manufacturing company. He'd thought then that his personal setback was only temporary and that one day he'd be up and running again and could get a head start with the two machines. Or did he think them merely trophies that he might take out from time to time to remind himself of another life, the one in which he'd been, for a time, successful? "Look, I'm in the city working in a filthy, noisy hell-hole from six in the morning until five at night," Sexton says. "And then five nights a week I go back to a rat-infested boardinghouse and sleep in a room with four other guys like some kid at camp, and all this so that you can sit here reading books and looking for pieces of your goddamned sea glass."

She lays the dish towel over the lip of the sink—slowly and carefully, like someone trying to control herself. "That's what you think I do all day?" she asks.

"You have to let me handle business in my own way, Honora. I know what I'm doing."

"You know that Louis is a Communist," she says.

"The rest aren't."

"It could be dangerous," she says.

He leans in conspiratorially toward her face. "Look at this sweet deal we've got now. They're going to take care of the mortgage and feed us. What could be better?"

"What could be better?" she asks. "Having a husband who doesn't withhold information from me would be better," she says. "Having a husband I can trust would be better."

"I couldn't have sold those machines," he says. "It wouldn't have been legal."

"Since when have you cared about something being legal?" she snaps. And immediately he can see that she knows she's gone too far. She puts a hand to her forehead. "I'm sorry," she says. "I shouldn't have said that."

But that's all right, Sexton thinks. Because he's got the high ground now. He can make this sale.

"You let me handle this, all right?" he says, bending over and kissing her on the side of her mouth. "I'll see you," he adds. "Next weekend or earlier."

"Sexton," she calls to him, but by then he is already across the kitchen. He makes a conscious decision to pretend he hasn't heard her.

In the hallway, McDermott is standing by the front door. Has the man been waiting for him all this time? Did he overhear that little marital tiff in the kitchen?

Sexton stops, pulls a pack of cigarettes from his pocket, and slides one out. He takes his time lighting it, snaps his lighter shut, and reaches down for his sack of clean laundry where it sits by the front door.

"Sandwiches in there if you want them," Sexton says to McDermott.

McDermott

He is trembling as they stand on the walkway. He puts his hands in his pockets to stop the shaking.

"You all right?" Ross asks.

Mironson is taking forever to say goodbye. Alphonse and Sexton are already in the truck. McDermott takes one last look at Honora on the doorstep.

"Everything's jake," he says, turning to Ross.

Alice Willard

Dear Honora,

I have sent you three letters but am worried as I haven't had a reply in some time. I am glad that you managed to write to Harold. I can only assume that the strike has kept you and Sexton busy.

Aren't these days beautiful? I can hardly remember a longer stretch of good weather. I suppose we will all be complaining in the fall about the lack of water and how our grass is brown but for now it is lovely.

Bernice Radcliffe said the service for Harold was very nice, though I thought Rev. Wolfe could have been a bit more personal in his homily. What he said could be applied to almost anyone around here and I think he ignored some of Harold's unique qualities, like the fact that he did his best to live a full life even though he was blind. But at least the service wasn't maudlin like some I have been to. And Harold is no longer suffering. It is very quiet here.

The Concord newspaper is full of stories about the strike in Ely Falls, and I didn't like one bit reading about that woman who took a beating from the police when all she was doing was trying to get food for her family. You stay away from Ely Falls now. I know that Sexton has to go there and be on the picket line like everyone else, but I hope you are being sensible and are not getting caught up in any of the fighting. I saw the story about the state militia being called out, and that made me nervous too.

The garden is bursting, and it is all I can do just to keep up with the beans and the carrots and the whatnot. I can't stand to see a garden go to waste and besides I can give the food to the hobos who show up almost every day now. Women have begun to come to the door as well, and some of them I recognize from town, and I think they would rather come to my door than have to go to the town hall for relief money, which would then be public knowledge and get around. I feel sorriest for the women who have babies with them as the babies look absolutely emaciated.

Are you eating well? I will get Richard to drive me down to the post office again so that I can send you a box. You must take care of yourself.

Love,
Mother

Alphonse

Alphonse slips alongside the familiar line of picketers, thinking that their signs always look homemade and that maybe the strikers could do a better job of printing the words INTERNATIONALISM WILL FEED US and NO UNION WILL STARVE, because all you have to do is take one look at the mill signs—ALL STRIKING WORKERS WILL BE REPLACED—to see which is the spiffier organization. No hand-lettered signs there.

All the picketers look bored and hot and like they wish they weren't walking around in circles on the cement outside the mill gates. Even Alphonse has gotten used to the sight of the state militia in their peaked caps and their rifles with bayonets, and he thinks they must be dying of heatstroke inside those long brown coats. Once in a while someone from the picket line will throw a stone at one of the guards and all of the soldiers will point their bayonets straight at the crowd and threaten to charge, but only twice, as far as Alphonse knows, have people gotten pricked. Arnaud Nadeau's father had to go to the hospital, and one other man Alphonse knows, and he doesn't understand why they keep having these fights since one side has rocks and the other has guns and it is pretty obvious who is going to come out the winner.

Mironson says it's important that the picketers be peaceful and that he will not tolerate any violence, but you can tell that the picketers, especially the men, are just itching for a fight most of the time. Alphonse thinks the special deputies who go around in plainclothes and masks so you can't tell who they are are much scarier than the state militia. The special deputies fight with bricks and sledgehammers and go into the tent city at night and take men out and beat them, and someone said that they tried to poison the water supply, but the men who were in charge caught them and made them run away. Alphonse doesn't know if this story is true, because there are so many stories floating around, and he thinks that sometimes people just make them up when they are having a slow day. This is already the fourth week of the strike, and it is no longer even interesting to see furniture on the street or people standing in line for hours just to get flour and beans from the relief center. When Alphonse can't get food to his mother, she buys bones from the butcher. She boils them and takes the scum off the top of the pot and then makes a stew with the broth. The stew tastes terrible, and Alphonse doesn't dare ask her what kind of meat it is in case she says horse meat. He eats and sleeps at home four nights a week, but on weekends they all go to Mrs. Beecher's house, and even though there is a lot of work to do, it is paradise over there. Just paradise.

He slips into an alley to take a shortcut to the Alfred Street candy store, where the men are waiting for him in the back room. This is the fifth place they have had as a secret strike center, because every time they get set up, the special deputies discover where they are and come in and smash the furniture and even take a swipe or two at McDermott or Mironson, who is a very good boss but who is sort of pathetic at fighting back—he slaps like a girl—or Ross or Tsomides, who just got out of the hospital, or any of the other twenty or so strike leaders who might just happen to be there.

Every morning there is a meeting of the strike committee, and usually Alphonse is there to get his orders for the day from McDermott. Alphonse is by far the youngest person, though there are two older boys who are maybe sixteen who do some of the driving. Alphonse wishes he were old enough to do some of the driving too, because it would be great fun to be behind the wheel of Mahon's bread truck, even though you don't have a seat and have to stand up.

After the meeting, there is always a rally at one of the mill gates and usually there is a song session, which is supposed to pep up the picketers, though some of the songs are just too embarrassing to sing. And then one or two of the strike leaders will give interviews to the newspaper reporters who have been coming into town. One reporter was from a New York paper, which got everybody all excited, and when Alphonse went to the picket line that day he noticed that the women were dressed in their Sunday clothes and were hoping to be interviewed. Alphonse is himself dressing better these days, mainly because his mother doesn't have to go to work and has more time on her hands and made him a shirt out of good white cotton and a pair of pants that for once aren't too short for him that he sometimes wears to Mrs. Beecher's house. And Mrs. Beecher has knit him a pair of socks, though the weather has been too hot for socks lately.

And tonight, McDermott said, they will go to Mrs. Beecher's house because they have to get out another newsletter, you have to keep the spirits of the picketers up, and Mrs. Beecher said on Sunday when he left that when they all came back she would make fried chicken and corn and ham and peach ice cream, which he just can't wait to taste.

McDermott

He shuts down the printing press and walks into the front room, and he can see in the relaxation of faces and shoulders that everyone is glad for the break from all the racket the press is making. Thibodeau has to set the second page, so McDermott is, for the moment, unoccupied. He wipes his hands on a handkerchief that could use a wash and puts it back in his pocket.

Honora has her back to him, her hands doing that liquid thing over the keys, Mironson speaking in his halting dictation beside her. *"A socialist society is only possible if capitalism breaks down completely and commits suicide,"* he says. *"When we come together we will be unstoppable,"* he says. She types without glancing at the machine, though she sometimes bends forward to peer at the paper in the cylinder. Her hair nearly covers her neck now, even when she rolls it. She has four dresses that he knows of, which she wears in a kind of rotation that is a mystery to him. His favorite is the pale blue with the man's collar and the belted waist. She has, since the beginning of the summer, developed a faint tan, which is now the color of toast. Not like McDermott, who goes blotchy lobster pink if he even looks at the sun. *Luck of the Irish,* Ross said. *Fucking Irish,* McDermott said.

He stands on the threshold, not needing to go farther into the room, content merely to stand and watch Honora and smoke a cigarette. All the windows are open for a breeze, and he can feel the humid air that has just a touch of cool threading through it. She sits with her back straight, and occasionally she rubs a muscle at the top of her spine. He envies Mironson, who gets to sit so close to her, to smell her, possibly, when all McDermott can do is watch.

He can't even think about how much he envies Sexton Beecher.

Once when Vivian and McDermott were alone on the porch, she said to him, "You look a bit like Honora," as if they had been speaking of Honora just that minute, when, of course, they had not, and he couldn't help but wonder if Vivian had seen something that he had meant to keep to himself.

He studies that bare spot, slightly damp, at the top of Honora's spine, the spot she just rubbed, and thinks he would like to touch her there. He closes his eyes, imagining that touch, and then he pictures running his fingers up through her hair and watching the goose bumps rise on her skin. He imagines trailing his hand the length of her bare arm and maybe even following his hand with his mouth. He has imagined all of it, every single day since he first saw Honora coming down the stairs, and he has begun to wonder if there isn't something wrong with him that he so desires something he can never have. Last week he told Mironson that he had an errand to do, then he walked over to St. André's and went inside and sat with all the wayward Franco boys and old women and tried to pray for a miracle. But then he shortly realized that any miracle he wanted would have to mean the death or disappearance of Sexton Beecher, and obviously a man couldn't ask for that from God. So he tried to pray instead to be released from the terrible fist of desire—a desire that he is almost never free of, that takes away his appetite and makes him sleepless in the night—but, of course, he couldn't do that either, because in truth McDermott doesn't want to be released. So he gave up altogether and went outside and smoked a cigarette on the church steps and thought he'd probably lost the habit of praying in a church anyway; it made him feel like a fake.

Honora pushes her chair back, stands up, and stretches her arms high over her head, raising her dress an inch above her knees. Mironson throws his shoulders back a couple of times to unkink them. Honora relaxes her arms and turns, one hand on the chair, and sees McDermott standing in the doorway. He can feel her smile all the way down to the soles of his feet.

"Taking a break?" McDermott asks.

"A short one," Mironson says.

"Are you both hungry?" Honora asks.

"Sure," McDermott says, though he can hardly get anything down these days.

"Want to help me make some sandwiches?"

"Sure," he says again, reduced in her presence, it would seem, to one-word answers.

He moves out of the doorway to let her pass. Sometimes they speak for just a minute in a hallway, occasionally for a longer period when she is cooking in the kitchen or has moved out onto the porch. She is easy to talk to, and on good days he is able to convince himself that she is merely a friend, a colleague—a *comrade,* as Mironson would say. He has talked to her about Alphonse, about Eileen, and about the brothers who used to be a handful. About the farm in Ireland he's never seen but about which his father spoke incessantly. About the way Ross more or less cornered him into helping to organize the union that now seems to be his life. He talks to Honora while she peels carrots or sets the table or puts away the groceries. Once, he went with her on her sea glass walk and they played a screwy game in which they color coded the people in the house to match the shards of glass. Honora was blue, hands down, McDermott said, and she said then that he was green for Irish. And McDermott said okay, he'd be the bottle green if Alphonse could be the light green, how was that? And Honora said that made sense even if Alphonse was Franco, and McDermott asked what color a Franco would be, and Honora said she had no idea, and McDermott said, "Honorary Irish, then." But Mahon and Ross were definitely brown, they agreed, and Vivian—no question there—was lavender, and Mironson would be the opaque white, "for his prose," Honora said, and McDermott laughed. The only man who didn't get assigned a color was Sexton. "Oh gosh, I don't know what color Sexton would be," Honora said, and McDermott thought Sexton most resembled a slimy yellow with brown threads like those from a jellyfish running through it, a thought that made McDermott wince with the realization that he was as jealous as a schoolboy.

"How can I help?" he asks, following Honora into the kitchen.

"Talk to me," she says as she unwraps a loaf of bread. He watches her walk to the icebox and remove a packet of bologna and another of cheese. "You stopped the press."

McDermott situates himself so that he

can see her mouth. It is, he thinks, the most beautiful mouth he has ever seen. Sometimes it visits him in his dreams—the upper lip that peaks in a plumpness that seems more French than Yankee. "Thibodeau had to set up the second page."

"Where is Alphonse today?"

"Mironson has him distributing leaflets at social clubs in Portsmouth."

"Will he come at all this weekend?"

"I think you can count on it," McDermott says. "Even if he has to crawl. You said you would make him peach ice cream. He's been talking about it all week."

She laughs. "I've got all the ingredients."

"And he wants another swimming lesson."

"He's doing well," she says, spreading a dozen slices of bread with mayonnaise.

"When you get done with him, will you teach me?" McDermott asks, and immediately he regrets the question. It sounds like a line every sleazy guy he has ever known would give.

But Honora seems to treat the request as plausible. "Sure," she says. "If you really want to learn."

"I do," he says, though truthfully if it

weren't for Honora he would never go near the water.

"You'll need a suit."

"I'll get one."

"Next week, then."

"Good."

He watches her layer the sandwiches—a slice of bologna, a slice of cheese, a leaf of lettuce, another smear of mayonnaise. He wishes he were hungry.

"Louis says the mood of the strikers is low," she says.

"It is," he says, relieved to be on more familiar ground. "Carnival's over. Bill Ayers, who owns the Emporium Theater, said he had to run the projector day and night for the first week."

She smiles. "And now?"

"And now everyone's beat. They're hungry and they're tired. Some of the men have left their families to look for work elsewhere. You know about the evictions and the tent city. And the truth is, men don't picket well. Women are much better at it."

"Why?"

"More patience." More than once McDermott has been thankful that he is on the strike committee. He isn't sure he could stand the boredom of the picket line.

"You know," she says. "I went in there to have a look for myself."

"You did?" he asks, surprised.

"About ten days ago. On a Thursday. I wanted to see."

"And what did you see?"

"I felt like I had had a blindfold on. I felt cut off from the action. So I took the trolley into Ely Falls. As soon as I saw a crowd, I got off. About two hundred picketers stood outside a mill. One man carried a sign that said 'The Truth Is on Our Side.' And there was a child with a sign that said 'The Ten Percent Pay Cut Took Our Milk Away.' "

McDermott nods.

"I saw the militia with their fixed bayonets. I didn't understand why they felt they needed to do that. The women were in summer dresses and the men were in shirtsleeves and ties. The children were sitting on the curb. They had cloth shoes with holes where their big toes went. Someone had given the children eyeshades, which looked kind of funny."

McDermott smiles.

"I saw another line of picketers and then discovered they weren't picketers at all. They were all relatives waiting to get their kinfolk out of jail. One woman told me it cost two bucks to get your husband out, and another said that every day the police arrested so many picketers they had to hire trucks from other towns."

"That's right."

"I didn't actually see the tent city, but I could smell it. It smelled like raw sewerage. I walked for another hour or so, sort of thinking I might run into you and Sexton and Alphonse, but I didn't see you. I stopped in at a lunch counter and had a milk shake and went home. What do you think will happen?" she asks.

He leans against the counter and crosses his arms. "I think the strike leadership will do just what it set out to do—break the backs of the mills in New England. But where I part ways with Mironson is that I think the mills will then go out of business or move south, and no one will have jobs."

"I hope you're wrong," she says.

"Me too."

"What would you do if the mills went

south?" she asks. "Would you go with them?"

"Never," he says. "A good Irish Catholic like me? Be a fish out of water." He wishes he hadn't smoked his last cigarette. "What about your husband?" McDermott asks, unable to say the man's name, as if saying it aloud might cause him to appear, right here, now, in the room with them.

"I'm not sure," she says. "It was hard enough just finding the job he has now. We could always move, I guess; go live with my family."

"Where's that?" McDermott asks.

"In Taft. It's a small lake town north of here. Near Lake Winnipesaukee."

"Your folks still alive?" he asks.

"My mother."

McDermott watches Honora spread her fingers over the sandwich to hold it together, and then cut beneath her splayed hand. She has clean, precise movements in the kitchen, nothing extra, nothing wasted. He has never seen her flustered, even when there have been a dozen or more men in the house, a dozen or more mouths to feed.

"I sometimes wonder if I shouldn't be in there too," she says. "On the picket line."

"You're doing your part," he says. "More than your part, really."

"Still, though."

"Still, though," he says, and he wonders if she will remember this particular exchange from Christmas.

Honora looks up quickly and smiles at him, and the smile moves through him like a warm rush of water. "That seems like so long ago," she says.

He puts his hands in his pockets. "And to think this is where you came back to that night," he says.

He walks over to the window and glances out at the lawn and the hedge and beyond the hedge at the narrow road that leads, he now knows, to a tiny village with a fish shack and a general store. One day, a couple of weeks ago, itching for a walk, he set out on foot along the coast road, not knowing where it might lead. He stopped in at the general store, had a Moxie and a chat with the owner.

"Seems like you must get a lot of peace and quiet here," he says.

"Not lately," she says, smiling.

"It can't go on much longer," McDermott says. "This strike, I mean. The city is a powder keg."

"In your heart," Honora says, speaking of an organ that seems to have a life of its own these days, that has lately led him to places he thought he would never go, "do you believe that capitalism is evil? I mean, we both listen to this all day. I was just wondering how you feel. Deep down."

McDermott watches as she tears open another waxed packet of bread and cuts another dozen slices on the bread board. "There are basics I'd like to see everyone have," he says. "People like Alphonse's mother, for example. I'd like to see her have, minimum, hot water, indoor plumbing, food for the table, access to a doctor who isn't a quack, some kind of assistance since she's trying to raise a family without a husband—but I'm not convinced that overthrowing capitalism is the answer. Truthfully, I'm not very political. I like the job I've been given to do, but I hardly ever think about the stuff Mironson talks about."

"Can you understand it?"

McDermott laughs.

"I seldom see you laugh," she says. "It's nice. I like it."

He blushes and hopes that the sudden color will be hidden by his blotchy pink sunburn.

"How come you don't have a girlfriend?" Honora asks. "I would think you'd have lots."

"I had a girlfriend," he says, "but it didn't work out the way I hoped it would."

"What was her name?"

"Evangeline."

"Like the poem," she says.

"I guess," he says.

"You don't know the poem?" she asks.

"Eileen told me about it," he says. "I don't read too much poetry."

She smiles. "I didn't think so," she says.

"She got pregnant by another guy," he says, confessing a fact he has never told anyone.

Honora looks up from her work, her expression giving away her considerable surprise. "You didn't know?"

"I didn't know anything," he says. "I'd never even . . . I was completely in the dark. I was about to ask her to marry me."

She puts the knife down. “Oh, I’m sorry,” she says. “That’s too bad.”

“Just as well,” he says, shrugging. “I might have married her. And *that* would have been too bad.”

She turns away and picks up the knife again, and he wonders if she regrets anything about her marriage. Sometimes it drives McDermott crazy to be in possession of a fact about her husband that he can never tell her—the one piece of information that might serve him well, the one thing about her husband that would almost certainly break her heart and then possibly might one day set her free. Even McDermott, as out of touch with God as he is these days, understands that. He does his best to try not to think about it, though when he saw Sexton Beecher two weeks ago leaving the speak with the English girl, he was so furious (and yet so unforgivably elated) that he found it difficult even to talk to the man later that night. And it is all McDermott can do sometimes when they are riding in the truck together or working at the press or sitting at the dining table at the boardinghouse not to take the guy by the lapels and shake him hard and tell him to shape up. Doesn't he see what he has at home? Doesn't he know what he is jeopardizing? What is wrong with the fucking guy, anyway?

But, of course, McDermott knows perfectly well what is wrong with the fucking guy. He's a guy. He's lonely in town. He wants a girl. So what? If McDermott didn't know Honora, he doubts he'd ever give the matter a second thought. None of his business is what he would think.

"What are you making?" he asks.

"Coleslaw," she says.

Maybe he is a little bit hungry after all. He wonders if he's got his medicine with him. With all this coming and going—beach to city, city to beach—the medicine is often not where it's supposed to be.

"It's exciting, being part of this," she says.

"The city has come alive," he says.

"I don't know what I'll do when you all leave," she says. "I've come to hate being here by myself."

"I'd have thought you'd be glad to see the back of us," he says.

"I miss you guys when you're gone."

His heart, stupidly, leaps—willing to snatch at any crumb.

"I, for one, hate leaving here," he says after a minute. "This house. I've enjoyed it."

She licks a dollop of mayonnaise off her finger. "Thank you," she says.

"I wouldn't have an excuse to talk to you, for one thing," he says, trying to make it light.

From the front room, McDermott can hear Vivian calling, *Hey, doll.* A chair scrapes against a wooden floor. Mironson says, *I'm starved.* Through the window McDermott hears the sound of waves crashing. The printing press starts up again.

Honora stares at the platter of sandwiches in front of her. "There's a pitcher of lemonade in the icebox," she says, "if you wouldn't mind getting it."

Honora

"No guns," Mironson is saying.

Sandwiches and coleslaw make their way along the table. Vivian, in parchment batiste, fills glasses with lemonade. McDermott has not come to lunch. Through the doorway, Honora can see him leaning against the porch railing.

"But the picketers need to be able to defend themselves," Sexton says from the middle of the table. Louis, in a short-sleeved white shirt, sits sideways, as if he were there but not entirely there. In his posture, he gives the impression of a man who is indescribably weary—which Honora thinks is probably the case. She wonders how it is that he does this for a living. Moving from town to town, following strikes, starting strikes, moving out, starting all over again. When this is finished, he will leave Ely Falls and enter into an entirely new community. She wonders if he minds, if he is ever lonely.

"No guns," Louis repeats. "Militiamen cannot weave cloth. They instill fear, but they cannot by themselves break the strike."

"But we're getting the—excuse me, ladies—*shit* kicked out of us, and we have nothing to fight back with but stones."

Honora thinks her husband might have been better served if he hadn't used the word *we*—not only because Sexton himself clearly hasn't had a hand laid on him, but also because Louis never pickets.

"This has to be done without violence," Louis says. "It has to be this way. Yes, the bosses are just itching for a fight. They're just itching for an excuse to bring out the machine guns and mow us all down."

"Golly, I hope not," Vivian says, smoothing her pleated skirt.

"No, not really," Louis says. "But as good as. It won't be machine guns, but it will be rifles and bayonets. Tear gas. Vomit gas. You haven't lived until you've been under an attack with vomit gas."

"Do we have to talk about this at lunch?" Vivian asks.

"If we had guns," Sexton says, gesturing with military precision, his fingertips blue with Copiograph ink, "this thing would be over tomorrow."

"Oh, it would be over tomorrow, all right," Louis says.

"So then," Sexton says.

"Don't you see?" Louis asks, looking up at Sexton as if he were a particularly recalcitrant child. "If one of us got caught with a gun, what that would do to us?"

"The press is already portraying us as alien creatures destroying a way of life," Sexton says.

"What way of life?" Ross asks, picking his teeth.

"They're portraying us as Reds," Sexton says.

"They call us the Red Menace," Tsomides says. "Oooh, that's so *scary.*"

"We could scare the scabs at the very least," Sexton says.

"We *have* scared the scabs. And remember, the scabs of today are the strikers of tomorrow," Louis says automatically, as if it were a sentence he has repeated many times.

Through the doorway, Honora watches McDermott put both hands on the railing and bend his head.

"We need relief, not guns," Honora can hear Louis saying. "Relief supplies are inadequate."

"We always need relief," Mahon says. "It's never-ending."

McDermott pushes himself away from the railing. He turns and glances inside the house.

"Amber applejacks," Ross says to Vivian. "Fifty cents a shot. Three, you feel like a king. Four, you feel like a czar. Five, you feel like hell."

"Honora?" Sexton says.

"I'm sorry?" she asks, turning her gaze back to the table.

"I was asking you what you thought."

"About . . . ?"

"Guns," Sexton says with pained annoyance. "What your opinion is."

Honora glances from Louis, who still looks indescribably weary, to Ross, who is sucking his teeth, to Vivian, who is taking a delicate sip of lemonade. Tsomides and

Mahon are tucking into their second (or is it their third?) sandwiches. Sexton is waiting for her answer.

"No guns," Honora says finally, and Louis looks at her with frank admiration. "I believe the strike can be won without guns," she says. "And I believe, as does Louis, that relief is more important than firepower. As long as the strikers have food and a place to sleep, and the strike is over before the weather turns, I think they can force the mill owners to restore the wages to where they were before the last pay cut."

Sexton sits back in his chair with obvious disgust. Ross raises an eyebrow, clearly surprised that the woman who cooks and types has an opinion.

"We're making history here," Louis says, turning around to face the group, and Honora thinks, not for the first time in the last several weeks, how remarkable it is that such an unprepossessing man can command such respect. "Each of us is part of something much larger, something that cannot be stopped," he says. Honora watches his eyes travel around the table, pausing at each individual in turn. "Honora, you've been invaluable. *Lucky Strike* has already caught the attention of organizers in Boston and New York. I'm told *The Federated Worker* wants to take it over. We're printing over ten thousand copies a week." He pauses. "Vivian, you're a firecracker. No one would be reading the thing without you." Vivian waves the compliment away. "Ross and Mahon and Tsomides and Thibodeau, you've been jerks," Louis says, and everyone laughs. "And Sexton, this never would have gotten off the ground at all had you not led us to your machines, your beautiful house, and your even more beautiful wife."

"Hear, hear," Ross says. Honora smiles and turns quickly to catch yet another glimpse of McDermott through the doorway, but the porch is empty now.

"How we conduct ourselves in Ely Falls will be remembered forever," Louis says, and for just a moment it seems the ponderous weight of history itself floats and settles around the table. It is so quiet in the front room that Honora can hear Ross breathing through his open mouth at the end of the table.

"You know," Vivian says, tilting her head and peering at her plate with unusual interest, "I don't believe I've ever had a bologna sandwich."

Sexton

Sexton inspects another sheet and cranks the cylinder with more force than is probably good for the machine. He cannot believe that just an hour ago his own wife sat at the table and made a fool out of him by not supporting what he had to say about guns. It's perfectly obvious that without guns they cannot possibly win this thing, that it will go on forever.

And that's the interesting part, he thinks, because he cannot quite make out why he does not want it to go on forever. It's not having the men in his house—he likes that; it was always too quiet with just Honora and him. And it certainly isn't wanting to go back into the mill, because he doesn't expect ever again to work there. He's betting Mironson will be able to use him somewhere within his organization; or, better yet, maybe now he can get a job in sales. In January and February, when he went out looking for a job, he had a sorry attitude; he was defeated before he'd even begun. Now he feels anything but defeated. What he feels now is . . . Well, what he feels now is that he's just itching for something to happen.

He thought he could make that sale.

He was sure he could convince Ross and Mironson and Tsomides—Ross a kind of sergeant mobilizing supplies and troops, Mironson a tactical general, thinking things through in that droopy way of his, and Tsomides because he'd been injured. As for McDermott, Sexton isn't sure where he fits in, but McDermott wasn't there at lunch, so it was only Ross and Mironson and Tsomides Sexton really had to sell. But none of them was buying. Sexton argued that at the very least they should give guns to the strike leaders so they could protect themselves against the special deputies, who everyone knows are no more than thugs hired by the bosses. He was concerned that the special deputies might one day show up at Fortune's Rocks, he said, thinking that the image of a man protecting his home might sway the others. They couldn't keep this place a secret forever, he said, and, frankly, he was amazed they'd kept it a secret this long.

Still Mironson wouldn't bite.

Maybe McDermott is the guy to convince, Sexton thinks. No, McDermott would never go against Ross and Mironson. You can just tell the guy's not on board one hundred percent. Kind of a dreamy fellow, actually—probably because he can't hear too well. And that's another thing that's got Sexton stumped. Why do they have a deaf guy on the team? Seems like a big liability to him.

He cranks the sheets out as fast as he can now. It galls him that he prints only the agendas. Nobody reads the stuff anyway, as far as he can tell. The real juice is in the newsletter with that dopey name. Amazing how that thing has gotten so popular. It seems like they spend half of their supply money these days on paper. At least Mironson has got Sexton running the books. Mironson could hardly work the adding machine they bought, and no one else wanted to, so that job fell to Sexton, which was something. But it's a backroom kind of job, and Sexton wants to be out front, which is where he should be. Making sales.

As for Honora, he will deal with her later. Tell her to button her lip. Well, he won't put it quite that way, but he'll let her know that he didn't like it, doesn't want it to happen again. Although *when* he'll tell her this is a mystery. She's always doing the dishes when he goes up to the bedroom these days, and usually he is so tired—with a little help from the booze—he can't stay awake long enough to wait for her. And when he opens his eyes in the morning, she's already up and in the kitchen making breakfast. He'll have to corner her before he leaves, though he doesn't want another scene like the one they had in the kitchen that first weekend. McDermott heard that one, Sexton is sure of it.

A wife should be respectful. Not contradict her husband at the table. Not in front of the men.

He wonders if he should start looking now for a job, see what's out there in sales. Even if he has to go a little distance, say back to Portsmouth. Honora is used to living with him away for stretches at a time.

She could manage by herself; she's good at that. But who knows how long this strike thing will last? He can't see abandoning the team until it's over. It had better be over by October, he thinks, or those poor bastards will all freeze to death over there in that tent city. What a dump. He hates it when he has to go in there with Mironson and Ross. The place smells like an outhouse that hasn't been emptied in years.

He checks the height of the pile of printed papers against his other stack. He has to collate and staple now. Most of the time he feels like a goddamn secretary. The adding machine and the Copiograph are women's tools—not a man's. And he should be in the front office, not the back room. He should be making his sales.

Honora

On Friday evenings, when Sexton comes home from a week in the city, he is carrying a bag of laundry. The smell of metal is in the shirts, and sometimes it snows lint when Honora upends the clothing from the bag. On Saturday mornings, she washes the clothes against the metal rungs of the scrub board and puts them through the wringer. She hangs the clothes out to dry—six shirts, two pairs of pants, neither of which is really suitable for work in the mill (or picketing, for that matter), five pairs of underwear, and five pairs of socks. She doesn't mind the washing, though the winter washing was the worst. The clothes froze into stiff shapes on the line, and sometimes Honora had to bring them in to warm them over the stove one by one. She worried about fire, and she minded not having money sometimes for proper soap.

Since the strike, however, the laundry has been sporadic, and she gets it done when she can. Thus it is that shortly after she has finished the lunch dishes (every bit of the bologna sandwiches and coleslaw and oatmeal cookies eaten) and has shooed Alphonse, who arrived midlunch and who followed Honora into the kitchen (like a stray animal, she thinks fondly), out of the house, she takes Sexton's bag of dirty laundry from its place by the back door and upends it onto the porch. Nearly a week's worth of clothing tumbles out: the shirts, the pants, the underwear, the socks, and various assorted handkerchiefs. She looks at the pile of clothing, ordinary enough, and thinks how much easier the laundry is to do since Sexton has been out of the mill.

A blot of orange catches her eye.

She bends to pick up a handkerchief. Once before, she saw a similar smear of orange on the front of a blue work shirt, and she thought at the time, insofar as she thought of it at all, that it was a spill of food from the boardinghouse—squash or turnip, possibly, or Campbell's tomato soup. But this time, the imprint on the handkerchief is so distinctive that it cannot be mistaken for food of any sort. Honora's fingers open, and the handkerchief floats to the floor. She puts her hand to her chest, unable to make a sound—the sort of essential nonsound she might make if confronted by a man with a gun. When at last she can breathe, she picks up the handkerchief and fingers the blot. She knows precisely what it is. She even knows the brand. Ruth Shaw used to wear it to McNiven's on Saturday nights.

Honora walks upstairs to the bedroom and lays the handkerchief upon the bed, smoothing the corners as she does so. She sits on a chair and waits. She knows that Sexton will come. He had ink on the front of his shirt at lunch, and he will, sooner or later, want to change it for a fresh one.

She is sitting by the window when he enters the room. "What are you doing over there?" he asks, already pulling the tails of his shirt from his trousers.

The handkerchief is spread out upon the bedspread like a scarf displayed on a department store counter, the orange blot a price tag. She watches him study the handkerchief, the moment of recognition.

Of course he will feign ignorance, she thinks. He will try to bluff his way through. He is, after all, a salesman who has not entirely lost his touch.

"It's lipstick," she says.

"What?" He seems completely unconcerned as he unbuttons his shirt.

"It's lipstick," she repeats. "The orange bit."

"So?"

"So?" she repeats.

"So there's lipstick on a handkerchief," he says, slipping the shirt off and tossing it on the bed—almost but not quite covering the offensive handkerchief. "It must be yours," he says.

"No," she says, mildly astonished that he seems unaware of the fact that she hardly ever wears lipstick now.

"Maybe I lent the handkerchief to Vivian," he says.

"You'd have to shoot Vivian before she'd wear that brand of lipstick," Honora says.

"How would I know who used the handkerchief?" he says. "I could have lent it to almost anyone."

Neither of them moves—she by the window, Sexton peering down at the bed as if he stood at the precipice of the Grand Canyon.

"Honora," he says.

"What?" she asks, looking up at him.

"Are you all right?"

"Yes," she says, rubbing her eyes.

"You're exhausted," he says.

"Yes."

"Well, then," he says, pulling a clean shirt from a shelf in the closet. "I guess I'll just have to give you the benefit of the doubt."

"Benefit of the doubt?" she says, looking up.

"Today at lunch. That was uncalled for."

"That was my opinion," she says.

"But it was humiliating," he says. "A wife doesn't contradict her husband in public."

"It was merely an opinion," she says. "It wasn't meant to humiliate you. It's what I think. I think guns are a terrible idea."

"And what are you going to do when thugs show up here with sledgehammers and baseball bats?"

"I don't know what I'm going to do," she

says, "because most of the time I'm alone here."

"Just my point," he says.

"For heaven's sake, Sexton. Surely you don't expect me to carry a gun."

And, no, he does not expect her to carry a gun; it is he who wants a gun. "I really don't understand you," he says, turning toward her and tucking in the shirt. "First you make a fool of me at lunch, and then you suggest I've been . . . what? . . . playing around? You used to have more sense than this, Honora."

The marriage might so easily end, she thinks. It could end right this minute. It is both a frightening and a thrilling thought.

Her silence makes him anxious. And anxious, he isn't at all handsome. His eyes seem to settle closer together even as she watches. He puts a hand to his forehead, a man in anguish. "I've never given you a single reason to suspect a thing," he says, and perhaps he sounds a bit more righteous than he needs to.

Honora glances out the window and then back again. Is it possible she has made a mistake?

"Cooking and cleaning for all these people," he says, deftly collecting both the dirty shirt and the handkerchief in one swipe with his hand. She watches as he balls the shirt and throws it into a corner. Though she doesn't see him do it, she is almost certain that he has pocketed the handkerchief. "I'll tell them to leave," he says.

"Don't do that," she says.

"I probably just lent it to someone on the line," he says.

Is it possible she has misread the orange blot, that it's as innocent as he says?

"Come on, Honora," Sexton says, moving toward her. He touches her shoulder and she flinches. He stands behind her chair and begins to rub the back of her neck. "Why don't you take a nap?"

Perhaps it is only the strike, she thinks. Or the men in her house. Or the work on the newsletter. She is not herself. No, she is not herself at all.

Sexton walks to the bed and turns the chenille bedspread down invitingly. Honora can hear the printing press with its clunky, rhythmic movements, a high feminine laugh, men's voices on the porch. Out on the beach, McDermott and Alphonse are throwing a ball, with Sandy running back and forth between them. A gull swoops down in front of the window and flutters in place for a moment.

Honora stands and moves to the bed. She climbs inside and closes her eyes. She can feel her husband's lips on her cheek.

"I would never do anything to hurt you," he says.

She hears him crossing the room, opening the door and then closing it with a soft click. She rolls away from the door and sleeps as she has not slept in weeks.

Delicate fingers are smoothing the hair off her forehead.

"Hey, sweetie," Vivian says.

Honora struggles to sit up. "What time is it?"

"It's eight-thirty."

"Really? I slept that long? You've all eaten?"

"We've all eaten. Ross cooked."

Honora rubs her eyes. "You're kidding," she says.

"I kid you not. And it was good, if you can believe it."

"What was it?"

"Some kind of lamb stew. Irish, he says. But listen." Vivian sits at the edge of the bed. "Sadie's downstairs. She arrived before dinner. Ross says he knows of a dance hall in Rye, and Louis says we all deserve a night off. So how about it?"

"Now?" Honora asks.

"We'll wait for you," Vivian says.

"He doesn't look old enough. They won't let him into the dance hall," Ross is saying. He has combed his hair and has on red suspenders for the special occasion.

"Bet they will," Tsomides answers.

"If he can't get in, someone will have to come back with him," Ross says, a bit of a grumble in his voice.

"I'll wait outside," Alphonse says quietly, looking as though he wishes he could disappear through the floor.

"For crying out loud, he's taller than I am," Sadie Vassos says, and this is, of course, perfectly true. Sadie, barely five feet, stands next to Alphonse in her denim overalls and a white blouse. Often she wears a worker's cap, but not tonight. Tonight she is going dancing. She hooks an arm through Alphonse's. "You'll be my date," she says.

"Okay, that's settled," Sexton says, patting his oiled curls in place. He glances over at Honora and then away. "Let's head out, gang."

Ross, Alphonse, Sadie, Sexton, and Tsomides, who still wears a bandage on his head, ride in Mahon's bread truck, while Honora and Louis and McDermott slide into Vivian's wagon. McDermott has a bottle, and Louis, who is wedged between Honora and McDermott, takes a swig and wipes his mouth. He passes the bottle to Honora, who has a drink as well, at once realizing that this is probably a very bad idea; she hasn't eaten since lunch. "Gin?" she asks.

"Mahon's best," McDermott says.

"Good to blow off some steam," Louis says. The gin spreads slowly inside Honora and makes the idea of a dance hall in another town seem immensely appealing.

"I couldn't agree more," she says.

"Need a break once in a while," Louis says.

It is more roadhouse than dance hall, and no one looks askance at Alphonse. Next to the band, an area has been roped off, and at this early hour there are only three couples moving to the music. Ross and McDermott slide two round tables together, stealing chairs from other parts of the room. Alphonse, in his best white shirt, looks thoroughly pleased with himself. He orders a Coca-Cola, and Ross, while McDermott has his head turned, pours a dollop of rum from a bottle badly hidden in a paper bag into Alphonse's drink. The paper bags are everywhere, Honora notes, their necks twisted at the top, fooling no one. She thinks that the Rye police must have a generously blind eye; all the patrons seem relaxed, not expecting a raid anytime soon.

Theoretically one can get food at a roadhouse, though Honora has not seen a waitress pass by their table. She is hungry and shouldn't be drinking until she has eaten, and, well, she is just not a very good drinker anyway. But Alphonse is clearly so happy and Vivian is just hooting away and Sexton is locked in conversation with Sadie and McDermott has returned with two glasses and a bottle of tonic water and seems to be making drinks for both of them.

"'Embraceable yoooou . . .'" Ross sings to the music.

"Somebody shut the mick up," Tsomides says from the end of the table.

"Hey, Tsomides, I think a little brains spilled out when you got hit," Ross says.

"Marriage is bondage," Sadie Vassos is saying, holding a glass filled mostly with ice to her cheek. "The sexual act should not be subject to the state."

Honora glances quickly at Alphonse and notes that he is even more bug-eyed than usual. She is going to have to tell Ross to cut it out with the rum. "I'm sorry we missed our swimming lesson today," she says to the boy. "Maybe tomorrow?"

"*You* believe in free love, Louis," Sadie says emphatically. She spits tobacco juice into an ashtray on the table, and Vivian says *Really.*

"I believe in it," Louis says, "though I don't know that I've ever practiced it."

"Whereas I," Vivian says, "have practiced it and don't believe in it."

"Hey, baby," Ross says with a low whistle.

"I am, however, very, very discriminating," Vivian says, giving Ross the eye.

"Did you get to try the peach ice cream?" Honora asks Alphonse, who has his feet hooked around the rungs of the wooden chair.

"I had two bowls," he says.

"I was thinking about trying blueberry," Honora says, "since it's the season now." She takes a sip of her gin and tonic, which tastes unaccountably good tonight.

"I used to live on a blueberry farm," Alphonse says.

"Did you?" asks Honora, truly surprised. She knows so little about Alphonse. "When was this?"

"Until I was nine," he says. "The farm went bad."

"You say a vow, you make a commitment, and then you have to honor that commitment," Sexton, astonishingly, is saying from his place at the middle of the table. Honora has noticed that whenever they gather, whether for a meal or a meeting, Sexton manages to insinuate himself into the center of it. His hair is perfectly parted, the dark blond curls as sleek as a movie star's. His mustache is groomed and waxed. It would be impossible to tell, she thinks, looking at him, that he is a ring spinner in the Ely Falls Mill.

"What is this thing called love?"

"I'm not sure bringing Alphonse was such a good idea," Honora says, turning to McDermott.

"Do him good," McDermott says, looking at the boy. "Expose him to different ideas."

"I think it's called corrupting a minor," Honora says. "And anyway, it's not the ideas I'm worried about."

"Won't tell his mother," McDermott says, and she thinks he might be a little bit drunk already. She can feel the heat from the side of his body.

"Is it all right to tell you that you look very pretty tonight?" he asks.

"Perfectly all right," she says.

"You look very pretty tonight," he says.

From the center of the table, Sexton

shoots Honora a quick glance. "You make the vows to each other," he says, "and that's what's binding." Honora wonders if this speech is for her benefit. They have not spoken since the incident in the bedroom.

"But *why* should they be binding?" Sadie is asking.

"My baby just cares for me."

"What about you, Ross?" Sadie suddenly asks when Sexton doesn't answer.

Ross blinks. "Me?"

"Do you believe in free love?"

"Nothing's free," he says.

"Definitely brown," McDermott says to Honora.

"Hey, doll, give me a dance," Vivian says to Louis. She stretches her long graceful arms above her head. "My feet are itching."

Louis smiles and stands.

"Sadie, how about a dance?" Sexton asks. "We can finish our discussion on the dance floor."

"I'll dance with you," Sadie says, standing and dropping an ice cube back into her glass, "but I think you're a capitalist shit."

Honora watches Sexton and Sadie move

through the throng, which seems to have doubled already since they arrived—Sexton tall and broad shouldered and almost too impeccable in this slightly sleazy roadhouse, and Sadie, who barely reaches his chest, in her overalls. People turn their heads to stare.

"*He's* a good sport," McDermott says beside her.

"She's all right," Honora says.

"Oh, I like Sadie," he says. "I think she's great. I just don't know that I want to dance with her."

"The mustache bother you?" Tsomides asks from his end of the table. "We Greeks like our women with mustaches."

"Pretend you didn't hear that," Honora says to Alphonse.

"Hey, cockroach," Tsomides says to Alphonse. "Come over here so I can talk to you."

Alphonse pushes his chair back, and Honora notices that the boy seems a bit unsteady on his feet as he makes his way to the end of the table. Ross and Mahon, Honora notes, have disappeared. "I think Alphonse is tipsy," Honora says to McDermott.

"He'll be all right," he says. He pauses. "I should ask you to dance."

"Maybe you should," Honora says, flirting a little.

"Only I don't know how."

"On the sunny side of the street."

"You could tell me how pretty I am again," she says.

"Say, Honora, you look very pretty tonight."

She waves him away. "I should probably get something to eat," she says. The lights are low, and it is hard to see across the room. McDermott shifts his chair so that their elbows are suddenly touching, but Honora cannot bring herself to pull away. She glances over at the front of McDermott's shirt, unbuttoned at the collar. His sleeves are rolled as well, and she notes, as she has done often in the last several weeks, the fine dark hairs on the back of his wrists. There are sweat stains under his arms. The temperature has risen inside the roadhouse, and even the open windows and door aren't helping much. McDermott takes a sip of his drink. "What happened to you today?" he asks.

"I had a nap," she says. "Overslept."

"Your husband said you weren't feeling well."

"He said that?" she asks, surprised.

"Can this be love?"

"You believe that stuff?" he asks.

"What stuff?"

"What Sadie was saying. About free love and all."

"I missed the beginning of the conversation," she says. "So I'm not sure." She pauses. "But probably I don't believe in it, no." She watches him finger the condensation on his glass. "Shouldn't we have these in paper bags?" she asks.

"What? These innocent little glasses of tonic?"

"What if the police come?"

"They're here already," McDermott says, gesturing with his thumb. "See that bald guy over there?"

Honora looks in the direction McDermott is pointing, her eyes resting on a shiny pate.

"Chief of police," McDermott says.

Cigarette smoke curls upward in the beams of dim electric light. A blue haze hangs only a foot or two above their heads.

"I really need something to eat," Honora says, standing.

The sea air hits her face as soon as she steps outside. She removes her pumps, which pinch in the heat. She inhales as deeply as she can, hoping to clear her head with a couple of good breaths. From a jalousie back window, she can smell meat cooking. She thinks briefly of knocking on that window and asking someone to hand food out to her. Anything, she would tell them. She takes a few steps forward, hoping she is not staggering, as are some who are moving toward their cars. But because the parking lot is gravel underfoot, she turns and drifts toward the back of the building, enjoying the cool blades of grass on the soles of her feet. She moves into the darkness, away from the light, putting her hands out so she won't walk into a tree. She thinks perhaps she should sit down, or better yet, lie down, and when she has gone far enough, she does so, feeling the dew all along her back. Fireflies dart and tease with their light. She tries to follow them, but they are tricky insects and never where she thinks they'll be. She closes her eyes, and her head begins to spin. Above her, the leaves of a tree are making a sound oddly like water.

She smells cigarette smoke and soap. She opens her eyes.

McDermott

"You're following me," she says.

McDermott lowers himself to the grass beside her.

"I'm drunk," she says.

"I noticed."

"Not used to holding my liquor."

"You didn't eat."

"No excuse."

Beyond the seawall, he can hear the surf. There is a commotion in the parking lot.

"Is Alphonse all right?" she asks.

"Sadie has taken him under her wing."

"I guess he'll learn a thing or two tonight."

"He's incorruptible."

In the distance a woman says, *I saw the way you looked at her.*

A mist crawls in from the water. He can

hear the music from the open door. The lantern at the entrance to the roadhouse is furry with light. He smoothes Honora's hair off her forehead and worries that his fingers, with their calluses, will be too rough.

"Honora," he says. He brings her face around so that he can see it. "I have to see your mouth, remember?"

With a slowness that would give her time to turn away if she wanted to, he leans over her and kisses her mouth. Her mouth is open, as if surprised anyway. He kisses her again. She makes a small sound at the back of her throat. "I just . . . ," she says.

"Don't talk," he says, closing his eyes. "I have my eyes closed, so I can't see what you're saying."

He opens his eyes to see if she is looking, and she laughs.

He kisses her again quickly. He reaches down to the hem of her skirt. He slides his hand up the back of her leg. He has wanted to do this all night. He has wanted to do this for weeks.

She shifts, but does not entirely pull away.

"I wish . . . ," she begins.

Above them, the tree is making a sound like water. Their faces hover inches from each other. He can feel her breath.

"You wish?" he asks.

Honora

It would be so easy, she thinks. All she would have to do is turn a fraction of an inch toward him, and that would be that. They are hidden from the light. No one would ever know.

He smooths her hair with his fingers. He says her name and turns her face to his. "I have to see your mouth, remember?"

She knows that he is going to kiss her, and she wants it to happen. She wants to stretch her body the length of his and to arch her back. Her mouth is partly open, and she makes a sound at the back of her throat.

"I just . . . ," she says.

No one but she and McDermott would ever know, she thinks.

"Don't talk," he says.

And hasn't Sexton dishonored the marriage already?

McDermott kisses her again, and overhead the tree is again making a sound oddly like water running. A brook, maybe.

"I wish . . . ," she begins.

What does she wish? She wishes that she had again the pristine jewel that was once her marriage. She wishes she could let McDermott love her. She wishes that she did not care about honor or trust or the future. About how she would have to think about herself—day after day after day, week after week after week.

His face is so close to hers that she can feel his breath near her eyes.

"You wish?" he asks.

She presses her palms lightly against his chest.

McDermott

The moon, fuzzy around the edges tonight, creates a cone of light on the water. The surf is barely breaking at the bottom of the low-tide beach. Alphonse was snoring when McDermott left him in his bedroll—a barely audible sound, like that from a woman. The boy sleeps with his mouth open and his eyes rolled far back into his head. His eyelids flutter with his dreams. Dreaming of peach ice cream, McDermott hopes. Dreaming of flying airplanes.

He takes another pull from the bottle of whiskey he found on the kitchen table. He woke in his bedroll, mildly surprised that he felt hungry. In the kitchen, he stood eating leftover lamb stew and saw the bottle on the oilcloth. It hurts his stomach but will help with the sleeping. He can't remember when he last slept the night through. He wakes restless, and it isn't because of the bedroll on one of the thin mattresses that Mahon trucked in—it happens at the boardinghouse too. Only there he can't go downstairs looking for a bite to eat. Madame Derocher keeps a lock on the icebox.

He puts his feet up on the porch railing and tilts the wooden chair backward. In the morning, he will leave.

Sometimes he sees her in the hallway as he is on his way to the bathroom for a wash, and once in a while she is in her dressing gown, carrying a pile of clean laundry or a stack of towels for the men. She keeps the door to her bedroom closed, and he has not wanted to see the bedroom or to imagine what goes on behind that door. And, in a way, that is the hardest part of leaving her in this house: knowing that he is leaving her with Sexton Beecher. Ross told McDermott about Beecher going on at lunch about guns, and privately they agreed that the guy is as crazy as a bedbug. If it weren't his house, Ross said. If it weren't for the typewriter and the Copiograph. You couldn't use a man's home and then boot him out, McDermott surprised himself by saying, and, reluctantly, Ross agreed. Keep an eye on him, though, Ross said. And McDermott thought then that he ought to tell Ross about leaving in the morning, that Sexton Beecher would no longer be his problem. But he hadn't conferred with Mironson yet, and it was Mironson he had to tell first.

McDermott feels a hand on his shoulder. Vivian moves past his chair to another on the porch, Sandy trotting behind her. "Hey, doll," she says, situating herself so that her face is visible to him.

"I didn't know you were still here," McDermott says, reaching down and scratching the back of Sandy's neck. He takes his feet off the railing.

"I'm embarrassed to say I passed out on the couch," she says, yawning slightly. "I saw a light and wondered who was out here."

"Just me."

"Couldn't sleep?" she asks.

"Not really."

"Oh Lord, I'm a mess," she says.

"You look fine to me," McDermott says, and indeed she does. Vivian is always an expensive-looking package, all the bows neatly tied.

"I need my bed," she says.

"I could walk you home," he says.

She waves his gallantry aside. "I've got the beach wagon."

"Beautiful night," he says, leaning forward and offering her a cigarette. She takes one, bends for the light, and inhales. She removes a speck of tobacco from her lower lip.

"Been brooding about the universe?" she asks.

"Don't know enough about the universe," he says.

"How about your particular universe?" she asks.

"Not worth brooding about," he says. "Want a drink?" He holds out the bottle of whiskey.

"I think I've overdone it already," she says, putting a hand to her head.

"A wee one can't hurt you," he says. "Hair of the dog?"

Even swigging from a bottle of whiskey, McDermott notes, Vivian is elegant in her gestures. She hands him the bottle back, and he takes another swig himself. "Are you all going back tomorrow night?" she asks. "Well, I guess by now it's tonight, isn't it?"

"I'm going back this morning," McDermott says. "Early."

"What's the rush?"

"Things to do," he says.

"Alphonse going with you?"

For once, McDermott hasn't thought about Alphonse. The boy, having arrived at the house late into the weekend, will not want to leave. "No," he says. "He'll go back later with the others."

"He liked that peach ice cream," she says, smiling.

"He's dreaming about it right now," McDermott says.

Vivian laughs. She takes another pull on her cigarette, crosses her legs. "What do you dream about, Quillen McDermott?"

The question is so unexpected and so direct that for a moment McDermott cannot answer.

"No fair thinking about it," she says. "You have to answer right away."

"Whose rules are these?" he asks, stalling for time.

"My rules, of course." She smiles, crinkling the few wrinkles at the sides of her eyes.

"Don't remember my dreams," he says.

"I don't believe you."

"Why not?"

"I think you're a deep one."

"Don't bet on it."

He takes another drink and slaps a mosquito. Vivian never seems to get bitten, he has noticed. Must be something in her perfume. McDermott feels the booze going down, waits for the pain. He has to take it easy now; he's had far more than enough already.

"What do you dream about?" he asks her.

"Oh, everything," she says. "My Maggy Rouff gown. My Houbigant atomizers. My Van Cleef and Arpels sapphire-and-diamond bracelet. My room at the Plaza Hotel."

He laughs.

"I'm serious," she says.

"I know you are," he says.

"Working on the newsletter has been a hoot," Vivian says. "I wouldn't trade an hour of the time I've spent here."

"That's pretty generous of you," he says.

She bends conspiratorially toward McDermott. "Don't tell Louis or Sadie, whatever you do, but I think I'm being indoctrinated," she says, leaning back in her chair. "Once you see the world the way Louis does—once you *allow* yourself to see it—it's very hard to see it again the way you used to. My sort, I mean. We seem, well, despicable, really."

"I don't think you're despicable," he says.

"How come you don't have a girl?" she asks. "A handsome guy like you."

"I did have," he says. "Last year. She left me for a bricklayer."

"How sad," Vivian says.

"Not really."

In the moonlight, Vivian's coppery hair is a dull metal that has lost its color. "Were you in love?" she asks.

"Thought so at the time," McDermott says, lighting a second cigarette with the first. It's another thing he should be cutting back on.

"But now you don't," she says, studying him.

He flicks his ashes onto the porch. "Now I don't," he says. From the window above them, there is the sound of a man calling a name frantically in his sleep. *Rosemary.*

"That's Ross," McDermott says, pointing upward. "His wife's name is Rosemary."

Vivian smiles. "Hard for them all to be away from their families," she says.

"Wouldn't know about that," he says.

"It's more obvious than you might think," she says.

"What's more obvious?" McDermott says.

"The thing that's obvious," Vivian says.

McDermott bends to tie his shoe. He ties the laces slowly and deliberately. His fingers feel like thick sausages.

"Bit of a thorny problem, though, isn't it?" Vivian says.

"Don't know what you mean," McDermott says.

"The shady husband and all," Vivian says.

McDermott instinctively glances around as though someone might have heard.

"Don't worry," Vivian says. "The husband's obtuse. I just happen to notice things. I'm very good at it. I do it as a hobby."

"Lucky for you," McDermott says, his heart racing.

"Your secret is safe with me," Vivian says.

"Don't have secrets," he says. Vivian searches for an ashtray. "Just stub it out with your foot," he says.

Vivian puts the toe of a delicate high-heeled pump on her cigarette butt. "I think she feels the same, if it's any consolation," she says.

McDermott tips his chair back and puts his feet on the railing again.

"Nothing she's said, mind you," Vivian says. "I can just tell."

He studies the cone of moonlight on the water.

"I'm upsetting you," Vivian says, reaching across the space between them and touching him on the shoulder. "I didn't mean to do that."

"She's married," he says.

Vivian withdraws her hand and sighs. "And ain't that a shame," she says.

Mironson is padding softly along the hallway, a wet towel over his arm.

"You too?" McDermott asks, keeping his voice low.

"Thought a bath would help," Mironson says.

"Must be something in the air," McDermott says. "Vivian just left."

"We're all keyed up," Mironson says.

"I'm leaving early in the morning," McDermott says. "I'll see you back at the city."

"Why?" Mironson asks.

"Eileen needs me. I haven't been around for weeks."

"Sorry about that. Of course you should go. But listen," Mironson says, "there are about a hundred newsletters left that have to be put together. If you could do those before you leave, you could take them with you. Wake up Mahon. Get him to drive you in."

Alphonse stirs on the mattress, his bedroll having unraveled hours ago. McDermott takes off his shoes and pants and shirt and gently tries to nudge Alphonse off the diagonal and over to his side of the mattress. But Alphonse, in his sleep, is a dead weight and will not easily be budged. McDermott slides his bedroll onto the floor. He lies on top of it in his underwear, studying the eerie moon-glow on the white windowsill. Beside him Alphonse is still snoring, and down the hall, a thousand miles away, a woman he knows is sleeping.

I think she feels the same, if it's any consolation.

He folds his arms under his head and stares up at the ceiling. Even from that first day on Christmas Eve, he felt Honora getting inside him. He didn't know it that day, but he remembers the sense of giddiness when she drove away, his direct prayer to God. He thinks about what happened earlier on the wet grass. The way her skin felt under his hand. In his mind, he goes over the kisses again. Were there two or three? The sound she made at the back of her throat. He knows he will remember the precise sound of that moan all his life, that he will have to listen to it again and again—a record on a turntable.

Alphonse twitches on the mattress, and McDermott turns to look at him. He can make out the spindly frame in the moonlight. The boy, in his sleep, turns onto his stomach and stretches his arms out toward the wall. He seems to be growing, McDermott thinks, even as he watches.

Honora

Earlier, she heard voices outside the window, Vivian's and McDermott's on the porch, and then later, in the hallway, Mironson's gruff baritone. Beside her, Sexton sleeps in his guileless pose, his arms thrown up behind his head, looking exposed and vulnerable and content, and for a moment Honora has a dreamy and irrational desire to lay something heavy on his throat and crush his windpipe.

My God, she thinks, sitting upright.

She slips on her dressing gown. She closes the bedroom door with a soft click. She picks up her feet, trying not to scuff her slippers along the wooden floor. She doesn't want to wake anyone in the bedrooms off the hallway. At the bottom of the steps, she pauses for a moment and listens. She can hear the surf, never absent, and something else. A rustle of papers. Coming from the front room, she is sure of it.

"I'm just finishing this," McDermott says when she reaches the doorway.

"Oh," she says, surprised. "You're up early." A sliver of excruciatingly bright light slips over the horizon, and Honora winces away from it.

"I'm leaving," he says, turning his head away as well.

"Now?" she asks. She leans against the doorjamb.

"Yes."

"Why?"

"My sister needs me," he says, bending to collate the stacks of paper on the table.

"Everything okay?" she asks.

"Everything's fine," he says.

McDermott is a bad liar, she thinks. "It's because of last night, isn't it?" she says, moving a step closer. He bends to his task, not answering her.

"I wish . . . ," she says.

His head snaps up. "What do you wish?" he asks, and she cannot tell if he is hopeful or angry.

"I'll make you some breakfast," she

says. The sun slants in through the east windows, showing every speck of dust on the table. The side of McDermott's face is pink. She hugs her dressing gown around her.

"I'm not hungry," he says.

"How are you getting back?" she asks.

"Mahon's driving me."

"Is he up?"

"I'll wake him in a minute."

"I'll make *him* breakfast, then," she says.

"It's barely five, Honora. Go back to bed."

"He has to eat. You have to eat too, for that matter."

McDermott is silent.

"Suit yourself," she says.

She separates the strips of bacon with a fork, the grease sizzling in the cast-iron pan. She imagines the scent of the bacon wafting its way up the stairs and slipping under Alphonse's door and waking the boy and sending him pell-mell into the kitchen. Twice she has heard footsteps going up and down the stairs, but so far Alphonse has not yet appeared. She longs to see his goofy face, the iron-filing haircut, the bug eyes, the shirt misbuttoned in his haste. She has hardly ever made anyone as happy as she seems to make Alphonse. Today she'll make him swim twenty feet on his own. He can do it. Sometimes you have to push a child to make him learn.

She hears a rustle in the doorway. "Got four strips here with your name on them," she says.

"You ought to let me starve."

Honora, in a crouch in front of the ice-box, looks up in surprise. "I thought you'd gone," she says.

"I came to apologize," McDermott says.

"No need to apologize. A lot of men are cranky when they wake up," she says, standing and bringing a box of eggs to the stove. "My brothers were terrible."

"I never slept," he says.

"That makes two of us." She lifts the individual pieces of bacon with the fork onto an old newspaper to drain them. She holds an egg above the empty skillet, aware that McDermott has moved farther into the room.

"I won't be seeing you again," he says,

and she inadvertently punctures the egg with her thumb.

Her heart kicks up from its lazy morning beat. "Why is that?" she asks, trying to get the bits of shell out of the quickly cooking egg.

"Honora, look at me," he says.

She turns, a slime of egg white on her fingers.

"Take the pan off the burner," he says. "I want to talk to you."

She wipes her hands on a tea towel. McDermott takes a step forward. The kitchen, on the west side of the house, doesn't have the eye-wincing light of the front room in the mornings, but still it's enough to see his face—pale and grainy, the eyes as blue as the ocean when the sun is setting.

"Sit down," she says, her hands trembling now. "I'll get you some coffee."

He hesitates. "All right," he says. "I could use some coffee."

She brings the percolator to the table and shakily pours him a cup. Normally she adores the smell of coffee, but this morning it threatens to give her a headache.

She sits at the only remaining chair. "The others are asleep?" she asks.

"I tried to wake Mahon twice," he says, "but I can't budge him."

She folds her hands in front of her and waits.

"I'm not coming back," he says, "so I suppose I think that gives me the freedom to tell you all the things I might have said in another life."

"In another life," she repeats.

"I wish you were free," he says.

She puts her hands together and presses them hard against her lips. A sensation of heat rises and floods her limbs and face.

"I love your mouth," he says.

She shakes her head.

"I hate your husband," he says. "I'm sorry about that, but it's true."

She takes a quick breath.

"I love the way you are with Alphonse."

A feeling of panic rises within her.

"Last night," he says, "on the grass, I wanted to make love to you. I wanted it so bad I thought I would do almost anything to make it happen."

She closes her eyes. She releases a hand, and he seizes it.

"You were afraid," he says.

She shakes her head no. "Yes," she says.

He kisses the inside of her wrist. "I think that's it," he says.

Alphonse

He wakes dreaming of bacon and when he sits up he realizes there is actually bacon cooking and so he stands and hops on one foot to get his pant leg on. He is starved, or maybe he was only dreaming he was starved, and he is so glad he didn't get stuck in Portsmouth or Ely Falls and have to spend the night at home instead of coming here and going to the dance hall in Rye. He buttons his shirt and pats his hair forward and realizes that McDermott is already up and so he looks out the window. But no, the sun is only a little bit over the horizon; he hasn't overslept. He runs out into the hallway in his bare feet and hooks an arm around the post at the top of the stairway and takes the stairs two at a time and then slows down in the front hall because he doesn't want to look too eager, does he?

He takes a breath and listens for any of the others, but he can't hear a thing. And then he walks as though nothing in the world were ever important to him, and when he gets to the doorway of the kitchen he stops.

McDermott and Mrs. Beecher are sitting at the table. McDermott has his back to Alphonse, and Mrs. Beecher has her eyes closed and Alphonse thinks it can't be true but it is, Mrs. Beecher's eyelashes are wet. McDermott and Mrs. Beecher are holding hands in an awkward sort of way, and Alphonse wants to know why she is crying. It scares him and he wants to ask them, but he doesn't dare move or breathe because he understands that this is one of those private moments that adults sometimes have to have to themselves. And then Mrs. Beecher opens her eyes and smiles and makes a little choking sound and looks up at McDermott, and that is when she sees Alphonse, who wishes he could evaporate on the spot.

He watches Mrs. Beecher pull her hand away from McDermott's.

"Alphonse," she says.

Honora

She moves from room to room, scarcely knowing what she is doing or what time it is. It has been this way since Sunday, since the men left, and when she tallies up her accomplishments at the end of the day, she is always astonished at how little she has done. Sometimes she feels heavy limbed and slow and wants only to sleep. At other times, she simply sits down and weeps—brief squalls within a chartless sail. She eats leftovers from the icebox, a few bites when she can manage to get them down, always thinking she is hungry but then discovering she is not at all. When Alphonse entered the room on Sunday morning, McDermott stood and mussed Alphonse's hair and said that he would be leaving, and then the door was open and he was walking through it, and Honora never had a chance to say another word to him—which has left her feeling constantly poised on the brink of speaking a sentence she doesn't know the words to.

In her dressing gown, she cooked breakfast, everyone except Louis expressing surprise that McDermott had gone. She had not laundered Sexton's clothes (she would never again wash his clothes, she decided), leaving him to scrounge through his drawers to find shirts and pants to take with him. And that is, of course, where he made his biggest mistake. Had he been truly innocent, she thinks, he would have been more distraught that she hadn't done his laundry.

He might return midweek, he said as he left, kissing her on the side of the mouth as if nothing had ever happened. And then the men and Alphonse were gone, and she was alone in her house, and all she could do was wander from room to room, looking out the windows and replaying the few moments at the roadhouse and at the kitchen table over and over and over until she had extracted from them every possible nugget of meaning. At the time, it seemed to take place before her mind could comprehend what was happening, though it was clear her body knew immediately, and she thinks it is astonishing the way the body can respond all on its own, without the mind quite keeping up.

She wanders into the front room, which she has not cleaned in two days. She drifts here often, each time intending to throw away the balled-up trash that overflows the wastebasket, sort the stacks of clean paper on the table, empty the ashtrays, dust the Copiograph machine and the typewriter, pick up the glasses that are strewn under chairs, behind the couch, and on the windowsills. But each time she stands in the room, a sort of paralysis overtakes her so that she finds herself sitting on one of the available chairs, staring out to sea, remembering the conversations and gestures of the past several weeks. And then she wanders onto the porch and continues her daydreams, vaguely guilty, vaguely aware that she should be tending to her house instead.

A slithery movement at the side of the house catches her eye. Moments later, she hears a timid knock on the glass panes of the back door. When she walks into the kitchen to open it, a woman in a gray cotton dress is standing on the back stoop. Honora has heard that women who do not eat lose their hair and their teeth, and that this can happen even to women in their twenties. The woman before her has a bald patch on one side of her head.

"I'm sorry, miss," the woman says even before Honora has spoken.

The sight of the woman, in her misshapen sleeveless dress, brings Honora sharply to her senses in a way that nothing else since Sunday has done.

"You're looking for something to eat?"

"Yes, miss, if you would. My husband and I haven't eaten since Friday."

Honora calculates the time—four days without food. "Come in," she says quickly.

"Oh, no, miss, I couldn't do that. Please, miss. If you could just give me some bread or some soup, I will just go away."

"Come in and sit down," Honora says in a voice she does not often use, a commanding voice that is reminiscent of her mother's. The woman does as she is told, hunching her shoulders as she walks through the door. Honora sees now that the woman's hair is stiff; she has been bathing in the sea.

There is more food than Honora has remembered inside the cupboards and the icebox. She takes out the remains of a chicken, a bowl of baked beans, a peach pie that somehow did not make it back with the men. In a cupboard above the icebox are two dozen cupcakes that Mahon brought in that didn't get eaten. She finds green beans and tomatoes and half a dozen fresh peaches.

"Do you have water?" she asks the woman.

"No, miss."

Honora finds a pair of large crocks that came from Jack Hess's store. One had beans in it, she remembers, and the other dried peas. She washes them out and fills them with water and puts them on the table. The woman immediately bends forward and takes a sip.

Honora pours cold water into a tall glass and gives it to the woman, who gulps it down. "Not so fast," Honora says. "You'll get a stomach cramp."

She fixes a plate of chicken and baked beans and sets it in front of the woman while she packs up the rest of the food.

The woman whose hair is stiff begins to cry.

"Is it really so bad?" Honora asks.

The woman wipes her nose on the back of her hand, and Honora gives her a handkerchief. "My husband has been on the picket line since the beginning. He's been arrested twice," she says. "We got evicted from our apartment. He said we could come out to the beach and live in the abandoned cottages, but then the owners started returning and we keep having to move. We have five girls with us. We're at the other end of the beach, and we don't have water, and we are having a terrible time of it."

"Is it near the house that sits up on the dunes?"

The woman takes a bite of baked beans and is silent.

"It's all right," Honora says, "you can tell me. That cottage that has pale blue shutters, with a porch on the second-story facing the ocean?"

The woman, who can't be much older than twenty-eight or -nine, nods.

"If you go there, to that house with the

blue shutters, the woman who lives in it will give you water. Her name is Vivian."

"Thank you, miss."

Honora has hardly wrapped up the food and packed it in a paper bag when the woman finishes her meal and stands. "Take this with you now," Honora says. "I'll put the jars out by the back door and I'll cover them. You can come back for them later."

"I will, miss."

"You can use the jars when you go to fetch water at Vivian's. She won't mind. In fact, I think she has a faucet outside for showers. Just tell her that Honora sent you."

"You are a saint, miss," the woman says.

"Hardly," Honora says.

"I have to go into Ely Falls to get my emerald ring sized," Vivian, who is bandbox smart in nude silk shantung, is saying in the hallway. "I've been meaning to do it all summer, but somehow the time has just gotten away from me. Thought I'd drop by on the way and say hello."

"Come in," Honora says immediately, thinking that only Vivian would consider going into Ely Falls to get a ring sized when there is a strike on. "I just made a sandwich for lunch. Can I make you one too?"

"I ate before I came. I'll have a cup of tea to keep you company, though."

Vivian follows Honora into the kitchen and sets her silk-and-bone purse on the table. "Have you heard from Sexton? From any of the fellas?"

Honora shakes her head and fills the kettle. There's a slight commotion at the back door, and the woman of earlier, now with a man in tow, picks up the jars and begins to walk back to the beach with them.

"Who's that?" Vivian asks.

"Squatters living in one of the cottages on the beach. Near you, in fact. I hope you don't mind, but they don't have water, and I said they might ask you from time to time for water. Was that all right?"

"My dear, yes. They have no water at all?"

"None. And she said they have five girls with them. You wouldn't have believed how quickly she ate the plate of food I put in front of her. They're from one of the mills in the city. Got evicted and came out here looking for somewhere to stay."

"Good heavens," Vivian says, sitting.

Honora puts the kettle on and sits at the table with Vivian. Honora studies her sandwich as if it were a foreign life form.

"Eat," Vivian says. "You're looking very peaked, if I may say so. You take such marvelous care of everyone else, but sometimes I just wonder if you take care of yourself at all."

"I'm not sleeping well," Honora says, taking a bite. "And then, during the day, I seem to want to sleep all the time." She puts the sandwich down. Perhaps she is not hungry after all.

"Still no word from Sexton? No word from McDermott?"

"Nothing from Sexton," Honora says. And then, her heart kicking up a notch, "And why would I hear from McDermott?"

"Oh, I don't know," Vivian says vaguely. "He seems the sort of fellow who would make sure you knew what was going on."

Honora nods.

"Thought there might be big doings in there this week," Vivian says, "but Jack

Hess says the strike leaders are really trying to keep a lid on everyone's temper."

"I hope they do," Honora said.

Vivian takes a cigarette from her silver case. "Want one?" she asks.

Honora shakes her head. "I hear the owners are bringing in scabs from Dracut."

"That'll go over well," Vivian says, exhaling a long slither of smoke. Honora thinks of opening a window. A headache threatens at the front of her head, and she thinks it must be from the personal squalls she's been subject to. Her eyes feel swollen and heavy.

"Did they give you any indication when they would all be back?"

Honora watches the mailman pass by on his bicycle. No letter from her mother today, then. "Not really," Honora says. "McDermott isn't coming back."

Vivian tilts her head in considerable surprise.

"He says his work will keep him in the city."

"That's a pity," Vivian says, examining Honora closely. "I like him very much."

"Yes," Honora says.

"I hope this doesn't mean that Alphonse

won't be coming either. Wouldn't be the same without Alphonse."

"No," Honora says.

"He's mad for you, you know."

"He's a sweet boy."

"I meant McDermott. He as much as said so on Saturday night. When we were talking on the porch."

"He said that?" Honora asks.

"I think he was feeling quite hopeless."

Honora peels the bread away from the sandwich. Maybe she could just eat the bread.

"It's something that can't happen," Honora says.

"You have to do what your heart dictates," Vivian says.

"Do you believe that?"

"Not sure, actually. It's always annoyingly inconvenient, isn't it, the thing about the heart?" Vivian stubs out her cigarette. "Frankly, I don't think he's at all well."

"He has an ulcer." Honora tears a small piece of bread off the slice and experimentally chews it.

"Well, I think he's a doll," Vivian says decisively. "I'd snap him up in a minute if he were interested in me."

Honora manages to swallow a bite before a distinct feeling of nausea sweeps through her. She presses her fingers to her mouth.

"Excuse me," she says, rising.

She moves slowly at first, then with more speed, through the hallway, up the stairs, and into the bathroom. She flips the lid up on the toilet, bends over, and vomits. She sits back on the tile floor and presses a towel to her face. She must have caught the grippe this weekend from one of the men, she thinks. She tries to remember if any of them wasn't feeling well. That would explain why she has been so out of sorts, why she has not been herself.

"Bad tummy?" Vivian asks from the doorway.

Honora glances up at her. "I don't know what it is," she says, "but I feel as though I've had a mild grippe for a couple of days now. Just the sight of that sandwich . . ."

"Oh, my dear," Vivian says. She reaches for a clean towel and hands it to Honora.

"What?" Honora asks.

"This might come as a terrible shock."

Honora rises from the floor.

"I think you're pregnant," Vivian says.

* * *

Honora sits in the kitchen chair, trying to absorb the news.

"What can you eat?" Vivian asks. "What sounds appealing?"

"I don't know," Honora says. "Something cold, I guess. Maybe something salty?"

Vivian finds a box of crackers and a jar of peanut butter. She pours milk into a juice glass and then sets the plate of crackers and the glass of milk on the table in front of Honora.

"Of course I should have guessed," Honora says. "I haven't had the curse in two months. I just wasn't paying attention."

"I knew only because I had a friend once who got into trouble with a married man. She looked just like you do now."

Honora drinks from the glass of milk. She hadn't realized how thirsty she was.

"Well, in that case it wasn't a very happy realization," Vivian says, wiping her hands on a tea towel. "I remember she went quite hysterical, in fact."

Which is not so odd, Honora thinks, because she feels like going quite hysterical herself.

"You're as pale as a sheet," Vivian says. "Actually, you're worrying me. Shall I help you into the front room so you can lie on the settee?"

Honora shakes her head. The last thing she wants to see is ashtrays full of butts.

"Perhaps a cup of tea?" Vivian asks.

Honora thinks of the new life inside her. She should be thrilled. This is everything she has hoped for, isn't it?

"Vivian," Honora says. "I'm not sure when I'll be able to tell Sexton. So let's just keep this between us for now, all right?"

Vivian makes a gesture at her mouth of turning a key and throwing it away. Honora dutifully eats the crackers and peanut butter and drinks the glass of milk. The nausea of earlier is gone now, though the sleepiness that seems to have infused her limbs is still there. She pushes the crackers away.

"Oh, Vivian," she says.

Honora walks out onto the beach. It is too hot inside the house, and she needs to breathe.

She strolls, keeping her head down,

searching the sand for the telltale hints of color, the shapes that look like New York and Kansas and Louisiana. She is sweating beneath her dress and has to pull the rayon away from her body to cool her skin. She walks into the ocean, the icy water sending welcome shivers through her shins.

She remembers McDermott's face hovering close to hers. The smell of soap and sweat and gum and cigarettes mixed with the low-tide scent of the sea. The tree that sounded like water.

She bends to retrieve a shard of opaque white sea glass, but discovers it is only a shell.

He put his hand under her skirt, and it would not have mattered to anyone except McDermott and herself.

She digs her toes deep into the wet sand as she walks.

She said to McDermott, *I wish.*

She finds a piece of brown pottery with a ragged edge and drops it into the water.

He said to her that she was afraid.

She surveys the beach and the ocean and the cottages in the dunes, and she knows that she *was* afraid. Not of physical love, which she longed for. But of who she would become.

It might have been, she thinks now, the single worst decision of her life. Because now . . . because now she can never even think about being with McDermott. She is pregnant with her husband's child.

In two years or three years, she thinks, she will have a small companion on her walks. Honora can see, for the first time, an image of a child bending his head to the sand, looking for bits of treasure. He will have Sexton's dark blond curls, perhaps her own brown eyes. He will glance down and find an azure piece of sea glass, its edges smooth and safe, and will hold the prize up for his mother to see. And she will call him Seth. If it is a boy, Honora will call him after her brother, whose atoms she has imagined all these years floating just beyond her reach. Seth will be reassembled after all.

You got your wish, McDermott will say.

A shudder of regret, deep and obliterating, moves through Honora's body, as if a small quake were rolling along the beach. She kneels on the sand to let it pass through her.

In another life, he said.

An incoming wave washes itself up the drop-off and then slides out again. A wet speck of color catches Honora's eye. She staggers to her feet. She runs and puts her foot on the bit of glass. When a second wave has receded, she bends down to retrieve the treasure she has caught with the ball of her foot. She cannot believe her luck. A shard half an inch in diameter and an eighth of an inch thick lies in the palm of her hand. Hardly worth noticing if it were a brown or an ivory. She holds it up to the light.

Crimson.

Scarlet.

Bloodred.

Alice Willard

Dear Honora,

I am so happy about your news I hardly know what to do with myself. I am writing you straight back even though Mr. Pollop just brought your letter this morning. I just knew that when Harold went he was making way for a new life.

I will come to Ely Falls when the baby arrives. I wouldn't miss it for all the world. Your letter said that you thought you were two months along. Have you guessed at a due date? Will you go to a clinic? I think you should, and so does Dr. Kennedy. I know you said you weren't telling anyone just yet, but Estelle had Dr. Kennedy this morning for one of her spells (which are just a way to get attention if you ask me) and I could see his car outside, so I went over, and I had to tell him, didn't I? He said *straight away that you should have it in the hospital and that you shouldn't even think about having it at home because hospitals are so much safer these days. He said the hospital will cost you $45 for ten days, the gas will cost $2.50 and the drugs $1.25. He said that any decent hospital would take $35 and be happy to have it.*

I went up to the attic and found some lovely silk and cotton and lawn from which I will make baby clothing for you—little nightgowns and bunting and so forth. I know that it is bad luck to make the christening gown ahead of time, so I will not do that, though I will look at patterns.

Oh, Honora, I cannot tell you how much joy your news has given me.

Now remember, it is very important to eat right when a baby is coming. I had terrible cravings for donuts when Charles was on the way, and if it hadn't been for your father's good sense, that's all I'd have eaten for months.

Please write me often, dear. I am most eager for any news.

Love,
Mother

Alphonse

His breath is tight and there is a pain in his side that he knows will not go away. He sprints along the road that runs through the marshes and he is moving so fast that he keeps surprising birds and ducks, which squawk and leap out of the grasses and flutter for a moment in his face before flying away. It is high tide in the marshes, and he thinks it is amazing the way it can be so beautiful and quiet and calm here at the beach while in the city there was screaming and flying rocks and fires and smoke, and then the shots. And then they were all at Rose Street, and he is pretty sure he will never forget the expression on his mother's face, or the way Marie-Thérèse stood with her fists to her mouth and whimpered and carried on like it was she who was hurt and bleeding and not some stranger she had never met.

Mrs. Beecher is going to be very, very upset, and why oh why does it have to be Alphonse who has to tell her?

Run, Ross said when they had made it up the stairs, four men carrying the wounded man as if he were a rolled rug, one leg falling against a step and the man waking out of a dead stupor to scream that one time and all the smears of blood on the wooden steps as Alphonse brought up the rear.

Alphonse ran out to the Ely Road, thinking he could take the trolley, but then he realized that would take too long and so he stuck his thumb out and a rusted red vegetable truck came hunkering along and Alphonse got in the back and sat with the rotting cabbages and jumped off when the truck came to a stop near the beach road.

You could tell all day that something bad was going to happen. Ever since Monday morning, all of the picketers had been in a sulky mood, and last night it was so hot and so sticky you couldn't even breathe inside the house, never mind move or sleep, and you could just see this morning on the line how hot and annoyed everybody was, as if they'd just been insulted and hadn't been able to think of a snappy answer back.

First there were a few rocks and then there was some shouting and shoving, or maybe it was the other way around, and Mironson tried to get everyone's attention and said, *Hello there!* and *Hey!* and *Wait a minute!* and finally *STOP!* But no one was giving him any mind, and the militia and the police just stood on the other side of the street protecting the scabs, looking like a wall that was never going to move. The crowd was kind of surging forward and backward and growing thicker and thicker as people got the news that finally, thank God, something interesting was about to happen. And Alphonse remembers the girls, teenage girls in their summer dresses and their hats, all trying to get on top of cars and saying, *What's going on?* And then Mironson jumped up on the hood of a Model T that wasn't going anywhere, and this seemed to Alphonse like a very bad idea, making himself a target like that when everyone could see the militia and the police were about to die of heat prostration in their uniforms and wanted to get this thing over with, and that was when Alphonse heard the first shot.

A policeman dropped, just dropped where he was standing, nothing dramatic, no clutching of the heart like you see in the gangster movies at the Emporium, and that shut the crowd up for a second, and then another policeman raised his gun and fired off three or four shots, and Alphonse heard a man scream, and he thought it must be Mironson, but Mironson just looked stunned, as if he'd had a piece of really bad news, and Alphonse saw Tsomides jump up on top of the Ford and drag Mironson off and that was when Ross said, *Alphonse, is your mother in your house?* And then Ross said, *Oh shit, oh shit, oh shit,* and that scared Alphonse because Ross hardly ever showed any emotion about anything, and that's when they put the man in the Ford and drove away and the blood got on the stairs and the leg hit the step.

The stitch in his side hurts so much he isn't sure he can make it, but there, at the end of the road, he can see the house, and there she is, outside hanging up her wash, and Alphonse needs the run to be over because his breath feels like sandpaper in his lungs, but he doesn't want one single bit to have to tell Mrs. Beecher the terrible thing he has to tell her.

Honora

The wet sheet blows against her dress and sticks like a bit of newspaper flattened in a wind against the side of a building. She struggles with the sheet and lifts it onto the line and secures it with wooden clothespins. She glances up the road, a small movement catching her attention. A cricket hopping, a wheel rolling in the dust. She peers for a moment into the distance and then she moves a few steps closer to the road. A boy is running, his body and head bent forward, his hands slapping the air as if for purchase, the way sprinters swim at the air at the finish line. At first she can't identify the boy, but then something in the shape of the head, the spindly body, causes her to realize that it is Alphonse. She looks quickly behind him to see if he is being chased.

She is holding a wet towel, stiff from the wringer, when he reaches her.

He bends, gasping for breath, unable to speak. She drops the towel and takes hold of his shoulders and puts her head close to his while he coughs and tries to speak. She gives him a fierce hug and tells him to come inside, and he says, “It’s Mr. Beecher.”

She says, “What?”

And he says,“He’s been shot, he’s hurt, and Ross said I should tell you and then go get Miss Burton and she should bring you to where he is because he is calling for you and won’t stop.”

“Where is he?” she asks.

“At my house,” Alphonse says. “On Rose Street.”

McDermott

"He shot a cop," Ross is saying in the squalid kitchen. From the living room, McDermott hears Sexton Beecher grunting and then being quiet for a moment, and then yelling as if he weren't quite right in the head.

"What happened?" McDermott asks.

"The asshole had a gun."

"Where'd he get it?"

"He says he pawned a pair of earrings."

"Jesus Christ," McDermott says.

In the corner, a young girl is whimpering. The mother is in with Beecher. "I sent the kid's brother for the quack," Ross says. "Beecher's lost a bathtub full of blood."

There's a smear of crimson along the wooden floor, as if someone had dragged a freshly killed deer through the kitchen and into the living room.

"Where were you?" Ross says.

"On our way back from Exeter," McDermott says.

"I didn't know a man had so much blood in him," Ross says.

"Where was he shot?"

"In the leg. In the thigh. Isn't there some great big artery there?"

"If it had hit an artery," McDermott says, "he'd be dead by now."

The screen door opens and slaps shut. Mironson and Tsomides enter the kitchen. The girl in the corner begins to cry louder, as if the men had come to shoot her in the leg too.

"I wish she'd shut the fuck up," Ross says to McDermott. "She's getting on my nerves."

Mironson's face is white, a sheen of sweat on his forehead. He tugs off his tie and opens the first four buttons of his thin shirt as if he were asthmatic and short of air. "We need to get him out of here," Mironson says. "He's left a trail on the stairs a blind man could follow."

"Where's Alphonse?" McDermott asks, looking around.

"I sent him to get Honora," Ross says.

McDermott brings his hand to his forehead. "Jesus Christ," he says. "You didn't."

From the other room, Sexton Beecher roars his wife's name.

A bucket in the sink is full of red water. The sole of McDermott's shoe is sticky on the wooden floor. He glances around at the yellowing paper on the walls, the small white stove with a crusty pot on top of it, the cupboards that have no doors. "I've got to go," McDermott says, brushing against Ross. "They shouldn't come here. It's too risky."

But then a woman in a shimmery blue dress, her copper hair ablaze in a pool of sunlight, is standing on the porch behind the screen door. Alphonse sneaks around and under Vivian and opens the door. Honora, in her slippers, her blouse untucked from her skirt, her hair wild about her head, walks into the room.

McDermott knows that he will never again want anyone or anything as much as he wants this woman.

"Where is he?" she asks.

Alphonse

He wishes someone would shut Marie-Thérèse up, because she is being very annoying and is not helping the situation one little bit. His house is crowded with men looking sick and hot and wishing they were somewhere else. His mother is holding a bloody towel, and inside the other room Mrs. Beecher is with her husband, who is just howling like an animal with its leg caught in a trap. Alphonse is standing with Miss Burton in the doorway between the kitchen and the living room, and Miss Burton is being very calm and speaking to Mrs. Beecher and McDermott, and you can just see that in this kind of a situation women are much better than men.

Ross says, "Where's Wing?" and Alphonse thinks maybe he should have been the one to go for the doctor instead of

Gérard, and Mahon is telling Mironson, who looks as if he is going to throw up, to leave immediately, and it is then that Alphonse hears the cars in front of the house and the metal doors slamming, and the room goes absolutely quiet.

Oh, Jesus, Ross says.

Sexton

Someone is pressing an iron against his leg and it is just searing his flesh, burning his flesh, and he is trying to buck it off, but there are hands on his arms and he hears his wife's voice saying his name over and over, and he tries to sit up, but she pushes her hands against him, and for the sake of almighty God, will someone just get this fucking iron off his goddamn leg? He can hear his wife calling for someone to help her and then there are stronger hands on his, and when he looks up he can see a man's face, what is his name? he can't remember, he should be able to remember, and the iron is pressed against his skin again, and he screams his wife's name. He can hear her saying, "I am here, I am here," but it is hard to pay attention because the pain is so great, and then he looks up at her and tells her he is sorry, although he is not completely sure what he is sorry about. But he knows that he is and that he has hurt her, and that she didn't deserve to be hurt, and then there is a pressure on his chest. The girl, Vivian, is saying does Honora know that he has been hit twice, and Honora is leaning over him and telling him something he should be paying attention to and he tries to hang on so that he can make sure he has heard her right, but he is being carried away by a river and he really, really wants to let go. And then he hears the big guy, what's his name? the hulking beast from a fairy tale, say *Oh, Jesus* from the kitchen.

Vivian

"He's been hit twice," Vivian says to Honora, wondering if anyone has noticed that Sexton Beecher is bleeding from another wound just below the first one. It's perfectly possible no one has discovered this because there is so much blood. She feels a small movement beside her, and Alphonse sneaks under her arm to take a peek into the living room.

"I don't think you want to look at this," Vivian says, turning the boy toward her body and enveloping him. He is just a boy, after all, and he shouldn't be a part of this. As best she can make out, Sexton fired a shot at a wall of policemen, which seems like an extraordinarily stupid thing to do, and the police fired back, as well they might have. It is all unnerving, and she has to admit that even she started to tremble a bit when they drove into Ely Falls and saw all the rioting over by the mills and the fires that seemed to be popping up everywhere. But Alphonse just kept telling her, in that small, polite voice of his, to turn here, miss, and to turn there, miss, and then they were on Rose Street and climbing the stairs to the kitchen.

What a dreadful apartment, Vivian thinks.

"Is he going to die?" Alphonse asks, looking up at her.

"No, Alphonse, he is not," Vivian says emphatically, knowing that this is what one should tell a boy of twelve years old, though of course one cannot possibly know if a man is going to die or not, and frankly, from where she stands, it doesn't look very good for Sexton Beecher. Her mind leaps ahead in time and she sees that she will want to take Honora back to her own house and make her stay there until the woman is on her feet again, which could be quite a while.

Vivian hears the footsteps on the wooden stairs outside and thinks, irrationally, that the police have come to solve their problem, to mop up the mess, as they do in gangster movies. But then she realizes, with some dismay, that this cannot possibly be the case, can it? Because in this particular movie, she and Louis and McDermott and Ross and Sexton (especially Sexton) and even Alphonse and Honora are the gangsters. And then she sees, through the screen at the kitchen door, the white hoods over the faces of the men and thinks, *Something is very wrong here,* because everyone knows that the Ku Klux Klan operates only in the south. Yet even then, and ever optimistic (for Vivian scarcely knows how to be anything else), she imagines that these men in their ridiculous white hoods with dark round circles for their eyes and noses will somehow explain themselves and restore order to this hideous and frightful situation.

But then the first man enters the kitchen, and Vivian understands at once that it is not going to be like that. It is not going to be like that at all.

Honora

She bends over her husband and pins his arms. His face is mottled bright white and dark red, and this, even more than all the blood, frightens her. She calls out that she needs help. McDermott comes and then Alphonse's mother, a small woman Honora has wanted to meet. She has wanted to tell this woman that Alphonse is a sweet boy, but of course his mother must already know this. Sexton is yelling Honora's name and grabbing for his crotch, even though that is not exactly where he has been hit. He says *I'm sorry* over and over and over, and she keeps trying to shush him and calm him down. He grabs for his crotch again, and Alphonse's mother looks over at her as if to say, Who knows what a man will get up to when he thinks he is dying?

McDermott is standing behind her now,

and Honora knows that he is seeing this thing that Sexton is doing and hearing him say *I'm sorry* over and over.

"Sexton," she says, putting her face close to his. "Don't speak. Just rest. You're going to be all right."

She glances up at McDermott and then back down at Sexton, and for the first time since she entered the room she thinks that her husband might actually die. She bends close to him and says, "Hang on, Sexton," but she can see, in an ominous relaxation of his features, that he is drifting into unconsciousness. And then an urgent question rises within her, and she knows that she has only seconds to answer it.

The life inside her body is as much Sexton's as it is hers.

She looks at McDermott again and wishes that she could tell him that she is sorry, that if she had to do it over again, she would not have been afraid under the tree that sounded like water. She would have had no fear and would have let him love her, and if that one night was all they had together, well then, so be it, because, really, what honor was there in denying love?

Sexton jerks his body, as though, even semiconscious, he wanted her whole attention. She thinks, *I have to do this now.*

She bends to her husband's face. "Sexton, I'm pregnant," she says.

She can see him struggling to comprehend, as if he didn't quite catch all the words. His fingers scrabble against the wooden floorboards. And so she has to say it again. "Sexton, I'm pregnant. We are going to have a baby."

With her hand on her husband's leg, she turns to find McDermott's face. And it is all there, she thinks; she has become as good at reading faces as he is. The shock of the news. The wave of comprehension. And then regret. Terrible regret.

"I didn't know," she says, reaching for his hand.

There are footsteps on the stairs. In the kitchen, Ross is saying, *Oh, Jesus.*

Vivian, in the doorway, holds Alphonse to her breast. The men coming through the kitchen door have white hoods and guns.

Vivian executes a graceful dance step and slips behind a sofa with the boy.

In another life, McDermott says and turns.

Honora yells the word *no!* but McDermott cannot hear her.

Through the doorway, Honora watches Louis vault into the air in a way he could never do on his own. Ross, as if he had been pushed, sits heavily on a chair that tips over onto the floor.

McDermott spins like a child's top—already damaged, already broken.

A man with a hood is standing in the doorway. He raises the long gun in his hands and says, "This must be the guy."

A second man, also in a white hood, pushes his way into the room. "He's gone," he says. "Let's get out of here."

The first man, a faceless creature, holds his gun toward Honora for a long second, and then he lowers it to his side.

In the kitchen, a young girl is bleating like a sheep.

Honora moves on her knees to the place where McDermott has fallen. At first she cannot tell if he has been hit. He seems merely to be stunned, or even, oddly, to be sleeping. She puts her fingers to his face, calling his name. She cradles his head. And then she feels the blood, warm and sticky in his hair. She stares at her hand. The girl in the kitchen is making an inhuman sound.

Honora stands, bewildered. Her own blood drains from her head, and her vision begins to narrow. Strong hands catch the sides of her shoulders.

Wordlessly, Vivian leads her away from McDermott to a chair in the kitchen. Alphonse, white faced, appears in the doorway. Vivian shields his eyes from the carnage as she marches him through the kitchen to the porch. "Go for help," she commands. "And don't come back inside this room until I tell you to."

Honora gazes around her. Alphonse's sister is holding her arm and crying in a way that is frightening to listen to. It is the sound of pure fear—the pealing of a bell long after it has been struck.

Mironson is sitting on the floor, against a wall, a smear of blood behind him on the yellowing wallpaper.

Ross, in death, has the posture of a clown midprank—his bulk against the back of the tipped chair, his feet in the air.

Mahon seems no longer to have a face.

Tsomides is cradling his head, but his eyes are open and unmoving.

The worst, though—the very worst—is the unnatural way Alphonse's mother is bent backward over the sink.

Honora counts.

Six dead.

A massacre, she thinks.

She stands and moves back into the living room, where McDermott is on the floor. In the corner, Sexton calls for her. Honora kneels over McDermott's body and puts a hand on his chest. She minds that she cannot see the color of McDermott's eyes—that lovely turquoise blue. She lifts her face to a God she does not know very well, and a wail begins to rise inside her.

Honora

Honora sets her suitcase on the slab of granite. Alphonse, returning from the beach wagon, picks it up, his shoulder hitched for balance.

"It's very heavy," she says.

"I've got it," he says.

His face has filled out some around his eyes, so that his features are no longer quite as comical as they used to be. And there is something sad in his mouth that will never go away. Vivian has taken Alphonse to her own hairdresser, a woman named Irma in Exeter, for a haircut, but still the boy's hair grows forward and wants to spike.

The year is 1930. A September day. Not quite an ordinary day.

Vivian, in a milk blue wool dress,

emerges from the hallway with a wooden caddy of flatware. She holds it aloft, a hostess with a plate of hors d'oeuvres. "I left the kettle and the teapot and two cups in the kitchen," she says. "Thought you might want one last cup of tea. Or am I wrong? Do you want to go straightaway?"

"No," Honora says, "a cup of tea might be good. All the stuff is here in the hall. Alphonse can just keep making trips. The only thing that will be a problem for him is that rocker."

"What are you going to do about the piano?" Vivian asks.

"I'm going to leave it," Honora says. "It was here when I got here."

"Whose is it?"

"I think it belongs to someone who used to live in the house," she says. "I never felt that it was ours."

"Oh, and by the way," Vivian says, turning, "I couldn't find the letter from the school. Are you sure you left it by the sink?"

"It was there this morning," Honora says. "Maybe I put it in my pocketbook. I'll check."

In four days, Alphonse will begin classes

at the Ely Day School in Ely. It will mean a two-mile walk to school, but Alphonse doesn't seem to think that this will be a problem. Honora isn't so sure about how he will manage during the winter months, but they will just have to figure that out when the time comes.

Vivian said that she had always wanted a house sitter, though it was perfectly apparent to Honora that the thought had never crossed Vivian's mind until the very moment when she made the offer. The bank will take possession of Honora's house on Friday. Honora doesn't want to be here when it happens.

"Come stay with me until I go back to New York," Vivian pleaded, "and then stay on through the winter. When I come in June, you can type my plays."

A year ago, Honora would have refused Vivian's offer. A year ago, Honora would have been unable to accept such overt charity. But not now. Not since that morning when McDermott spun in the middle of the floor and Vivian slipped with Alphonse to safety behind a sofa. It was the only way Honora could keep Alphonse with her, she realized at once, and so she said yes. Without a second thought.

One morning in mid-August, Alphonse took the trolley to the end of the Ely Road and walked the rest of the way to the beach. His brothers and sisters had all been divided up among their relatives, he said when Honora opened the door. He himself was being sent to his uncle Augustin and his aunt Louise in Lowell. He wanted to live with Honora instead, he said, and would that be all right? The boy's chin was trembling, and Honora knew how much it had cost him to have to ask her this. She hugged the boy, and the two of them wept like infants on the granite doorstep.

Alphonse had lost his mother and McDermott—the two people he had loved most in the world. Sometimes it seems to Honora scarcely possible that the boy is still standing.

Honora fills the kettle and sets it on the stove, remembering the first day she entered this kitchen and found her way to the window and opened the shutters and saw the glass coated with a year or two of salt. The filmy light, like that from frosted glass, lit up an iron stove, its surface dotted with animal droppings. The oven door opened with a screech and bang that startled her.

She waits for the water to boil. She remembers how Sexton fixed the tap and how the faucet retched and spattered brown water into the sink.

For ten days in late July and early August, Honora took the trolley to the Ely Falls Hospital. She said hello to the policeman who guarded Sexton's door—a man named Henry. She sat beside Sexton's bed and knit a pair of socks. Though his leg was healing, her husband never spoke a word. Honora, after two or three days of frantic questioning, finally gave up trying. Sexton's eyes had moved so close together that it seemed that only a thin bridge of bone separated them. He did not comb his hair. When his leg was healed, he would go to jail.

On the morning of the eleventh day, before Honora had had a chance to leave the house, two policemen came to her door. She gasped when she saw them, thinking they had come to shoot her. They searched every inch of the house and wanted to know where her husband was. She told them she had no idea.

Sexton Beecher had escaped from the hospital, they said. He had stolen a Ford.

Don't ever buy a Ford.

He's taken the open road, she thought but didn't say.

She pours the boiling water into the teapot. "Alphonse, do you want some milk?" she calls into the hallway, eyeing the half pint of milk that is left.

"In a minute," he says. "I'm almost finished."

"I'll come for the trial," Vivian says, leaning on the counter.

"They don't know when it will be," Honora says.

"Only the two men have been charged?"

"They won't give up the other names. They're said to be protecting Jonathan Harding."

"The bank president."

"Yes."

"Not the Klan, then."

"No, not the Klan."

"Have you heard from Sexton?" Vivian asks lightly.

Honora shakes her head. She does not

believe she will ever hear from Sexton Beecher again. In her mind, she sees a map with threads of blue and pink roads, a small round dot moving along them.

The two women stand in the kitchen—Vivian against the lip of the sink, Honora by the icebox. "I don't know if I'll get back for Thanksgiving," Vivian says. "It's likely that we'll have rehearsals."

"Oh, that's all right," Honora says. "I'm thinking that I might take Alphonse to Taft to see my mother."

"Will you be able to travel then?" Vivian asks.

"I'll be seven months along. I think it will be fine. If not, I won't go."

"I might come for Christmas, though."

"Oh, would you?" Honora asks, brightening. "Alphonse would love that."

"And your mother will come for the baby?" Vivian asks.

"I think so. She wants me to have it in a hospital."

"Well, I should hope so," Vivian says, slightly aghast.

Honora puts her cup in the sink. "You know," she says, rinsing it, "there ought to be a word for when one's most exciting—

one's most *joyful*—moments take place during a time that is grim and hard for others around you. I've been trying to think of such a word all week, but I haven't found it yet."

"You mean this summer?"

"Yes. Everyone in Ely Falls was suffering because of the strike, and we . . . well, we were having so much fun, weren't we? And were living so well. Relatively." She thinks a minute. "Well, not relatively at all. We were living well, period. Every weekend was a party."

"War is like that," Vivian says. "Men often speak about how they felt most alive—and most in love, for that matter—during wartime."

"I loved McDermott," Honora says.

"I know you did," Vivian says.

"He was so good with Alphonse," Honora says.

"Yes, he was."

"He would be glad, wouldn't he, that Alphonse is—"

Honora stops. She cannot go on. She takes Vivian's cup and rinses it in the sink.

"I thought I would make an oyster chowder tonight," Honora says. "Does that sound all right to you?"

"Sounds peachy." Vivian lights a cigarette. "Want one?"

"No, thanks. I had to give them up." She points to her stomach. "They make me nauseous."

"Good," Vivian says. "Filthy habit. I read in the paper today that the Ely Falls Mill is closing."

"McDermott said that would happen."

"Ironic, isn't it?" Vivian says.

"The strikers win and then they have no jobs."

"I can take Alphonse to school in the beach wagon for the first week," Vivian says.

"That might be good. I think he's very nervous about it."

"As well he might be," Vivian says. "We have to take him shopping. He needs clothes."

"He certainly does," Honora says.

"So do you, for that matter," Vivian says.

"Actually," Honora says, "I'd like to get some fabric and make maternity clothes. My mother is sending me patterns."

"As long as I get to edit them," Vivian says.

Honora smiles. "I don't know what I'd have done if you hadn't been here," she says.

"Nonsense," Vivian says. "You're the strongest woman I know. That's why Alphonse has come to you."

"You know," Honora says, "you read a word like *massacre* and you think, I know what that means. It means the slaughter of innocent people. And then you go on. You read another fact. You read the word *trial.* Or *conviction.* But then . . . when it happens to you, when you live the word, you realize that the word itself means nothing. It tells you nothing at all. It doesn't begin to convey the horror, does it?"

"No," Vivian says. "It doesn't."

"It was a bungle," Honora says. "Just a terrible bungle."

"Yes, it was."

"There was nothing noble at all about what happened. About their deaths. No sacrifice. No honor. It was just a *bungle.* We should never have been there in the first place. It was a disastrous decision on Ross's part. In that apartment, we were just sitting ducks." Honora remembers the way the men in masks came through the door with their guns. The way Ross said *Oh, Jesus.*

"You can't do this," Vivian says, crossing the room and taking Honora into her arms. "You have to stop. You simply have to stop."

"I know," she says.

"You can't let Alphonse see you like this," Vivian says.

Honora rubs her eyes with the heels of her hands. "I know. I won't."

"Well," Vivian says.

"Well," Honora says. She looks around at the kitchen, nearly empty now. "Alphonse, come get your milk," she calls into the hallway.

Alphonse enters the kitchen, swinging his arms to unkink them.

"We packed the glasses," Honora says. "Just drink it from the bottle."

Alphonse lifts the bottle of milk to his face. He wipes his mouth with his sleeve.

Alphonse

He carries the last carton to the beach wagon, which is so full that you can't even see out the back, and Alphonse thinks how strange it is that there is so much stuff when the house has always looked, well, kind of empty. But now he will have his own room at Miss Burton's house, though she has said he will have to sleep in the cellar if he keeps calling her Miss Burton and so he is trying to remember to call her Vivian. But he will still call Mrs. Beecher Mrs. Beecher and he is relieved that she hasn't asked him to call her Honora. Mrs. Beecher slides into the front seat, a carton of books on her lap. Alphonse crawls into the backseat and lies down over all the blankets and boxes with his head nearly touching the top of the car, and Miss Burton, Vivian, gets in and starts the beach wagon and then Mrs. Beecher says, “Wait, I nearly forgot,” and sets the carton on the front seat, gets out of the car again, leans in, and says to Vivian that she’ll be right back, she just left it on the landing. And then she is kind of running up the walkway and opening the front door, and Vivian turns to him and says, “Are you all right?” and he says he is just fine, though there is a sharp corner of a box sticking into his side, and then Mrs. Beecher is standing in the doorway with a white platter in her arms, and even from the beach wagon Alphonse can see how beautiful all the glass is in the sunlight.

Author's Note

The city of Ely Falls is fictional. The details of violent labor unrest, however, are culled from numerous incidents in New England and elsewhere during the late 1920s and the early 1930s in which hundreds of striking mill workers and their children were killed or seriously injured by state militia or vigilantes hired by mill owners. As an interesting footnote, the Ku Klux Klan did indeed flourish in northern New England during the late 1920s. Its victims were Catholics, Jews, and ethnic minorities.

The following works were consulted while writing this book: *The Strike of '28* by Daniel Georgianna and Roberta Hazen Aaronson; *The Great Depression* by Robert S. McElvaine; *Working People of Holyoke* by William Hartford; *Ordinary People Extraordinary Lives* by Debra Bernhardt and Rachel Bernstein; *La Foi, La Langue, La Culture* by Michael Guignard; *Working-Class Americanism* by Gary Gerstle; *A World Within a World* by Gary Samson; *Ethnic Survival in a New England Mill Town: The Franco-Americans of Biddeford, Maine* by Michael Guignard; *The Great Depression* and *The Hungry Years* by T. H. Watkins; *The Town That Died* by Michael Bird; *The Parrish and the Hill* by Mary Doyle Curran; *Down and Out in the Great Depression: Stories and Recipes of the Great Depression of the 1930s* by Janet Van Amber Paske; *Amoskeag* by Tamara Harveven and Randolph Langenbach; *Gastonia 1929* by John A. Salmond; *Hard Times* by Studs Terkel; *The Last Generation* by Mary H. Blewtt; *Saco Then and Now* by Peter N. Scontras; and *Let Us Now Praise Famous Men* by James Agee and Walker Evans.

I would like to thank Jewel Reed and Bill Newell for supplying details of life during 1929 and 1930. I would also like to thank my agent, Ginger Barber; my editor, Michael Pietsch; and my husband, John Osborn, for their support and guidance.